Praise for Georgia Beers

Dance with Me

"I admit I inherited my two left feet from my father's side of the family. Dancing is not something I enjoy, so why choose a book with dancing as the central focus and romance as the payoff? Easy. Because it's Georgia Beers, and she will let me enjoy being awkward alongside her main character. I think this is what makes her special to me as an author. While her characters might be beautiful in their own ways, I can relate to their challenges, fears and dreams. Comfort reads every time."—*Late Night Lesbian Reads*

Camp Lost and Found

"I really like when Beers writes about winter and snow and hot chocolate. She makes heartache feel cosy and surmountable. *Camp Lost and Found* made me smile a lot, laugh at times, tear up more often than I care to share. If you're looking for a heartwarming story to keep the cold weather at bay, I'd recommend you give it a chance."—*Jude in the Stars*

Cherry on Top

"*Cherry on Top* is another wonderful story from one of the greatest writers in sapphic fiction…This is more than a romance with two incredibly charming and wonderful characters. It is a reminder that you shouldn't have to compromise who you are to fit into a box that society wants to put you into. Georgia Beers once again creates a couple with wonderful chemistry who will warm your heart."—*Sapphic Book Review*

On the Rocks

"This book made me so happy! And kept me awake way too late."—*Jude in the Stars*

The Secret Poet

"[O]ne of the author's best works and one of the best romances I've read recently…I was so invested in ['   book in one sitting."—*Melina Bickard,* (UK)

Hopeless Romantic

"Thank you, Georgia Beers, for this unabashed paean to the pleasure of escaping into romantic comedies…If you want to have a big smile plastered on your face as you read a romance novel, do not hesitate to pick up this one!"—*The Rainbow Bookworm*

Flavor of the Month

"Beers whips up a sweet lesbian romance…brimming with mouth-watering descriptions of foodie indulgences…Both women are well-intentioned and endearing, and it's easy to root for their inevitable reconciliation. But once the couple rediscover their natural ease with one another, Beers throws a challenging emotional hurdle in their path, forcing them to fight through tragedy to earn their happy ending." —*Publishers Weekly*

One Walk in Winter

"A sweet story to pair with the holidays. There are plenty of 'moment's in this book that make the heart soar. Just what I like in a romance. Situations where sparks fly, hearts fill, and tears fall. This book shined with cute fairy trails and swoon-worthy Christmas gifts…REALLY nice and cozy if read in between Thanksgiving and Christmas. Covered in blankets. By a fire."—*Bookvark*

Fear of Falling

"Enough tension and drama for us to wonder if this can work out—and enough heat to keep the pages turning. I will definitely recommend this to others—Georgia Beers continues to go from strength to strength." —*Evan Blood, Bookseller (Angus & Robertson, Australia)*

The Do-Over

"You can count on Beers to give you a quality well-paced book each and every time."—*The Romantic Reader Blog*

"*The Do-Over* is a shining example of the brilliance of Georgia Beers as a contemporary romance author."—*Rainbow Reflections*

The Shape of You

The Shape of You "catches you right in the feels and does not let go. It is a must for every person out there who has struggled with self-esteem, questioned their judgment, and settled for a less than perfect but safe lover. If you've ever been convinced you have to trade passion for emotional safety, this book is for you."—*Writing While Distracted*

"I know I always say this about Georgia Beers's books, but there is no one that writes first kisses like her. They are hot, steamy and all too much!"—*Les Rêveur*

Calendar Girl

"A sweet, sweet romcom of a story…*Calendar Girl* is a nice read, which you may find yourself returning to when you want a hot-chocolate-and-warm-comfort-hug in your life."—*Best Lesbian Erotica*

Blend

"You know a book is good, first, when you don't want to put it down. Second, you know it's damn good when you're reading it and thinking, I'm totally going to read this one again. Great read and absolutely a 5-star romance."—*The Romantic Reader Blog*

"This is a lovely romantic story with relatable characters that have depth and chemistry. A charming easy story that kept me reading until the end. Very enjoyable."—*Kat Adams, Bookseller, QBD (Australia)*

Right Here, Right Now

"[A] successful and entertaining queer romance novel. The main characters are appealing, and the situations they deal with are realistic and well-managed. I would recommend this book to anyone who enjoys a good queer romance novel, and particularly one grounded in real world situations."—*Books at the End of the Alphabet*

"[A]n engaging odd-couple romance. Beers creates a romance of gentle humor that allows no-nonsense Lacey to relax and easygoing Alicia to find a trusting heart."—*RT Book Reviews*

Lambda Literary Award Winner *Fresh Tracks*

"Georgia Beers pens romances with sparks."—*Just About Write*

"[T]he focus switches each chapter to a different character, allowing for a measured pace and deep, sincere exploration of each protagonist's thoughts. Beers gives a welcome expansion to the romance genre with her clear, sympathetic writing."—*Curve magazine*

Lambda Literary Award Finalist *Finding Home*

"Georgia Beers has proven in her popular novels such as *Too Close to Touch* and *Fresh Tracks* that she has a special way of building romance with suspense that puts the reader on the edge of their seat. *Finding Home*, though more character driven than suspense, will equally keep the reader engaged at each page turn with its sweet romance."—*Lambda Literary Review*

Mine

"Beers does a fine job of capturing the essence of grief in an authentic way. *Mine* is touching, life-affirming, and sweet."—*Lesbian News Book Review*

Too Close to Touch

"This is such a well-written book. The pacing is perfect, the romance is great, the character work strong, and damn, but is the sex writing ever fantastic."—*The Lesbian Review*

"In her third novel, Georgia Beers delivers an immensely satisfying story. Beers knows how to generate sexual tension so taut it could be cut with a knife…Beers weaves a tale of yearning, love, lust, and conflict resolution. She has constructed a believable plot, with strong characters in a charming setting."—*Just About Write*

By the Author

Visit us at www.boldstrokesbooks.com

PEACHES AND CREAM

by

Georgia Beers

2023

PEACHES AND CREAM
© 2023 By Georgia Beers. All Rights Reserved.

ISBN 13: 978-1-63679-412-9

This Trade Paperback Original Is Published By
Bold Strokes Books, Inc.
P.O. Box 249
Valley Falls, NY 12185

First Edition: August 2023

Credits
Editor: Ruth Sternglantz
Production Design: Stacia Seaman
Cover Design by Inkspiral Design

Acknowledgments

It's been a couple of books since I've had a food-focused story, so I figured it was about time. When I wrote *Dance with Me*, something about Adley Purcell spoke to me, and I decided pretty early on in that book that she deserved her own story. Plus, ice cream! Toss in a bit of an homage to one of my favorite rom-coms, *You've Got Mail*, and the book practically wrote itself. I really wanted to be Adley's best friend. I still do. I hope you will too.

As always, thank you to Bold Strokes Books and everybody on staff for being such a professional, dependable organization that continues to grow and change with the landscape of publishing. I'm lucky to be a part of it.

I have a small but very valued circle of support, both friends and family, both writers and non-writers. They keep me grounded but help me fly. I couldn't do what I do without each and every one of them. They know who they are.

And finally, I've said it a hundred times, but I'll say it again: If you're holding my book in your hands or reading it on your e-reader or listening to the audiobook, I want to thank you. It's not dramatic to say I wouldn't be where I am today without you, so thank you from the bottom of my heart. You keep reading and I'll keep writing.

Stop worrying so much.
Have the ice cream.

CHAPTER ONE

From the gentleman on the other side of the bar."

The bartender's voice was low and gravelly, and she had to lean in very close to Sabrina in order to be heard, which Sabrina didn't mind because the bartender was also super hot. Tall, piles of dark hair, and she smelled great—like strawberries and something woodsy—which she wouldn't have known if she hadn't had to get so close. A glass of bourbon, neat, was slid in front of her. She shifted her gaze to meet the eyes of the guy across the bar who held up his beer in salute. Handsome enough, tall, dark hair short on the sides and a little floppy on top. Younger than her, clearly. Tie pulled loose and askew over his white shirt.

She thanked the bartender with a nod and finished the bourbon she currently had, then slid the empty glass in and grabbed the new one. And stifled a sigh because men constantly hit on her. Women never did. She hadn't been able to quite figure that one out yet.

She took a sip, and her gaze went not to the guy who'd sent the drink, but to the brunette sitting at the two-top table behind him. She'd caught Sabrina's eye the second she'd arrived. She'd been alone for a good fifteen minutes, and Sabrina was working up the nerve to go talk to her when a cute blonde arrived, kissed the brunette on the cheek, and took the other seat. Sabrina had sighed internally. *If they're not straight, they're taken.* That had been her experience for the past several months as she'd traveled from city to city. Not that she was looking for a relationship. Who had time for that? And while she loved the idea of some soft conversation, a shared bottle of wine or a meal, maybe a warm body for the night, she wasn't really that person. Picking up a stranger and taking them home? She wished she was built to do that, but she just wasn't. She had been aching for longer than she cared to admit, and she looked with longing at the brunette again. It would be lovely to at least *talk* to somebody, though. Sadly, getting in the middle of something like the two women at the table wasn't on her list of things to do today.

Resigned, she sipped again, feeling the zap of the bourbon as it warmed its way down her throat and settled in her stomach. And lower. It was one of the reasons she loved bourbon. It settled far south, created a comfortable, subtle buzz between her legs.

Aaaand here he comes. As she knew he would, the guy who'd sent the drink was making his way around the bar.

"Hi there," he said, sidling up next to her and holding out his hand. "Eddie."

"Hi, Eddie." She shook it, making sure to do so firmly, like her mother taught her. Something useful for business, as was typical of her mother. "Sabrina."

"Sabrina. I like that."

She had to force herself not to roll her eyes. Which she felt bad about because Eddie wasn't doing anything wrong. Truth was, she was tired, she was bummed about the brunette, and she didn't have the energy to play nice with this guy who had no idea how wrong the tree he was barking up was.

And then something surprising happened.

A tall, gorgeous woman came into the bar, crossed to the two-top table, and kissed the blonde on the mouth. Then she pecked the brunette on the cheek and stood next to the blonde's chair with her arm around her as the three of them talked.

Well, well, well, isn't that an interesting turn of events?

"I haven't seen you here before," Eddie said, yanking her attention back to him.

"No, you haven't." She didn't offer any details, which she knew was rude, but seriously, why let him waste his time? "Listen, Eddie, thanks for the drink," she said, doing her best to be polite, but not inviting. "I really appreciate it, but—"

He sighed, crestfallen. "You're married. Have a boyfriend. Both."

She laughed softly—she couldn't help it. "I'm sorry," was all she said, because outing herself to strange men wasn't something she did if it was possible to avoid it.

He shrugged and gave her a boyish grin. "Can't blame a guy for trying, right?"

"Not at all. And seriously"—she held up her drink—"thank you."

He nodded once, then turned and headed back to his side of the bar. As she followed his retreat, her gaze was snagged by the table of women.

All three of them were looking her way.

She swallowed hard. Her heart began to pound in that anticipatory way it does when somebody you find attractive notices you. Her lower body tightened deliciously as she wet her lips, then pulled her gaze away and sipped her bourbon.

Allowing herself only surreptitious glances for the next few moments, she almost jumped up and cheered out loud when the blonde and her girlfriend said their good-byes to the brunette and headed for the door. Sabrina gave it another moment. Two. Waited to see if the brunette was in a hurry to leave, but she didn't seem to be. She signaled the bartender.

"That woman over there by herself, what's she been drinking?"

"Pinot grigio," the bartender told her.

With a nod, Sabrina ordered a glass.

❖

Adley Purcell worked too much.

Her best friend Scottie told her so all the time, and she had known her since they were kids, so if Scottie said she worked too much, Scottie was probably right. She worked too much—she needed to get out, find a hobby, meet other people, get laid for God's sake, maybe even find that special someone. Easy for Scottie to say. She'd met Marisa almost a year ago and had been floating on a cloud ever since. While Adley wasn't against cloud floating—seriously, who would be?—she just didn't have the energy to go looking.

Which was why it was so weird when the blonde at the bar who had caught Adley's eye the second she walked in—the blonde that both Scottie and Marisa had noticed and pointed out to her—approached her table with a half-drunk glass of what looked like whiskey in one hand and a full glass of white wine in the other.

"Hi," the blonde said, and holy shit, she was even more beautiful up close. Small, but with big energy. Adley could feel that right away. The bluest eyes she'd ever seen and just the barest hint of dimples when she smiled at her. "I'm afraid I'm about to be really presumptuous, but I haven't been able to take my eyes off you since I got here. You're gorgeous. And I brought you wine." She set the glass in front of Adley and waited.

Adley knew she was blushing. She could feel the heat in her face, her ears. She swallowed down the ball of nerves that had taken up residence in her throat. "I mean, if you brought wine, you already get points." She indicated the other chair. "Please. Sit." She reached for the wine, took a sip. It was exactly what she'd been drinking. "Thank you for this."

"You're welcome." The blonde held her hand across the table. "Sabrina."

"Adley." Adley took her hand. It was warm and soft, her shake firm, confident.

"It's nice to meet you, Adley." Sabrina held up her glass. "Cheers."

Adley touched her wine to the rocks glass in Sabrina's hand and felt snared by her gaze. "Your eyes are *so* blue." *Oh my God, did I say that out loud?* She gave her head a quick shake and closed her own eyes for a second. This woman had her off balance in a big way. Not something she was used to.

"Well, you have incredible hair."

There was a beat of quiet, and then they both burst into laughter, which eased the tension considerably, thank fucking God, but did nothing to quiet the buzz of sexual energy that so clearly ran between them like an electric current. "You know, it's weird," Adley began, completely aware that she was about to say things to Sabrina Whose Last Name She Didn't Even Know that she probably shouldn't. Things she'd never said to anybody. Because she'd never been in this situation. "I am not somebody who picks people up in bars. I don't even hit on them. But you…" She tipped her head and studied Sabrina, who was watching her closely, a small smile playing at her full lips. "I don't know what it is. I want…I want to…"

"So do I." The small smile grew, and Sabrina stood up. "Come with me," she said, holding out her hand.

And the absurd thing was Adley didn't even hesitate. She slid off her chair, put her hand in Sabrina's, and let herself be led. Past the bar and the poor schmuck who'd tried to pick up Sabrina as Adley had watched. Past the end of the bar and through the back hallway to the ladies' room. It was a Wednesday, and maybe that's why the bar wasn't terribly busy, but there was nobody else in the ladies' room—though Adley wondered if that even would've mattered. Sabrina spun around and stepped toward Adley until her back hit the door, and then they were close, so close. Sabrina's eyes had a dark ring around the blue— she could see that now. Her lashes were thick and dark, her brows a bit lighter, her hair lighter still. And her lips…God, her lips. Full and pink and shiny and—

And then there was a kiss.

Oh, dear sweet Jesus on a unicycle, what a kiss.

It started slow. Soft. Not tentative, but not demanding. Not yet. Sabrina was slightly shorter than Adley. She tasted like bourbon, strong and a little sweet, and Adley's hand was in her hair before she even knew she was lifting it. Silky hair, thicker than expected, and Adley grasped the back of Sabrina's neck and pulled her closer and that's when *demanding* entered the chat. Sabrina pushed her tongue into Adley's mouth, and Adley welcomed it, brought up the other hand, selfishly pulling Sabrina in as far as she could, and they played that delicious game of push-pull, of give-and-take, of top and bottom.

Adley was instantly wet, everything south of her waistband tightening, and God, when was the last time she'd been this turned-on this fast? Ever? Had that ever happened? She wasn't sure she believed in love at first sight, but she certainly believed in *lust* at first sight because that had happened tonight, just now, and she was living it.

Everything faded into the background. Her job, her job worries, what Scottie would think, the rest of the bar—everything softened into a blur, and the only thing that stood out in sharp relief was Sabrina. Her body against Adley's. Her tongue doing things to Adley's mouth that made her feel like her knees were about to give out. Her hands… God, her hands were everywhere, strong and sure, and what if Adley just melted? Just gave in and became a big puddle of nothing but sexual bliss? Could she do that? Because holy mother of dragons, she wanted to.

How long did they make out? Yeah, *make out* was the right choice of words. They had blown right past *kissing* and shot straight to *making out*. Like teenagers. It was ridiculous. This was ridiculous, but so, so good. Had Sabrina been kissing her all her life? Oh my God, had they been together in another life? Adley had a friend who believed in that sort of thing, and after this, Adley might believe in it too because how was it possible for a stranger to know her body so well? Thank God they were standing up and making out in a bathroom because if they'd been in bed, Adley might never let this woman leave. Like, ever.

With no idea how much time had passed, Adley slowly pulled her head back and looked into those blue eyes. They'd gone dark and hooded, Sabrina's ragged breathing matching her own.

"Hi," Adley whispered.

"Hey there," Sabrina said back, her face barely two inches from Adley's.

"So, yeah, um, I don't do this." Wow, could she say something sadder? Yikes. She closed her eyes. "Oh, that was pathetic."

To her credit, Sabrina laughed softly. "Not at all, because I was going to say the same thing." She toyed with the collar on Adley's shirt, ran her fingertip across her collarbone, back and forth. "I'm only in town temporarily, so…"

Well, that figured. Not that Adley was surprised. She wasn't somebody that was well acquainted with good luck. "Ah, I see." She cleared her throat and did her best to find some bravado she didn't feel. "I mean, I'm super busy and don't have a ton of time anyway…" She shrugged. Actually shrugged.

Sabrina tipped her head to the side, and it was weird that Adley had just met her but could already read her face, could already tell she had an idea. "What if…" Her gaze moved from Adley's collarbones up to the ceiling. "God, this is nuts." She blew out a breath. "But I'm just gonna say it. Fuck it. I'm gonna say it. What if we did this every so often? My job is out of control. Intense. Stressful. And sometimes…"

"You just want to blow off some steam with no strings attached." Adley said the words without even thinking about them.

"Yes! With somebody who's not tied to my job and doesn't know a thing about it."

"I so get that." And she did. While she'd never thought about it exactly, it was an idea she could totally get behind. "It could be a drink. It could be a walk." She swallowed. "It could be a make-out session in the bathroom of a bar."

"I mean, it could be a make-out session just about anywhere," Sabrina whispered, and then her mouth was on Adley's again, and all Adley's thoughts flew right out of her head.

CHAPTER TWO

A re you kidding me?" Scottie shouted, eyes wide with clear disbelief as she sat on a stool at the stainless steel back counter of Adley's ice cream shop, Get the Scoop. It was late on Thursday morning, and she'd stopped by to say hi on her way to work at the salon she owned with her two friends.

"I'm not. We exchanged numbers and will periodically let each other know where the other is if we need some"—Adley grinned and gave her shoulders a little shimmy as she said the next words— "recreational activity."

"Sex?" Scottie whisper-hissed the word, which only made Adley laugh because there was nobody else in the shop.

"I mean, maybe? Who knows? And what if we do that? It's the twenty-first century, Scooter."

"No strings, huh?"

"No strings. She's only here in town temporarily anyway."

"But..." Scottie dipped her spoon in the bowl of fresh vanilla bean ice cream Adley'd just made. "Don't you want strings?"

Adley held out her arms, indicating the whole of the shop. "When do I have time to date? It's almost May. Busy season is coming. And I'm scrambling to keep my business afloat in this shitstorm of an economy. Things aren't good. Fucking Sweet Heaven is opening a new shop not two blocks from here. I haven't got the time, let alone the energy, to give to somebody else. You know?"

"But some making out here and there..."

"*That* I have time for. Listen, I've got needs."

"Well, I *did* see her, and she *is* astonishingly good-looking, so I'd probably make time for that, too."

"So gorgeous," Adley said, and then, as it had so many times since the bar last night, her brain carried her away on a floating raft of sense memories…Sabrina's mouth on hers, her hands in Sabrina's hair, tangling her fingers in it, their bodies pressed together hotly…

"Earth to Ad," Scottie was saying with a laugh. "Man, you've got it bad. Your face is red. Are you all hot now?"

"It's been almost two years for me, Scoot. I'm always hot."

Scottie's eyes widened a bit. "Has it been that long?"

Adley nodded.

"And there hasn't been anybody since?"

Adley shook her head.

"Not even to make out with in a ladies' room?" Scottie rolled her lips in and bit down on them to stifle a smile.

"No!" Adley laughed through her own disbelief. "I have never in my life done that, made out with somebody I met five minutes before. What is wrong with me?"

Scottie was laughing openly now. "What happened to *It's the twenty-first century, Scooter?*"

"That was me, faking nonchalance! It's ridiculous! It's *so ridiculous!*" She was laughing but also still kind of flabbergasted at the whole thing. "What the hell is happening to me?"

Scottie smiled at her, that warm, gentle smile she had that made Adley feel loved. "Sweetheart, I think what's happening is that you're taking care of you. There's nothing wrong with that." She ate the last of her ice cream and took her dish to the big industrial sink. "If you and she have an understanding, then who am I to judge? Who is anybody to judge, right?" She rinsed her bowl, set it in the dishwasher, and turned to face Adley. "I just want you to be happy."

Adley knew she was telling the truth. They'd known each other since they were in school. Scottie was the twin sister Adley'd never had. "I know."

"So if sucking face in random public places with the devastatingly sexy woman from out of town you just met makes you happy, you have my full support." Scottie grinned and pulled her into a hug before Adley could playfully slap at her. "Okay, gotta go cut the hair of the world," she said, grabbing a handful of Adley's and examining it. "You're overdue, by the way. Stop by Saturday, and I'll trim your ends."

"Yes, ma'am."

"Thanks for the ice cream. The vanilla bean is still one of your best. Simple and delicious." And she was out the back door and gone.

The quiet settled over the shop then. It was early in the season, and they didn't open until midafternoon, so this was the time she loved. Nobody there but her, in a place she'd loved so much as a kid.

Get the Scoop was opened by her grandfather in the early eighties, one of only three places in Northwood at the time where you could get ice cream. Cones, sundaes, sandwiches. Her grandfather wasn't the most creative—his menu consisted of the basics—but he grew a following. And Adley had practically grown up in the shop, coming in after school, working there before she had even reached a double-digit age. But scooping ice cream wasn't what fascinated her. It was the *creation*. So when her grandfather started to give her some leeway to make new and unique flavors, teenage Adley ran with it. She learned to blend flavors, to churn in more or less air for a lighter or more dense ice cream. She went to college and earned herself a business degree with a minor in culinary arts so she could understand the chemistry and creation behind ice cream. And when her grandfather decided to retire and sell the shop because Adley's parents weren't interested, she begged and pleaded and got herself a small business loan and bought it from him, changing it into an *artisan* ice cream shop.

People loved her ice cream. They did. They talked about it. They waited in line. But what Adley hadn't counted on were things like convenience, expense, desire for tradition. Ice cream was for kids, or so the world would have her think. And kids didn't want a honey ice cream called Baby Bear or mango pineapple with coconut called Tropical Dream. They wanted chocolate or vanilla or a swirl, dipped in a candy shell or covered with sprinkles. She had those things, yes, but some parents didn't want to wait in line behind the senior couple or the young newlyweds who wanted to take their time tasting different flavors before deciding. So they'd head over to Skippy's, a place that had soft serve in exactly three flavors. That wasn't ice cream, as far as Adley was concerned. Ice cream had to be scooped by hand, out of the big tub it was just put in a few hours before when it was made.

She sighed. Loudly, so it echoed through the empty shop. Then she mixed the batter for the waffle cones she made by hand right here on the premises every couple of days. The smell alone was heavenly, warm and inviting. Somebody should bottle it, make it into a lotion, she always thought. And people loved those cones. Get the Scoop did have a very loyal following. Tons of great Yelp reviews. There'd been a local news story on it. But the economy wasn't great, and people didn't have the extra money to spend on expensive ice cream so much right now. She had a meeting scheduled with her CPA next week to see how bad it was.

She didn't like to think about it.

So she wouldn't. Not today. Instead, she shifted her train of thought and turned it to the super hot and super sexy Sabrina and all the super hot and super sexy things they did to each other last night.

Oh yeah, that was way, *way* better…

❖

Sabrina had gone back and forth a million times already today. Last night: Crazy hot and sexy fun? Or the dumbest thing she could've done on her first night in a new town?

Back and forth. Back and forth.

But, wow, Adley was simply intoxicating. It was the best word she could find. She'd literally felt a little drunk around her. A little tipsy. Slightly off balance, but in the best of ways. It had been years since she'd been that attracted to a woman. Actual *years*. Surprising, completely unexpected, and—if she was being honest—invigorating.

"And temporary," she said quietly to herself. "Let's not forget that part."

She didn't have to be anywhere today until two, so she took her time getting up and ready. She was in temporary housing arranged by the company, a small Airbnb just on the edge of the city's most popular area, Jefferson Square. A city girl at heart, she generally preferred to be in an apartment of some kind, but this place was different. There was something about the neighborhood…the quiet, the nice yards, the close proximity to everywhere she'd need to be. She'd actually walked to and from the bar last night. Yeah, she liked it here. She could expense a standard four-door rental car, but she always upgraded it. If she had to continually drive around to learn a new city, she could at least do so in luxury. Her baby-blue BMW was parked in the driveway, and she glanced out the window at it, then blew it a kiss.

"Good morning, beautiful," she said.

The house was nice, a one-story ranch with two bedrooms and a huge fireplace in the living room. Sad that she wouldn't need it, being here during the late spring and summer months. By the time it got cool enough for her to want that kind of heat, she'd be off to the next city. But it was pretty to look at.

Showered and dressed, she took her second cup of coffee out onto the small open porch and sat in the white rocking chair with the striped cushion. A young couple walked by with a golden retriever on a leash and waved to her. She sighed inwardly as she waved back, wishing she could get a dog. She'd always wanted one. Never had one. Maybe one day, when she didn't travel so much. If she didn't travel so much. She never thought of herself as a person who wanted roots, but not having any for so long was starting to wear on her.

Her phone pinged from the small table next to her and she picked it up—Bryce Carter, coworker and asshole of the highest order, letting her know where to be and when for their first meeting. As if she didn't already have this information. As if she didn't already check directions and drive to the meeting location yesterday to make sure. Bryce Carter, king of mansplaining. You'd think her influence with the president of the company would be worth more when she told them Bryce was a misogynistic jerk, but instead of being reprimanded, he was promoted.

"Yeah, yeah, yeah," she muttered, even as she typed a return message that was much more polite. Then she scrolled through her texts and saw the one from Adley. They'd exchanged numbers last night, and she'd sent an emoji with heart eyes when they did so. It made her smile.

Adley.

Sabrina wanted to know everything about her and also nothing. Nothing at all. Nothing was safer, wasn't it? She couldn't get tied down, didn't have time for that, not to mention she never stayed in one place for more than a couple months. Long enough to scope out the city, do research, oversee the construction and grand opening of the store, and then she'd be off to the next one. That was the rhythm of her life, and getting to know somebody like Adley just didn't fit.

But spending a little bit of time with her here and there, maybe making out some more, maybe spending a night together? That did fit. That fit perfectly. And it was hard to find somebody who was in a position in life where the same thing worked for her. So the last thing Sabrina wanted to do was squander an opportunity. She opened a new text.

Probably a late night for me, but I'm sure I'll need a cocktail after. If you're around, I'll be back at Martini's around nine...

There. Open-ended. A little vague. Not so much an invitation as a report of the weather. A *Here's where I'll be* and nothing more. No expectations. No demands.

She read it over once, twice, corrected a typo, then sent it before she completely lost her mind.

Pushing herself to her feet with a sigh, she knew it was time to get moving. She downed the last of her coffee and took the mug inside to change from her joggers and hoodie to the black pinstriped business suit hanging from the closet door in her bedroom. It was time to get to work.

For the rest of the day, visions of the tall, gorgeous brunette with smiling eyes, soft lips, and a tiny dimple low on her left cheek filled Sabrina's mind, keeping her body tingling and her panties damp.

CHAPTER THREE

A dley couldn't go out two nights in a row.

Could she?

It was unheard of, for her anyway. First of all, Scottie's head would explode from the shock. She was always trying to get Adley to come out with her, and Adley was always finding reasons not to. Being tired was her most-used excuse, but it was rarely a lie. She worked hard, and she worked a lot. And by the time the shop closed at nine and she took care of the register and got things cleaned up and ready for the next day, it was usually after ten before she got home. Twelve-hour days or longer were regular for her.

Now it was nine fifteen, her employees were gone, and she was alone in the locked Get the Scoop, staring at what was left to clean up and wondering if anybody would care if she left it to deal with in the morning.

"I mean, I *am* the boss," she said out loud to the empty back room with a shrug. "The only person who'd care is actually me."

She held up both hands, palms to the ceiling, and pretended to be a scale. On one hand: cleaning up, having things sparkling the next morning. On the other: drinks with a beautiful and intriguing woman who kissed like nobody's business and had occupied more of her headspace all day than she cared to admit.

She dropped her hands and, with a shake of her head, took off her smock and grabbed her purse, muttering, "Scottie's gonna kill me."

So apparently, Thursday nights were pretty busy at Martini's. Who knew? It took Adley a good ten minutes of creeping along in her car before she found a parking spot. She checked her hair in the rearview mirror, regretting that she didn't go home to change into something a little more presentable than her jeans and deep green button-down top with the capped sleeves. But she knew if she'd gone home first, she likely would've chickened out and would now be in her pajamas in bed watching *American Ninja Warrior* or some other mindless show while she decompressed from her day, probably with a glass of wine. So she'd stayed in the same clothes, and here she was, in the parking lot of Martini's. She could get a glass of wine here, right?

"What am I doing?" she whispered to her reflection. And she thought about jamming the car into reverse and just leaving. Just going home. But something wouldn't let her. Before she even thought about it, she'd reached for the door handle and pulled it open. And then she was standing on the asphalt. And then her feet were moving. And then she was pulling on the door to Martini's. And then, even through all the people standing and talking or sitting at tables or walking across the room, she could see her. Sabrina. Sitting at the bar, rocks glass of amber liquid on its way to her lips just as their eyes met. The glass stopped, hovered. And Sabrina's face broke into a gorgeous smile that had Adley's knees going slightly weak. "Jesus Christ, what am I doing?" she muttered to herself. But that didn't stop her feet from carrying her right toward Sabrina.

"You made it," Sabrina said, and even though Adley didn't know her well, she did know that this gorgeous blonde was happy to see her.

"I did. I almost didn't. But I did."

"Saved you a seat," Sabrina said, indicating the barstool next to her. "What can I get you?"

Adley took the seat, hung her purse on the little hook under the bar, and made eye contact with Clea, the bartender she'd met once or twice through Scottie. "Sauvignon blanc, please." She inhaled quietly, let it out slowly, and willed herself to relax. The nerves had kicked in, the butterflies in her stomach morphing into fighter jets that felt like they were ramming into her internal organs. She turned to meet those big blue eyes, and then something strange happened. She relaxed. Everything in her eased. Her shoulders dropped, the tension in her jaw released, her hand stopped trembling. One look from this woman she didn't even know did that? What the fuck was actually happening? "How was your day?" she asked Sabrina as Clea slid the glass of wine in front of her. "Did you work? What do you do?"

Sabrina looked down into her glass and seemed to be contemplating something. After a moment, she met Adley's gaze, her eyes soft. "My job is stressful and—honestly?—doesn't bring me a ton of joy lately. How would you feel if I didn't talk about work?"

And something about that honesty wrapped itself around Adley and gave her a gentle squeeze. "You know what? My work is normally something I love but has been really stressful lately, too." She held up her wine. "To not talking about work."

"I will totally drink to that." Sabrina touched her glass to Adley's. They sipped, and could Sabrina feel the sexual tension that ran between them? Because Adley was pretty sure she could reach out and touch it.

"So, no work talk. Where are you from?" No work talk was fine, but Adley wanted to know everything else she could find out about this woman.

"Atlanta originally. If I had to consider someplace home, it would be Atlanta. But I travel a lot."

"For the work we're not talking about."

"Exactly."

Adley sipped. "Atlanta, huh? I might have to call you Peaches now."

Sabrina's soft laugh had a musical quality to it, like tinkling piano keys. Adley liked it. A lot. "My grandpa called me that. And so does my dad."

"And there go my points for originality." Adley let go of a dramatic sigh.

"You want to call somebody from Georgia *Peaches* and think you're due points for originality?"

"Valid." Adley grinned.

"What about you? Are you from here?"

A nod. "I'm a Northwood girl, born and raised."

"Siblings?"

"I have an older sister. Brody. She's an architect. My dad grew up here, and my mom moved here from the Philippines when she was just a toddler. What about you?"

"No siblings. Only child. My parents tried for years to have a baby with no luck so finally decided to adopt. They brought me home when my mom was forty and my dad was forty-five."

"Was it lonely? Being an only child? I've always wondered that. I mean, Brody and I would beat the snot out of each other when we were kids, but she was always there for me."

Sabrina seemed to think about the question. Adley watched her face, how her eyes shadowed as she seemed to go far away for a moment. Then she sipped her drink. "I guess maybe a little. The bonus was that, with no siblings, I got all the attention." She signaled to Clea for a refill.

Adley laughed quietly. "Yeah, I guess I can see that. I had to share everything with Brody. Even if she didn't really want to play with something I had, she'd pretend she wanted to just so I'd have to share."

"I did often wish I had a brother or sister, though. Those stories make me wonder what it would've been like, how different my life might be now."

They grew quiet, but it was a comfortable silence, not one Adley felt she needed to fill. She sipped her wine, and when she looked at Sabrina, Sabrina was looking at her. And they stayed like that, just holding eye contact, and that was another thing that surprised Adley— the prolonged eye contact didn't make her feel squirmy or like she needed to tear her gaze away, like it usually did. She simply sat there, wine in hand, and looked back at Sabrina. Her skin was flawless. Creamy. A little on the pale side, especially compared to Adley's year-round tan, as Scottie called her skin tone. Sabrina's eyebrows were expertly shaped, her eye makeup light but flattering.

"I think you're beautiful," she said softly, and the words were out and floating between them before Adley even registered that they'd been in her brain. And as she watched, two subtle splotches of pink blossomed on Sabrina's cheeks.

"Well," Sabrina said and then sipped her drink without looking at her, "thank you. And right back atcha." That's when she turned back to meet Adley's gaze. "Because, damn."

Adley laughed, then turned back to face the bar, her own smile plastered on her face. "Glad we got that established."

"Right?"

There was a moment of silence between them before Adley spoke again. "Seriously. What is happening? I don't understand it." Her words came out both light and heavy at the same time, even though that didn't seem possible.

"I think…" Sabrina wet her lips, and that alone did very sexy, sensual things to Adley. Sabrina seemed to gather her thoughts, then finally met Adley's gaze. "Here's what I think. We are two people who find each other super attractive, who are both very busy and very stressed, and maybe…maybe we just find the solace we need in this wild sexual chemistry we have. And maybe we don't need to analyze it any more than that." A beat went by, and she blinked and looked slightly mortified. "I realize that *so* sounds like I don't care to get to know you, I just want your body, and that's not at all what I'm saying, I—"

Adley stopped her with a hand on her knee. Because you know what? Sabrina was right. It was 2023, and if she wanted a sexual relationship with no strings attached, she was allowed to do that. Maybe instead of being horrified, Scottie would be impressed with her modern way of thinking. Because yeah. She could do this. More than that, she wanted to. For the first time in her life, no strings attached sounded downright *perfect*. "How long are you in town?"

"My next city is Denver, and that's…" Sabrina pulled out her phone and scrolled to her calendar. "Sometime in mid-August."

"Okay, so it's the end of April. That gives us all of May and June and likely most of July."

"Two and a half solid months. And change."

"I think we could have a lot of fun in two and a half months and change." Oh my God, who was she? Who was saying these things? But honestly, the more they hammered out what they were, the better Adley felt about it. And that was *so* not her.

"I think so, too." Sabrina said it so softly, with her eyes on Adley's mouth, and suddenly Adley hopped off her stool.

"I need to get home. It's getting late." She looked pointedly at Sabrina, who caught on immediately.

"Me, too." She signaled to Clea and closed out her tab like she was in a contest to do so as fast as possible.

Adley held out her hand, Sabrina took it, and together they left Martini's and walked quickly to the parking lot, which wasn't dark but was only dimly lit. Very bad for a woman walking to her car alone. Absolutely perfect for two people who were about to kiss like their lives depended on it.

And they did. Sabrina's back against her car, Adley pinning her there, bodies touching from breasts to thighs. Adley kissed her, softly at first, tentatively. Yes, they were ridiculously attracted to each other, but they didn't know each other's bodies. *Yet*, Adley thought as she explored Sabrina's mouth with her own—soft, warm, the slightly sweet nuttiness of the bourbon still lingering on Sabrina's tongue, and Adley wanted more. Hand in Sabrina's hair, she pulled her in closer—as if that was even possible—and pushed into her. One of them let out a whimpered sigh, and then hands were moving, stroking. Adley felt Sabrina's on her ass, even as she slipped her own under Sabrina's top, felt the heated softness of her stomach, her skin almost impossibly soft, and she wrenched her mouth away. Stood there, breathing raggedly, her forehead against Sabrina's.

"Holy shit," she said quietly.

"I was just going to say the same thing," Sabrina whispered on a grin. "You're sure you don't do this all the time?" Her voice was teasing, but there was a glint of seriousness in her eyes that Adley could see even in the low light.

"I promise." She toyed with a chunk of Sabrina's gorgeous hair, like silk between her fingers. "Listen, if one of us should be concerned about how common this might be, it's me. You're the one who travels from city to city. Maybe you have a girl in every port."

"I would be insulted if that wasn't a very valid point." Sabrina held her gaze and nibbled on her bottom lip for a second before saying, "I promise you, I don't do this. I don't have a girl in every port. I don't have a girl in *any* port. Mostly, I just go to a new city, keep my head down, and do my job."

"And I raised your head this time?"

"You so did." Sabrina caught her mouth again with hers, kissed her hard and deep, and Adley knew that it wouldn't be long before the kissing wasn't enough. But she kept that to herself.

For now.

CHAPTER FOUR

Sabrina always told herself she'd sleep in on weekends. Ever since she began as VP of new markets for Sweet Heaven, she'd promised herself she'd try. Here was the thing with her job—she had time between cities. The traveling, the shipping of her stuff, the setting up in her temporary new home. There was time off there for her to acclimate and settle in. But once work began, it was intense. Ten-, twelve-, fourteen-hour days sometimes. Paperwork and meetings and phone calls. And even though she didn't technically have to work on weekends, she often did. What else was she going to do alone in an unfamiliar city? She could explore, yes, and she would. She did. But first, she always promised herself she'd get some extra sleep on the weekends.

So when her eyes popped open at five fifty on Saturday morning, she groaned, rolled over, and pulled a pillow over her head. Yesterday had been a whirlwind. Fourteen hours of meetings and phone calls and email and more meetings. Zoom meetings and in-person meetings with fucking Bryce Carter. She lay there, staring at the ceiling. She really needed to learn to just accept him. Dealing with him was one thing, but he wasn't going anywhere, and they had to work fairly closely at times. She had to find a way to not clench her jaw the entire time they met about something. She'd crack a molar.

As she lay in the warmth of her bed, her thoughts drifted to Adley. She didn't even know her last name, but holy good God, did she have an effect on Sabrina. Yesterday had been too busy to see her, and honestly, that was okay. It was probably good because…well, because. Apparently, Adley had been busy, too, and Sabrina didn't ask with what. That wasn't what they were about.

What they were about was purely physical, and just like that, Sabrina was thrown back in time to Thursday night in the parking lot of Martini's. Pinned against her car by Adley, who was a little taller and a little broader in the shoulders, and Sabrina liked to think of herself as a big thing in a small package. A little bit of a top. Somebody who liked to take and have control. But letting Adley take the lead Thursday night, letting her trap Sabrina between her car and Adley's body? That was too many levels of hot for her to count.

The next thing she knew, she'd slipped her hand into her panties, totally surprised but not surprised at all to find herself very, very wet. Her entire body went tight in less than three minutes as her orgasm ripped through her, visions of Adley above her filling her head.

Even though she'd woken up early and gotten herself out of bed by six thirty, she allowed for a leisurely morning—coffee, scrambled eggs, then a walk around her neighborhood. It was bright and sunny, but still the tail end of April in upstate New York, so kind of chilly. She donned her super soft joggers and her favorite dark blue hoodie, piled her hair into a messy bun, and wandered the streets near her house. Nicely maintained homes, small but cozy. Not much in the way of flowers yet. A few crocuses or daffodils peeking their heads up, tiny pops of color in an otherwise somewhere-between-brown-and-green world. But the fresh air was heavenly, and she breathed it in, filled her lungs with it, let herself bask in the quiet sunshine of the crisp morning, nodding to a dog walker and his Cavalier King Charles spaniel. She liked this place, this Northwood, New York. It had charm. She'd been to… God, she'd lost count of how many cities she'd traveled to since she'd taken over the position four years ago. Ten? Fourteen? They kind of blurred together after a while, though Asheville was nice. But there was something about this current city. She was going to see more of it later today, and she was surprised to realize she was looking forward to it.

It was early afternoon when she left a little ice cream shop called Earl's. Not bad. Well, not bad, but not great. Very dated as far as decor went—scarred and scratched tables, foggy glass on the display case showing its age. The flavor choices were in tubs purchased from a well-known national ice cream supplier, which was fine. The selection wasn't bad, though the flavor she chose—chocolate almond—was slightly freezer burnt, and her cone was just this side of stale. The pricing was decent, and there were only a handful of patrons. She'd visit again next month when the season was closer.

In her car, she pulled out her phone and scrolled to the form she had there. She typed in her notes, her observations, her thoughts on the ice cream itself. When she finished, she typed the next address into her GPS, then chose a little Billie Eilish as her driving soundtrack and pulled out of the parking lot.

On to the next.

❖

It's not May yet.

Adley kept telling herself that, every day for the last three weeks when she did the books. Profits were abysmal. But it wasn't even May yet. It would be in a couple days. But not yet.

Saturdays were the exception to the bad business lately. Saturdays were busy. Her location probably helped. Get the Scoop was not far from Jefferson Square, a part of town known for its shops, bars, and restaurants. It was a bit of a walk, but you could do it if you were up for it. Adley could've walked to Martini's on Thursday night to meet Sabrina, but she'd chosen to drive because the walk would've taken a good fifteen minutes. And she was tired. And she was nervous. And driving helped her chill the fuck out.

Of course, that whole train of thought brought her to Sabrina.

Mother Mary on a trampoline, what was she doing?

She'd asked herself that same question about a hundred times since meeting Sabrina four days ago—oh my God, had it only been *four days*?—and she never had an acceptable answer, other than the one that made no sense. *Enjoying myself.* How had she lived for thirty-four years and never realized this was something she could do? That having a purely physical relationship—could it even be called a relationship?—with somebody she barely knew would bring her comfort and confidence and fill a void she hadn't even realized she had? How?

"Did I miss something?" Mandy asked. She was one of Adley's most reliable employees, the only one over thirty, and she had breezed into the back room of Get the Scoop in her pink logoed T-shirt and baseball hat. Now she was looking at Adley expectantly.

"I'm sorry. What?"

"You're shaking your head with a mysterious smile on your face." She pulled open the door to the walk-in freezer. "Just wondered what I missed." She disappeared inside, then came out carrying a large tub of freshly made chocolate almond ice cream. "All good?"

Adley didn't have to force a smile. It was already there, plastered on her face, the way it always seemed to be now whenever she flashed back on her time with Sabrina. She wondered if she was also blushing but was pretty sure Mandy'd call her out if she was. "Yeah. All good."

"Good." A nod toward the front. "Busy out there." She headed back up. A few years older than Adley, she was the only employee who wasn't college or high school age. Most of Adley's staff came and went with the seasons, but Mandy was a fixture. She wasn't full-time, but she was close, and Adley was thankful every day. Mandy was reliable and terrific at customer service, and she kept the younger employees in line. She also looked out for Adley, though Adley pretended she didn't know that and Mandy pretended she wasn't doing it. It had become a sweet friendship that was important to Adley.

Refocusing her attention, she turned back to the stuff she'd been working on before thoughts of Sabrina had crowded her mind. She poured batter into the waffle iron for cones, then turned to the bowls on the counter. She'd been experimenting with a new flavor. Peach cobbler ice cream. Gee, wonder where the idea to use peaches had come from. She shook her head, felt that unfamiliar feeling of happiness, and did her best to concentrate on work. When the waffle iron beeped, she removed the waffles and rolled them while they were still warm into cone shapes. God, was there anything better than that smell?

When the alarm on her phone went off over an hour later, she jumped, literally. She'd been so intent on mixing flavors and trying to get the right ratios. It wasn't quite right yet. Plenty of peaches, not enough cobbler taste. Plus, the texture was off. She put everything in the walk-in freezer, then met Mandy's eyes through the opening in the wall that looked out into the shop. She motioned to the back door, letting Mandy know she was leaving for a bit. Mandy shot her a thumbs-up and nodded, then went back to the customer she was helping.

Feeling confident things would be looked after, Adley took off her apron and hat and left through the back door. Once in her car, she headed toward the east side of town.

❖

Get the Scoop was much busier than Earl's, if the parking lot was any indication. And it was a bit of an odd blend of old and new.

Sabrina pulled her BMW into a spot and sat for a moment just looking. The building itself was clearly old, maybe from the seventies or eighties? The paint was chipping on the corners, the drainpipe was sagging a bit on the left, and the shape of the building itself screamed *I was built a good forty or fifty years ago!* But the sign seemed newer, more modern. And under *Get the Scoop* was *Artisan Ice Cream* in a pretty swirly font. And then under that, *small batches made by hand.*

"All right, Get the Scoop Artisan Ice Cream, let's see what you've got." She exited her car and headed for the door.

Once she got past the wondrously delicious smell of homemade waffle cones that floated on the air and made her mouth water instantly, she noticed an interesting mix of customers. Not just kids, as you'd expect at an ice cream shop. There were some, of course, but there were also couples, both young and old, and a handful of twentysomething girls at a corner table. A mix was good. A mix meant the product appealed to more than just one demographic.

Sabrina waited in line, scanning the menu on the wall, which was the most modern thing of all in the whole place, electronic and large. And easily altered, she knew. Good for changing flavors, prices, descriptions, all done with a few keystrokes. She really wanted to see the back room, see what kind of equipment they used to make their artisan ice cream. Oh well. She returned her focus to the flavors, which were interesting and unique, and she wanted to taste them all. Maybe she'd have to make a few trips.

The staff was made up of mostly young kids, college or high school aged. Typical for an ice cream shop that was seasonal. The redhead was older, maybe in her thirties, and Sabrina wondered if she was the owner. She seemed to be in charge.

"Hey, what do you guys think of the new Sweet Heaven going in?" the man in line ahead of her asked the redhead as she scooped his chocolate almond ice cream into a waffle cone.

The redhead didn't even look up as she lifted one shoulder in a half shrug, making Sabrina think she'd gotten this question a hundred times already. "It is what it is, right? We'll still be here. With our handmade, artisan ice cream." She stood up with the cone and handed it over with a smile.

"I hear their ice cream is manufactured in a big facility, then shipped." He wasn't wrong about that, Sabrina thought. "I bet it's not nearly as good as yours." He lifted his cone in a subtle salute and moved on down the line to pay.

When it came time to place her order, she asked for a kiddie size of three different flavors in dishes to go, and one small chocolate almond in a waffle cone because there was no way she wasn't getting one of those. It was a bit too busy in the shop for her to concentrate, so she took all her purchases out to her car to taste.

"Holy shit," she said as she chewed a bite of the waffle cone. It was sweet and decadent, with a hint of vanilla in the batter. The chocolate almond ice cream was dense and creamy, with the perfect blend of sweet chocolate and salty almonds. After a couple bites, she propped the cone in her drink holder and turned to the kiddie dishes. "Holy shit," she said again as she savored a spoonful of what was called Baby Bear. It was honey ice cream with pieces of doughnuts in it. Honey ice cream was tough. It could be cloying and overly sweet. But not this. This was super subtle, just a hint of honey. And the doughnut pieces were just the right size and texture. God. Fabulous. From there, she shifted to the bowl of Berry Blast. Pretty straightforward name, but there was nothing straightforward about the flavors. Vanilla ice cream—which, on its own, was creamy deliciousness with a complexity that vanilla rarely had—dotted with blueberries, blackberries, and raspberries. Not berry flavored, but actual berries. Some fresh. Some freeze-dried, which gave it some periodic crunch. Sabrina shook her head, trying to remember the last time she'd been not bored by ice cream. The third bowl was called Zingaling, and it was simply dark chocolate ice cream with cayenne. A third *holy shit* was muttered, and Sabrina let the flavors play on her tongue. The chocolate alone was complex, deep, dark, and almost mysterious. Then a zing of cayenne would come along and wake up her taste buds before fading into the background. Eating it was an experience.

After a bite or two of each flavor, she snapped the lids back on and returned to the waffle cone. And damn if she didn't sit there in her car and eat every last bite of it.

"Fucking delicious," she said quietly to the emptiness of her car as she wiped her mouth. Whoever made the ice cream here at Get the Scoop not only knew what they were doing but had a love for the stuff. It was clear in the depth of flavor in each one she'd tasted. Already planning to come back and try more, she started her car up and headed home. She wanted to make notes while it was all fresh in her mind. A new Sweet Heaven ice cream shop would most likely impact Earl's and not in a good way. But Get the Scoop was unique. It was hard to predict—Sweet Heaven was nationally known, a hot commodity—but maybe Get the Scoop would be spared.

She kind of hoped it was.

❖

"You're so much happier here." Adley said it while meeting Scottie's eyes in the mirror in front of her chair at Trio, the salon Scottie had recently opened with her good friends and fellow hairstylists, Sebastian and Demi. "It's so clear in everything, from the way you look cutting my hair to the way you move."

"Really? I mean, it's totally true, but I didn't realize it was obvious." Scottie had a comb in one hand and her scissors in the other and was trimming away Adley's split ends.

"Maybe it's because I know you so well, but…yeah. It's nice to see." The place was adorable, much smaller than Scottie's previous salon where she'd rented a chair from a woman she couldn't stand, along with about eight other stylists. This salon only had three chairs. The color scheme was black and white with some occasional pops of red or silver. Very sleek and modern, but somehow, it had a warm feeling to it. Modern could be cold, but Trio was inviting. "How's Marisa? And my favorite little boy, Jaden?"

At the mere mention of her girlfriend and girlfriend's kid, Scottie's entire demeanor went all soft and mushy. "They're great," she said, her smile wide.

"Oh my God, look at you," Adley said with a laugh. "You're all gooey." Then she pulled the teasing tone away and said softly, "I'm so glad you're happy, Scoot. You deserve it."

"Yeah? Well, so do you." Scottie stopped cutting and met Adley's gaze in the mirror again, then put her hands on Adley's shoulders and leaned closer. "You do."

"I know. One day…"

"Well, it's probably *not* gonna be the chick from the bar who's literally just passing through town, you know."

"I know that."

A squeeze of her shoulders. "Do you?"

Adley snorted a laugh. "Of course. I'm not stupid. This is just some fun. I'm having some fun. That's all."

Scottie held her gaze for an uncomfortably long time before giving one nod and going back to Adley's hair. "Okay. Good. I'm just checking. I know you and I know your heart, and I don't want you getting hurt by this woman because you have expectations she can't meet."

"I know. I've got my eyes wide open. This is just a bit of fun, which I also think I deserve. I work hard."

More nodding. "You do. I know it. I'm just looking out for my favorite best friend."

"Hey!" came Bash's voice from his station. "I heard that."

"Me, too," called Demi from her station. Both their clients sitting in their chairs laughed.

"Uh-oh," Adley said, grinning at Scottie. "You're in trouble now."

CHAPTER FIVE

A rtisan ice cream, huh? That's not something I expected to find in a city as small as Northwood, New York." Tilda James gave a little chuckle into the phone, and Sabrina could picture her, short silver hair perfect, tailored business suit, sitting behind her mahogany desk in her large office back in Atlanta.

"It's a really cute little place," Sabrina said. She was sitting in her rented house at the small dining room table, paperwork spread out all over it. "I tasted a few flavors. Really good. Lotta depth."

"Really." It was a statement, not a question. "Send the flavors to me, and I'll toss them over to innovations."

"I also visited a couple other places." Sabrina wanted to move the subject away from Get the Scoop, though she wasn't sure why. Something about the place…she just liked it. And most small ice cream businesses didn't survive the arrival of a Sweet Heaven. Her mother seemed to thrive on that fact, gain energy from it. Sabrina didn't, and she certainly wouldn't be sending the flavors to Sweet Heaven headquarters so they could copy them. But she didn't tell her mother that.

She filled her in on the four other places she'd visited yesterday. Poor Earl's didn't stand a chance. She'd known it as soon as she'd seen it. The phone call lasted another fifteen minutes, and then she finally got to hang up. God, talking to her mother could be stressful. You'd think she'd be used to it by now, but the tension hit her shoulders about three minutes in and didn't leave until well after the call had ended. Always. It had always been like that.

She sat there for a moment, talking herself into relaxing the way her father had taught her. Then she glanced at her watch. Ten fifteen on a Monday morning. Her father would be doing his rounds at the hospital in the palliative care unit. He'd long since retired from his nursing career, and now he volunteered at various hospitals in Atlanta, talking to terminally ill patients, listening to them, helping them make peace with their mortality. How he did it, she had no idea. He was a special man. She picked up her phone again.

"Well, hello there, Peaches." The nickname had nothing to do with Atlanta or Georgia at all, as she'd sort of implied to Adley. It was one he'd given her as a baby because she'd had barely any hair for her first year, just some peach fuzz on her head. His voice was warm and soothing, and Sabrina's shoulders instantly relaxed.

"Hi, Dad. Am I interrupting anything?"

"Nope. Just playing gin with Mr. Caldwell here." She heard the snap of a playing card.

"Is he kicking your ass?"

"He is *very soundly* kicking my ass."

She laughed, just the sound of his voice making her world feel better.

"How's things in…where the heck are you again?"

"Northwood," she said. "Upstate New York. Cute little city, actually."

"Just get off the phone with your mother?"

She blinked. "How did you know that?"

"You have that tone. The one you always get after you've talked with her. A combination of irritation and frustration with a little bit of sadness thrown in."

"Yeah. I'm sorry."

"Sweetheart, you have nothing to be sorry for. I'll take any opportunity to chat with my best girl. So, tell me all about this Northwood."

Sabrina made a mental note to make sure to call her father on other occasions besides just after she'd talked with her mother. She hadn't realized she'd been doing that, but it made sense. Her father was like a soothing balm spread on her skin after she'd been rubbed raw with sandpaper. Her mother being that sandpaper.

Which wasn't fair, really. Her mother wasn't a bad person and Sabrina loved her very much. But she could be…cold. Stoic. Unfeeling.

All Sabrina had ever wanted in life was to get her mother's approval. And so often, it seemed almost elusive…

Giving her head a shake, she did her best to rid her brain of those thoughts. She didn't want to deal with them now, not when she had to head over to the new Sweet Heaven site. She was the boss here. Well, she and Bryce Carter. Why her mother had to send him, too, she wasn't sure, but she could either let it bug her endlessly or she could suck it up and do her job. She chose the latter. They were expecting her at the site by lunchtime, so once she finished talking to her father, she headed into her bedroom to change into something that wasn't joggers and a hoodie.

Dressing for a construction site-type location was always a little weird. She needed to dress the part of boss, but a suit would definitely be overkill, not to mention get ruined by construction dust and debris. She chose dark jeans, a white button-down top, and a burgundy jacket. She rolled the sleeves of the top around those of the jacket and pulled the collar out. Black ankle boots with a small heel completed the outfit. She pulled her hair back in a simple ponytail in case she had to don a hard hat. Some foremen were sticklers about that, as they should be.

She gave herself the once-over in the full-length mirror in her bedroom. A nod of approval later, she was about to turn away when Adley popped into her head. Again. That had been happening more than she cared to admit. Would she be up for seeing her on a Monday evening?

"There's only one way to find out." She pulled out her phone.

❖

Adley had promised herself she wouldn't bother giving Sweet Heaven any of her attention. At all. Nothing. Nada. Zip. Zilch. She'd go about her business, continue to make her ice cream and serve her customers, and Sweet Heaven? What Sweet Heaven?

Yet here she stood, on the sidewalk in front of the building with the enormous vinyl banner.

Coming Soon! Sweet Heaven Ice Cream and Dessert!

Probably a good thing it was too high for her to reach because she had the sudden, almost irresistible urge to rip it down.

The windows were covered, so she couldn't really see inside. Only light and shadows moving, so there were definitely people working in there. A glance up at the sign again and Adley was horrified to feel her eyes well up. This place could be the end of her business. The end of Get the Scoop. If it wasn't already struggling, maybe she'd be okay, but now? The way things were? She had that sinking feeling in the pit of her stomach when she knew something bad was on the horizon. She blew out a breath.

"Goddamn it." She said it quietly, only for herself, and then felt her phone buzz in the back pocket of her jeans. An incoming text. She pulled it out, looked, and just like that felt a hundred times better.

How do you feel about burgers and fries?

Adley smiled at the timing, how Sabrina seemed to show up just as she was wallowing, making her instantly pull herself out of it. She typed back.

We are bffs. Me, the burgers, and the fries. Very tight. She sent it and watched the dots bounce as Sabrina typed.

I hear there's a lake around here. Was thinking of inviting them to dinner there, at the shore.

"Seriously?" Adley stood there for a moment, surprised. *Have you been spying on me?*

What? No. Why? And then a wide-eyed emoji.

Turning back toward her car, she walked as she typed. *Because sitting in my car with a burger and fries and watching the water is one of my fave things to do...*

And then Sabrina sent three emoji with hearts around them. *In the spirit of our agreement, that's where I'll be. Just FYI.* And a wink.

Adley laughed softly through her nose. *Maybe I'll be there, too.*

Feeling considerably lighter on her feet, she got in her car and headed toward her own ice cream shop. Sitting at a red light near Jefferson Square, she looked around and was surprised when her eyes landed on a familiar tall, dark-haired woman in a blazer and jeans. Her big sister, Brody, clearly laughing. The door was being held for her by a handsome red-haired man, and Adley was just about to honk her horn to get her attention when the man bent down and kissed Brody. Square on the mouth. The red-haired man who was not her husband.

"Oh my God," she said aloud, her hand hovering in midair over her horn. Brody and the man went into the restaurant, the door closing behind them. A light honk sounded, the guy behind her letting her know the light had turned green. She swallowed hard and continued to the Scoop, wondering what the hell was going on.

❖

The evening was chilly. Overcast. Not rainy, not yet, anyway. All of this meant that the parking area Sabrina had chosen to sit and watch the water while she ate her burger was empty, save for her car. And then Adley's slid up alongside her on the right. Glancing at her through her driver's side window, Adley smiled softly, waved at her, and everything in Sabrina just...settled.

And then she was there. Adley. Opened the car door and slid inside and, without preamble, leaned over and kissed Sabrina on the mouth. Then she grabbed a fry and popped it into hers. "Hi."

"Taking your life into your hands there, stealing my fries," she teased.

"You wanna make out with me later. I'm not worried." Adley grinned at her.

Sabrina laughed and reached into the back seat. "You're not wrong. Here." She handed over a second bag containing a burger and fries. "As ordered. Lettuce, tomato, mustard, no pickles, you weirdo."

"Listen, I love pickles." Adley took the bag and hauled out her own fries. "Just not on my burger."

"I'll say it again—weirdo." She gestured to the center console where two large sodas sat. "Drinks are here."

Adley unwrapped her burger and took a bite, then hummed in what sounded like relief and fell back against the seat as she chewed. "Thank you so much for this. It's perfect. I really needed it."

"Bad day?"

Adley hesitated for a second or two, staring out the windshield at the water before answering. "Kinda? Not work stuff, though." She turned her head against the headrest so she faced Sabrina. "Can I talk to you about it if it's not work stuff?"

"Of course." It was odd, their no work rule, right? But being near Adley, Sabrina just wanted to be somebody else. Somebody other than who she was from day to day. And right now? She wanted to hear all about whatever was causing that cute little divot of worry between Adley's dark eyebrows.

"So, I'm sitting at a stoplight today on my way to work—which I'm not talking to you about." She winked and popped a french fry into her mouth. "And I look toward this cute little restaurant and see my sister, Brody, laughing and clearly happy, heading into a restaurant, the door being held for her by some guy."

Sabrina nodded. She was watching Adley's mouth as she talked. She couldn't help it. Those full lips…goddamn. She gave herself a mental shake. "Okay."

"And I'm thinking she's having lunch with a coworker. Or a client. She's an architect."

She nodded again, watching the passion and emotion build in Adley's face. In her body, the way she moved her hands as she spoke.

"But then he kissed her. Like, *kissed her*-kissed her. On the mouth." Adley's gaze met hers. "But he wasn't her husband."

Sabrina flinched. "Oh. Wow. I didn't see that coming."

"Yeah, neither did I."

"Yikes." Sabrina took a sip of her soda. "Did she see you?"

Adley shook her head and held her finger and thumb scant millimeters apart. "I was this close to honking my horn at her, but when the guy kissed her, I just froze."

"I bet." Silence reigned in the car for a beat or two. "You gonna say something to her?"

Adley sighed, ate the last bite of her burger, then shrugged. "I honestly don't know. Should I? I mean, I should, right?"

Sabrina inhaled and crumpled up the wrapper from her burger. She put it in the bag and held it open for Adley to deposit hers. "What's her marriage like?"

"I mean…" Adley stopped and seemed to really think about the question. Outside, the sky grew grayer, impending rain approaching over the lake. "It's not something I ever really thought about. Nathan—her husband—is nice enough. I wouldn't call him warm and fuzzy, but he's nice enough."

"Look, I don't know your sister or her husband. Or you, all that well." She grinned and Adley gave a small chuckle. "But I do know that nobody really knows what goes on behind the closed doors of others. I can't begin to understand the marriages of some people. My dad is the sweetest man on the planet. He loves everybody. He was a nurse. Now he volunteers at a hospital helping dying patients. He's just the kindest, gentlest man I've ever known. My mother? The exact opposite. She's the head of a large corporation, and she's very successful. She's also cold and driven, and I'm surprised she ever agreed to be a mother."

"Wow," Adley said, her eyes wide, and Sabrina realized she really should dial it back a bit.

"Okay, that's *maybe* a little harsh. She loves me. I know she does. But I think they adopted me because my dad wanted a kid."

"You're close to your dad?"

"Very." A splat of rain hit the windshield, followed by another and another. "All this to say that maybe you don't know what's happening with your sister's marriage. And maybe she could use somebody to talk to."

"So your vote is yes, I should say something to her." Adley chewed a fry thoughtfully. "I think I should, too."

"Yeah?"

"I just needed somebody else to give me a nudge." Adley met her gaze and held it.

"I get that."

They were quiet as the rain increased, and then the sky opened up, dropping buckets. The car became rhythmic, and Sabrina felt somehow safe and protected, ensconced inside with Adley next to her, the scent of french fries still prevalent in the air.

"Why do you think your mom didn't want kids?" Adley asked softly. It was growing darker by the minute, deep gray clouds rolling in off the lake, but Adley's eyes somehow stood out as she focused on Sabrina.

Sabrina inhaled and let it out slowly. "I heard her talking once. To her secretary. I'd stopped by after school to say hi, and she didn't know I was there. I had a basketball game that night, and I wanted to remind her, make sure she was coming." She swallowed, the memory stinging her more than she'd expected it to, though she wasn't sure why. "And as I approached her office, I heard her secretary remind her of a meeting, but then tell her she couldn't run it too long because I had a game that night. And my mom sort of made this scoffing sound and then a groan like my game was the biggest hassle she'd have to deal with all day. Then she said—and I'll never forget it—*Do yourself a favor, Jeannie, don't have kids until you're over thirty and have a better handle on life. They are little energy vampires.*" She kept her eyes on the storm through the windshield and had to work really hard to keep her eyes from welling up. Why? She'd replayed those words in her head a thousand times in the twenty years that had passed since. Why were they affecting her so deeply now? And then she felt it. Adley's hand on her forearm.

"Oh, Sabrina, I'm so sorry. That's awful." And what Sabrina appreciated most—besides the physical touch, which she was starting to understand she craved more than she'd realized—was that Adley didn't try to make her feel better. She didn't make excuses for her mother, try to suggest she was having a bad day or something. Though maybe she had been. She just touched her arm, rubbed it softly, and sat with her. Several quiet moments went by before Adley spoke again. "I'm curious about something, though."

Sabrina turned to look at her, but Adley continued looking straight ahead. "What?"

Adley faced her, and there was a glimmer of something in her eyes that Sabrina couldn't quite make out in the dark. "How did somebody as short as you actually make the basketball team?"

A beat of silence went by as their gazes held before Sabrina gasped loudly. "How dare you?" She playfully took a swipe at Adley, who laughed and dodged away, and then they were grabbing at each other in the small front seat of the BMW. "I'll have you know I was scrappy and *very* fast."

"I bet you were. Tell me, how fast can we get into that back seat?"

And before she even realized she was doing it, Sabrina hauled herself between the front seats and plopped into the back in a matter of about four seconds.

"Wow," Adley said, eyes wide, clearly impressed. "You didn't even spill the drinks." Again, their gazes held, but there was something primal this time. Something raw.

"Get your hot little ass back here," Sabrina whispered, and then she watched Adley swallow, her eyes going impossibly darker.

"Yes, ma'am." But instead of crawling over the console, she popped her door open, then opened the back door, and launched herself onto Sabrina. Five seconds in the pouring rain had nearly soaked her, but Adley didn't seem to care and neither did Sabrina. In the next second, Adley's mouth was on hers, her tongue pushing in, kissing her hard and deep.

Yes...

In that moment, Sabrina realized this was what she'd been waiting for all day. This woman's body. This woman's mouth. This woman's hands. This woman.

This woman.

Chapter Six

B itch, where have you been?"
Teagan's voice was cheerfully teasing over the FaceTime screen, their smile wide, their hair high and not as perfect as usual, since it was early for them. Sabrina missed them so much it made her chest hurt.

"Where have *you* been?" she tossed back.

"Listen, I am *very* busy." Teagan winked at the phone—they were the only person Sabrina had ever met who could wink and not look like a dork doing it. She wished more than anything that Teagan was there in the room with her. "I kid. I've been working nonstop on that fuck—er—freaking nursery."

"Nice dodge on the profanity."

"You have no idea how hard it is, but I promised Kyra I'd try."

Sabrina laughed but stopped abruptly. "Wait…I thought you'd finished the nursery. Like, last month." Sabrina was making herself some eggs for breakfast before she had to go to the new site. The frying pan at her Airbnb was awesome, heavy and nonstick, and she made a mental note to jot down the brand and order herself one for home.

Teagan scoffed. "Yeah, so did I."

A knowing smile crept onto Sabrina's lips. "Kyra change the color again?"

"This is the *third* time, Bri. I may have to kill her if it happens again."

"Sadly, you can't kill her. She's carrying your child."

"A minor technicality. I could figure it out." They laughed and talked colors and how the nursery had gone from pale yellow to sage green to the current lavender gray that Teagan had just finished up this week.

"At least you've probably become really great at painting," Sabrina said. "Bright side?"

"There is that. I could probably hire myself out now. Start up my own painting business." Teagan had moved into the kitchen as they talked, and now Sabrina could see them pop a K-Cup into the Keurig and wait for it to brew. "Tell me what's up with you. Where are you now? Remind me."

"Northwood, New York. Upstate. It's a super cute little town. Work is fine. Same old same old. Fucking Bryce is here with me again, though."

Teagan groaned their frustration, and Sabrina again felt an amazing sense of gratitude for this person who had once been her partner and was now her dearest friend in the world. "I don't know why your mom finds it necessary to saddle you with him. Seriously, what's the deal?"

Sabrina shook her head as she slid her eggs onto a plate, then took the phone with her to the dining room and propped it against a fake plant that doubled as a centerpiece. She sat down to eat as she answered. "I don't know. It feels a lot like a babysitter."

"Or a spy," Teagan offered with an apologetic shrug.

"Or a spy."

"Tell me about this Northwood." Teagan also sat, sipped their coffee, and focused on the screen.

"As I said, it's super cute. Small, but not teeny. It's got a lake. I found a fun bar called Martini's. My Airbnb is nice." She shrugged as she forked some eggs into her mouth. "I haven't had a ton of time to wander and explore yet."

Teagan was staring at her through the phone. They were silent for a beat. For two. Three. Then they gasped and pointed a finger at the screen. "You met someone!"

Stupid fucking FaceTime.

"I hate you." Sabrina knew better than to try to deny it. Not to Teagan. She couldn't. Teagan would see right through her. They always did.

"You do not hate me. Now tell me. She hot?"

Sabrina laughed. "Right to the important stuff, I see."

"Absolutely. She hot?" Teagan repeated.

PEACHES AND CREAM

This time when Sabrina sighed, it was soft. Dreamy. "Ridiculously." She shook her head, lost in the memory of Adley in her back seat. "So ridiculously hot."

"How'd you meet her?" Teagan propped their elbows on the counter, their chin in their hands. "Tell me the story."

"I met her in a bar."

"Original."

"Ha."

"The aforementioned Martini's?"

Sabrina nodded.

"And?"

"And…I don't know." In that second, she knew she wasn't ready to talk about Adley. But she also *needed* to talk about Adley. Because there was most definitely something a little different here. Something.

"You don't know…what? I'm not following here. Talk to me like I'm a child."

"Like you're a child or like you act like a child. There's a difference."

"You're hilarious."

Sabrina laughed softly, then took a deep breath. "Okay. So, I meet this girl, Adley is her name, at a bar the first night I'm here. And I swear, Teag, the chemistry? Oh my God."

"Off the charts?"

"Off the charts. Like, the second I saw her, I was drawn to her. And I watched her with her friend—I actually thought she was with her until another girl came in and kissed the second girl. Then they left together, and Adley was alone at her table. So I bought a glass of wine and took it to her."

Teagan sprang up and comically spun in a circle, clearly shocked. "You did what?"

"I know! It was so unlike me. But I didn't hesitate. I just did it, and I took it over to her, and she invited me to sit. And, Teag, I swear to God, I've never been so physically attracted to somebody in my life. In. My. Life."

"Gee, thanks." But before Sabrina could backpedal, Teagan grinned through the phone. "I'm teasing you. So then what happened?"

"It was like serendipity. She complimented my eyes. I complimented her hair. And then…"

"And then what? *And then what?* You're killing me with this story, you know."

"And then we went into the ladies' room and made out."

Sabrina's blunt delivery had the intended effect because Teagan gasped loudly and then burst into hysterical laughter. "You did *not*."

"Oh, I most certainly did. And it was incredible. I…" She looked around the room as if the right words were hiding behind the couch or something. Then she shook her head and shrugged toward the phone. "I don't even understand it. Any of it."

"Any of it…wait. Has there been more? More making out?"

Sabrina sighed, knowing how this all was going to sound. "Okay, you can't judge me. I mean it."

Teagan's face grew serious. They looked directly through the screen at her. "Babe. No judgment. You know me. I don't judge."

That was a very true statement, and Sabrina nodded. "Okay. There have been two other times. We text when we're free. We don't talk about our jobs. I don't even know her last name. We were so weirdly on the same page with this. We both just wanted…" She shook her head, again struggling to find the right descriptions to explain to her best friend what was happening in her life right then.

"You both just want some release."

Sabrina blinked, then slowly began to nod. "Yeah, I think that's a good way of describing it. She seems to be as stressed as I am over her day-to-day, so we meet when we can, we talk a little, we have a make-out session, we go on our merry separate ways." Another shrug. Just to prove how very nonchalant it all was, right?

"Listen," Teagan said, their eyes boring into her through FaceTime, "all I want is for you to be happy. If this is helping with that, more power to you. Just…watch yourself, okay? I don't want you finding yourself in a place you didn't think you were. I don't want you getting hurt."

"Like I said, I don't even know her last name."

"Yet."

It was a fair response, and Sabrina nodded her understanding. "I promise to watch myself."

"Good. Now." Teagan sat back and propped their socked feet up onto the table. "Tell me about the new store."

"I'm going over there today to see how things are going." They spent the next half hour chatting about the new Sweet Heaven shop—the location, the few local ice cream shops she'd visited, especially Get the Scoop and its super creative flavor combinations. Kyra also made an appearance over Teagan's shoulder, kissing them on the cheek, then showing Sabrina her baby bump.

Sabrina had had that once with Teagan. That partnership. That loyalty. That camaraderie. But she hadn't been ready for it then.

What about now? Was she ready for it now?

❖

This was where Adley was happiest, alone in the kitchen of Get the Scoop, experimenting with new flavor combinations. Nothing thrilled her more than coming up with something that worked. Sometimes, it was subtle and lovely, coated her tongue, and gently made itself known. Sometimes, it exploded in her mouth like a symphony of tastes, blasting her with flavor. Either way worked, and she never knew which direction a new combination would go until she tried it.

Her speaker played soft tones of classical music. That was her choice today. She listened to everything, but her mood always dictated the style for the day. She was pretty sure it was Vivaldi playing right now as she chopped up some figs and then put them in hot water on the stove to cook them down into a chutney of sorts. What she was going to mix it into, she wasn't sure yet. Vanilla? Caramel? Apple? All three?

A sharp knock on the back door startled her, but only because she was so focused. Chuckling at herself, she went to push the door open, expecting Scottie for her very common before-work visit. She was surprised to see it wasn't Scottie, but Brody.

"Hey," her sister said, giving her a hug in the doorway, enveloping her with the woodsy scent of her perfume. "I hope I'm not bothering you. I had a little free time before a client meeting so thought I'd stop by and say hi."

"Not bothering me at all. Come in."

Brody walked past her in her work clothes. Black pantsuit, pumps, her dark hair up in a twist. She looked every bit the professional woman she was. She headed into the giant kitchen, complete with large stove, industrial dishwasher, ice cream churners, and a walk-in freezer. A big stainless steel table took up the center, and Brody's eyes roamed over all the ingredients and equipment spread over it. Then she lifted her head slightly and sniffed. "Oh, wow, that smells fantastic. Figs?"

Adley nodded. "Thinking about some fall flavors. Assuming I'm still open in three months."

"Still struggling?" Brody knew things had been rough financially, knew much more about it than their parents did.

Adley sighed. "Yeah. And there's a new Sweet Heaven shop going in over on Fox. They started prepping the building this week."

"But your ice cream is so much better." Brody set her purse down on the table and took a seat on a stool she pulled close. "Theirs is… artificial tasting. Boring. Factory-made."

Adley sat, too. "Yeah, but it's also cheap and convenient."

"I guess." Brody knew the score. She was the only one besides Scottie who understood how much Get the Scoop meant to her. Not even their parents seemed to get it. "Still." She grabbed a spoon and aimed it at the bowl of ice cream nearest Adley. "Can I?"

Adley nodded. "Go for it." It was just an experiment. "Vanilla with fig jam."

"Oh my God," Brody said, her fingers in front of her mouth. "That's fantastic."

"Yeah?"

"Like…Thanksgiving if Thanksgiving was just dessert."

"You don't think it's too bland? I was thinking I might add a little bit of cinnamon."

"Ooh, that might work."

Adley jotted notes on her phone, then looked up at her big sister, who was helping herself to another spoonful. She was happy, Brody was. She could tell. There was smiling, even when nothing was being said. And she seemed kind of light on her feet. It occurred to Adley then that she hadn't seen her like this in a long time. In fact, when was the last time she'd just popped into the Scoop unannounced, just to say hi?

Brody looked up and caught Adley watching her. "What?" She wiped at her mouth. "Do I have ice cream on my face?"

Adley shook her head. "How are you, B?"

Brody blinked at her, slight confusion clear on her face. "I'm fine. How are *you*?" She laughed softly, like she was pretending to understand a joke that eluded her.

"No, I mean really. How *are* you?" Adley set down everything and focused on her sister. "Really."

"I'm *fine*. I'm *great*. Really. Why?"

"Because I saw you."

Brody squinted at her and gave her head a small shake. "Saw me...what?"

"I saw you. With the redheaded guy. Monday. In Jefferson Square. He kissed you."

For the first time in her life, Adley understood what it meant when all the color drained from somebody's face. She watched it happen to her big sister, as if all her skin pigment was being sucked out of her body, leaving her pale and stunned. "I...um..." She stood up, swallowed audibly, turned away, then back, and it looked very much like the three or four spoons of ice cream she'd just eaten were threatening to make a reappearance.

Adley did her best to keep any judgment from her voice. "Talk to me. Are you unhappy? With Nathan?" She watched Brody's face flinch at the mention of her husband, and in only a few seconds, she went from animal-caught-in-headlights to complete defeat. Her shoulders slumped. The rest of her body sort of...fell. She dropped her chin to her chest and sighed.

"I haven't been happy with Nathan in a really long time, Ad. Not in a really, really long time. And Paul...he..." She raised her gaze to the ceiling, and Adley could see how her face seemed to light up, that happiness returning just in the few seconds her mind was on this Paul. "He *sees* me. You know what I mean?"

Adley shook her head slowly.

A deep breath. Brody sat back down, her forearms on the table. "Your partner's supposed to notice you," she began. "Pump you up when you need it. Make you feel special. Tell you whatever you need to hear at any given time. Right? That you're sexy. That you're a good person. That they love you, etcetera, etcetera. They're supposed to want to spend time with you. Do things with you. Ask you to do things with them. I've been married to Nathan for almost six years, and for about four of them, I've felt like I have a roommate."

This was news to Adley, and she found herself almost entranced by the words her sister was saying.

"He does his own thing with his own friends. We hardly spend any time together. He doesn't ask me about work. He hardly notices me anymore..." Her voice trailed off, and Adley knew by her sudden swallowing that she was close to tears. And seriously, how did somebody not notice Brody? She was gorgeous. Fun. Kind. Nathan was a lucky man, but if what Brody was telling her was true, he didn't know it. Or he knew it and just didn't care.

"So...what are you gonna do?" she asked, stirring the fig compote as it simmered on the stove.

Brody inhaled, then blew it out. "I don't know."

"Are you in love with this Paul?"

"I don't know that either."

Adley nodded. "Fair enough." She took the pot off the heat and set it on a different burner to cool. "Have you talked to Mom and Dad about it at all?"

Brody's snort was loud and almost comical. "So Mom can tell me I'm being selfish? No, thanks. I can do that all on my own."

Adley nodded, knowing she was right about their mom. "Is there something I can do to help you?"

"Tell me about you. Take my mind off this." Brody glanced at her watch. "I have about twenty minutes."

"Okay. So, I'm doing something weird," Adley said, then glanced over her shoulder to see Brody's reaction.

A tip of the head and a narrowing of the eyes, a small chuckle. "All right. What's weird?"

And she spilled. Like an overly full bucket of water, she just tipped a little and it all came pouring out. Meeting Sabrina, kissing her within the first fifteen minutes of talking to her, subsequent making out after that.

Brody sat quietly, but with her eyes wide and her mouth hanging open. When Adley finished talking, she simply said, "Holy shit."

Instead of feeling judged, it made Adley laugh. "I know, right?"

"Wow, Ad, this is *so* not you."

"Oh, I know it." She went back to stirring the fig compote—which didn't need any more stirring—just to give herself something to do with her hands.

"And no work talk?"

She shook her head. "We are both stressed by our jobs, and we joked that first night about not talking about them, and it's just...stuck. Which is kind of refreshing, if I'm being honest, because I worry enough during the time I'm here." She set the spoon down and met her sister's gaze. "It's kind of nice to set it aside in my free time, at least for a while."

"You know, I can see the benefit in that. Also, if her tongue is in your mouth, you can't do much talking anyway." Brody shot her a look and waggled her eyebrows, and that made her laugh, and she suddenly felt lighter, like Brody got it and it was safe to talk more.

"My God, Brodes, she is so fucking hot. I've never met somebody that can turn me on from across the room the way she does. It's nuts." She brought her fingers to her mouth and stared at her sister, slightly shocked that she'd admitted such a thing out loud.

Brody looked at her for what felt like a really long time before she said softly, "And you're okay with this...casual arrangement?" She took another bite of the ice cream, clearly over the possibility of getting sick, then watched Adley as she swallowed it. "Because I know you, little sister, and casual has never been your thing."

"Well. Maybe it is now." She lifted one shoulder. A half shrug. Yup, totally nonchalant. *Casual...see?*

Brody did not look convinced, but she held up a hand, palm forward. "Could be. Okay. I'm just looking out for you. You know that, right?" She waited for Adley to nod, then she gave her a tender smile and in a soft tone said, "I just don't want to see you get hurt, that's all."

Adley knew that. She did. Her sister was always on her side. From the time Brody was two and Adley was born, Brody had been her own personal protector. All through school, when she came out to their parents, the first time she had her heart broken, Brody was always there, arm around her, keeping the world at bay, and telling Adley everything was going to be okay. So it was no surprise that her situation with Sabrina concerned Brody.

"I know. I appreciate that." Another thought occurred to her. "And Jesus, please don't say anything to Mom and Dad."

Brody snorted a laugh. "And don't *you* say anything to Mom and Dad about *me*."

"The Purcell sisters, covering each other's asses for the past thirty-four years." Their gazes held for a moment before they both burst into laughter. "You know, for something wild and kind of secret, I've told both you and Scottie about Sabrina when I didn't actually intend to tell anybody."

"I haven't told a soul about Paul."

She decided telling Brody that she'd mentioned her dalliance with Paul to Sabrina probably wasn't the best course of action in that moment, and instead, she shifted the topic back to ice cream and business and stupid Sweet Heaven and their stupid new ice cream shop.

All the while, though, her brain kept tossing her images of big blue eyes and soft blond hair and the most amazing lips she'd ever kissed.

Yeah. Uh-oh was probably right.

❖

The afternoon picked up slightly. Again, Adley tried to remind herself that it was still kind of early in the season—not even technically summer yet—and she just needed to be patient. Business would pick up. That being said, she sent two of her employees home and took their place behind the counter. It was one thing she'd promised herself when she'd opened, that she would never be above getting behind the counter and scooping ice cream herself. Plus, it was good for people to see her face.

So it would be she and Mandy and one high school boy, Jeremy, until closing, and Mandy was on her break.

"It's my birthday," the little girl in line said as her turn came up.

"It is?" Adley asked. "How old are you today?"

The little girl struggled, then held up four fingers. "This many."

"Four? You're four? Wow, that's big. What kind of ice cream would you like to celebrate this very important birthday?" She lifted her gaze to meet the eyes of the man she assumed was the girl's father.

He looked down at the girl. "Final answer?" She nodded her head enthusiastically. He looked back up at Adley. "One banana split, please, with…" He gestured to the girl to go ahead.

"Strawberry, chocolate chip, and cake batter." She glanced up at the man, who raised his eyebrows in expectation. "Oh. Please."

"One banana split with strawberry, chocolate chip, and cake batter ice cream, coming right up. Go have a seat after you pay, and I'll bring it out to you." While Adley loved creating new flavors and new desserts, there was something comforting about making a classic. She scooped the three flavors into the boat-shaped bowl, split the banana, and drizzled her homemade chocolate sauce over it. Then she added a squirt of whipped cream—also homemade—on each scoop, added three maraschino cherries, and then stuck a candle in the center scoop. Mandy grinned over her shoulder as she returned from her break and sent Jeremy to his, and Adley lit the candle, then carefully brought it to the girl, singing "Happy Birthday." Mandy joined in from behind the counter, and it was only a couple seconds before most of the shop was singing. The little girl's grin was so wide, and she clapped her hands together when Adley set the dish in front of her, and then the whole place clapped when the song was finished and she'd blown out her candle. And the sheer joy on that little girl's face made every worry of Adley's vanish.

"Thank you so much," the father said quietly to Adley as the little girl dug in. "This means more than you know. She lost her mom about eight months ago, and this is her first birthday without her."

"Oh God, I'm so sorry." Adley brought her fingers to her lips, and her heart began a painful aching.

"I know she's only four and this probably isn't going to be super memorable years from now, but..." He shrugged and looked Adley in the eye. "It means more now than you know. Thank you."

She nodded and squatted down so she was eye level with the little girl, who already had whipped cream on her chin. "Good?"

The girl nodded, eyes big and wide.

"What's your name?" Adley asked.

"Madison."

"Well, Madison, my name is Adley and this is my shop. You come in anytime you want, okay?"

More nodding. "I wanna try all the flavors." Madison drew out the word *all* so it had about four syllables.

"I bet we could arrange that." She pushed herself to standing and ruffled Madison's blond hair. "Happy birthday, Madison." She returned to the counter to help Mandy, suddenly feeling lighter. Less stressed. Just...better.

The next person in line was a gentleman of about forty or so, with sandy hair, a bright orange tie, and way too much aftershave.

"Hi there. What can I get for you?"

"What's your policy on tasting? Like, sampling?" There was only one person in line behind him and Mandy was taking care of her, so Adley leaned her forearms on the top of the display case as she spoke.

"I'm happy to give you a little taste of anything you're interested in. Or we have our sample platter, which is three quarter-scoops of three flavors of your choice for two fifty. What do you like? Maybe I can help?"

And for the next nearly twenty minutes, she gave the man taste after taste. Sometimes, he let the bite roll around in his mouth and looked like he was thinking. Others, he'd ask her questions about ingredients, ratios, shelf life. Soon, there were a good eight or ten people in line behind him. Thank God, Jeremy came off his break to help Mandy.

Finally, the man asked if he could take a pint of Baby Bear to go, so she scooped it up and sent him on his way.

Mandy must've heard her relieved sigh, because she sidled up close and said quietly, "He reminded me of a guy that comes to my friend Lindsay's wine bar. She calls him Mr. Can I Taste That because he samples enough wine for free to fill an entire glass before he ever actually buys one."

Adley nodded. "I think he sampled enough for a medium two-scoop cone." Then she shrugged. "Ah, well. Nature of the business, right?"

By the time she closed up that night and got everything cleaned and put away, she was very nearly dead on her feet. So tired that not even the text from Sabrina asking if she wanted to meet for drinks was enough to entice her, and that said something.

Really want to, but soooooo tired, she texted back. *Rain check?*

The response came immediately. *I'll miss you but no worries. Next time. Sleep tight.* And a kissing emoji.

Her tired eyes focused on those first three words. *I'll miss you.* Would she? Would she actually miss Adley? It's not like they saw each other every day. And it's not like they were in a relationship, right? Well. Not an actual one. It was a relationship of convenience. Of need-filling. Perfectly acceptable. Totally allowed. And…maybe missing was allowed. Because if she was being honest with herself, she missed Sabrina, too.

CHAPTER SEVEN

That Sunday afternoon in June was gorgeous—not too warm, not too cool, sunny, a blue sky filled with puffy cotton ball clouds— the best kind of summer day to Adley. She didn't love high heat and humidity. Neither did she love super cold, with piles and piles of snow. But she could appreciate a day like this, especially after spending her entire day inside, scooping, selling, creating ice cream and ice cream desserts. There'd been a time when she wouldn't leave the shop before nine or ten on a summer night when they were open late, but over the past several months, Scottie had convinced her that it wouldn't matter if her business survived this downturn if she wasn't alive to care because she'd worked herself into the ground.

It was a valid point.

So, here she was, weirdly buzzing with a nervous energy that had become an almost regular thing for her with regard to her business, closing the door of her car and then walking toward the fenced-in dog park section of the larger Ridgecrest Park. She could see Scottie in the back corner, talking to another woman and watching as her new puppy, Blue, ran himself ragged with four other dogs. Another person came up behind Adley with a key card and held the gate open for her.

"Hey, Scooter," she said as she approached Scottie.

"You made it." Scottie's face showed genuine glee at the fact, which told Adley that a large part of her probably thought she'd blow her off.

"I did. How's the doggo?" She watched as Blue got rolled by a larger dog but got right back up and shook himself off, then jumped back into the fray.

"He's a maniac. I may have to bring him here a couple times a week to run off some of his puppy energy or he's gonna eat our house." The mix of worry and giddiness on her face really was kind of cute.

"Backyard's not doing the trick?" Adley asked, as the dogs tore past them in one furry blur of legs, heads, and flapping ears.

"I was just telling Grace here that he doesn't run like this when he's alone in our yard."

The woman standing next to her was pretty, with dark hair pulled back and a black T-shirt. She smiled at Adley and held out a hand to shake. Adley introduced herself, and Grace used her chin to point out a black and brown dog that looked like a large beagle mix of some kind. "Delilah's a little older, but holy crap, she becomes a puppy again when I bring her here." She watched for a minute, then asked Scottie, "So, you just started coming here?"

"We got him for our kid a few months ago, and he was just a love. Still is." Scottie followed Blue with her eyes as she spoke. "Now that he's six months old, I can almost see his energy levels written on his adorable furry face. Decided to give this park a try, even though I've heard many a dog park horror story."

Scottie and Grace kept talking, and Adley only partially listened. Her brain was too full, and her entire body was thrumming. Excess energy, worry for her business, guilt about standing in a dog park instead of behind the counter at her shop, desire to have a pet of her own, all of these things combined inside her to turn her into a big ball of nervous energy. Not a person who enjoyed jogging—or who had ever voluntarily jogged in her life, at all—she absently wondered if she needed to go for a run. Or take a hike. Or go mountain biking. Skateboarding? Should she drop in on a half-pipe? Would that level of adrenaline surge then calm her? Because seriously, she felt like a walking stick of dynamite whose fuse was burning precariously low.

As Scottie and Grace continued their in-depth discussion about the dogs they loved and the bowel movements of said dogs, Adley scanned the rest of the park, beyond the dog park's fencing. Two guys playing Frisbee. A couple on a blanket, a picnic basket between them. A woman on a bench under a tree, reading. Two women pushing a stroller. A man—hang on. She backed up to the woman reading under the tree. She squinted, then felt a surge of warm happiness. With a quick stroke down Scottie's arm, she said, "Be right back," and headed for the exit of the fencing.

Once outside the dog park, she glanced down at herself. She'd come right from the shop and hadn't had a chance to change. And hadn't really thought about it. It was just Scottie. It was just the dog park. But there was a chocolate ice cream spot on her jeans, and she had three rainbow sprinkles stuck to her left forearm. Brushing them away, she fixed her hair under her hat with the word *Scoop* on it—which she did not dare take off because she'd had it on all day and hat hair was a serious thing. She smoothed the ponytail sticking through the hat and hanging between her shoulder blades, straightened her white V-neck T-shirt that had stayed surprisingly clean under her apron, took a deep breath, and headed for the tree.

"I would never in a million years have pegged you for a true crime fan," she said when she got close enough for Sabrina to hear her. She was in lightly washed jeans and a black Henley with the sleeves pushed up to reveal her forearms and what looked like a fresh manicure, her nails a deep burgundy. And when she looked up from her book, the happiness to see Adley was so clearly written on her face that it nearly made Adley swoon right there in the grass where she stood. *Aaaaand I'm wet.* Bam. Just like that. Did Sabrina have any idea of the power she held?

"Oh, I am not just a fan. I'm a full-blown junkie. True crime books. Podcasts. *Dateline. 20/20.* Netflix documentaries. Give them all to me." Sabrina put her bookmark in her book and closed it. "What in the world are you doing here?" she asked as she scooted to make room on the bench.

Adley sat, feeling suddenly warm and relaxed and utterly turned-on, all at the same time. She gestured vaguely toward the dog park. "My friend is there with her dog and asked me to come by and say hi. I just happened to see you sitting here—with your I'm sure super relaxing, not-at-all stressful book—and thought I'd come say hello."

Sabrina laughed, a low, throaty sound that did nothing to alleviate that dampness between Adley's legs. "The anxiety is worth it when the bad guy gets caught and justice is done."

"What if justice is *not* done?"

"Then I usually throw the book across the room."

"Interesting," Adley said, and it was her turn to laugh.

Sabrina squinted across the park toward the dogs. "If I'm not mistaken, that's the same friend who was at the bar with you the night we met."

Adley nodded. "It is. Scottie. She's my BFF. We've been friends since we were kids."

"And the other woman who walked in that night and kissed her?"

"Marisa. Her girlfriend. Between you and me? I think Scottie's gonna propose soon."

"Really? That's awesome."

"Yeah, she's hinted here and there about how Marisa is The One, with a capital *T* and a capital *O*. So I'm just waiting." She gave a sigh that came out a little dreamy. "I'm so happy for her. She deserves to have somebody like that." She could feel Sabrina's eyes on her and worried she might've taken things over the line of *casual* right into the forest of *serious*. But what the hell? She was here—she might as well own it. She turned to Sabrina, who was still gazing off into the distance. "Do you ever think about that?"

"About what?" Those blue eyes turned to her, glanced up a bit as if looking at her hat, then back down to meet her gaze.

"Settling down. Being in one place with one person."

A half shrug. "Sure. Sometimes. I do get tired of traveling all the time."

Not exactly what she meant, but Adley didn't push. She just nodded, and then they sat in silence for a moment before Sabrina spoke again.

"Hey, do you have dinner plans?"

Adley made a show of thinking hard, tipping her head from one side to the other, tapping her lips with a fingertip, until Sabrina laughed softly. "I, in fact, do not have dinner plans."

"Wanna come to my place?" Her gaze held Adley's. Solid. Clear. Adley knew exactly what would happen if she said yes. Exactly.

So she didn't say it.

She nodded.

❖

Sabrina zipped around her house, cleaning like she was a human Roomba. It wasn't terribly messy, but she had crap lying around all over the place—papers, books, her laptop, a jacket here, a pair of socks there, three pairs of shoes in various rooms. She wasn't used to having company when she traveled for work, and Adley was going to be here in less than an hour.

Adley. What the hell was it about her?

She'd racked her brain since leaving the dog park, trying to figure out what it was about this woman that drew her so strongly. It was physical, yes. Definitely. Without a doubt. But it was more than that, and that was the scary part. Whenever she saw Adley, whatever setting or situation they were in, she just wanted more. More time. More conversation. She wanted to know more. She wanted to feel more. Like, literally feel. She wanted her hands on Adley, and she knew it, and she owned it, and she was no longer afraid of it. It just was.

Did Adley feel the same?

She was pretty sure she did. There was always something in her eyes. Those deep, dark eyes that were shockingly expressive. Sabrina was reasonably sure she could read Adley's mood in just about any case. Today, they said how happy Adley was to see her. And when Sabrina had invited her over for dinner, Adley's eyes said she knew exactly what Sabrina was suggesting, and she was in.

She'd never really had that. Well, maybe with Teagan. But they'd both known pretty early on that they were destined to be friends and not partners. But since then? No. She'd never felt so connected to another woman. Not like this. Not like Adley.

And yet, they'd mutually limited things to the physical. Because clearly they each had reasons to do so.

Maybe it was time to rethink that. To actually get to know each other on other levels. On every level. Maybe...

The doorbell rang, startling her enough to make her flinch, then chuckle at herself. She was nervous, she realized. A glance down to check her jeans, her royal-blue shirt that buttoned down the front. As she headed toward the door, she checked her hair in the mirror. Soft, wavy, down around her shoulders. She closed her hands into fists, then relaxed them, annoyed at herself for being so nervous, but also laughing about it.

"I am officially ridiculous," she whispered aloud before reaching for the doorknob and pulling the door open. The sight that greeted her stole her breath, just reached right into her lungs and took all the air. Adley wore dark jeans that could not possibly have fit her tall frame any more perfectly. Her short-sleeve top was a deep emerald green, which only served to accentuate the rich tan of her skin and the shiny waves of her dark hair, which was down completely for the first time since Sabrina had met her. Waves and waves of midnight that she wanted to dive into and swim through. She smelled like sugar and vanilla, and Sabrina inhaled quietly through her nose, taking it in.

"Hi," Adley said, then held out a bottle of wine to her. She leaned forward and kissed Sabrina softly on the lips before pulling back, saying softly, "You look gorgeous," and sidling past her and into the house. Sabrina stood there, bottle of wine in hand, and just watched her move.

"This is so cute," Adley said, standing in the middle of the living room and turning in a slow circle. "It's an Airbnb, you said?"

Sabrina shut the door and nodded. "Yeah. When I'm going to be in a city for a stretch of weeks, I usually get one instead of staying in a hotel. Feels a little more like a home, you know?"

"Totally." Adley wandered some more, peering in this room and that. The place wasn't that big, but she strolled along, and it wasn't until this had gone on for several moments that Sabrina realized maybe Adley was nervous, too. Sabrina let her wander, waited patiently.

"I think I'll open this," she said, holding up the bottle.

"Perfect." Adley followed her. "Are you cooking?" she asked as they entered the kitchen.

Sabrina snort-laughed, then waved an arm out to encompass the area that was clearly *not* being used to make a meal. "I thought we'd order in." And then she suddenly grew serious because what if Adley had expected her to cook? "Is that okay?"

"Of course it's okay," Adley said, crossing to her and wrapping her arms around her. "I'm a big fan of ordering in, too."

"Perfect," Sabrina said, using Adley's earlier word as she toyed with the hem of Adley's shirt. It was snug, hugged her torso softly, subtly putting her breasts on display. "I like this," she said, her voice husky.

"Yeah?" Adley pressed herself closer. "I like yours, too. Buttons. Buttons are sexy." Her fingers began toying with them.

"Are they? How come?"

"Because they tease. They hide what's underneath, but you can get a little peek if you want." With that, she unfastened one, then another, then pushed the sides of Sabrina's shirt apart just enough to bare more skin.

"I see. I didn't realize this." She swallowed hard as Adley's fingertips skittered across her flesh. Her body was suddenly on fire, her underwear instantly wet. God, how did Adley have such power over her?

"Now you know."

Sabrina nodded. Their lips were mere millimeters apart, but they didn't kiss. No, this was something else. This teasing. This playing. It was hot, God, so hot, and she was so turned-on, she worried she might burst into flames. Reaching around, she cupped Adley's ass with both hands and pulled so their bodies were pressed together, hers trapped between Adley and the counter. "I happen to love these jeans."

"Do you?" Adley's voice was barely a whisper. "How come?"

Sabrina tightened her grip, flexed her fingers into Adley's flesh. "Because they leave zero to the imagination."

And with that, Adley threw her head back and laughed. Of course, that exposed the long column of her throat, and Sabrina took advantage of that, running her tongue up the side, immensely satisfied when Adley's laughter morphed into a moan.

Oh God, they were going to set the bed on fire.

Adley brought her head back up, and her gaze met Sabrina's as she took her face in both hands. She held them there for a long moment, just looking into Sabrina's eyes, and Sabrina couldn't look away, not even if she wanted to. Which she did not.

"I want you, Adley. I need you to know that."

Adley nodded, still holding Sabrina's gaze.

"Also? I want food."

Adley blinked at her for a beat before another laugh shot out of her. And then they were both cracking up, laughter filling the kitchen, the two of them doubled over until tears leaked from their eyes.

"At least I know where I stand," Adley said, still smiling that smile.

Sabrina grasped her chin in her hand. "No." That one word was adamant. Serious. Adley stopped laughing. "I want food because I plan to keep you up all night, and I need sustenance to do that. See?"

Adley nodded again, her eyes wide. "I do see," she whispered. "So? What should we order?"

❖

Chinese food always arrived so quickly. She closed the front door with a hip, then scanned the small house.

"Let's eat in here," she said, indicating the living room with her chin. "We can sit on the floor. Have a little floor party."

Sabrina grinned at her. "That sounds perfect. I'll get forks and drinks."

"Forks?" Adley held up two pairs of disposable wooden chopsticks.

"Yeah, um…" And Sabrina's face turned a lovely shade of pink. "I can't use those."

"Challenge accepted," Adley said, pointing a set at her. She set down the food and snapped the chopsticks apart.

Sabrina returned with plates, napkins, and two glasses of wine, set them all down on the table, then took a seat on the area rug next to Adley. They opened containers of lo mein and egg rolls and rice and cashew chicken and dished them out onto plates. Then Adley took a set of chopsticks and scooted closer so she was sitting right next to Sabrina.

"Okay, give me your hand." Sabrina obliged, and Adley took it in her own. She tucked one chopstick into the web between Sabrina's thumb and forefinger, then tucked it between her middle finger and the base of her thumb. "This one is stable. It stays still." She demonstrated with her own chopstick before setting it down and placing the second one in Sabrina's hand. "God, your hands are soft," she said quietly, then cleared her throat. "Okay. This one does the work." Again, she demonstrated with her own to show Sabrina how to move them.

"Like this?" Sabrina asked, and she just about had it. She tried picking up a piece of broccoli, but the ends of the chopsticks crossed and she dropped it.

"Hold them a little higher. A little closer to the ends of the sticks." She adjusted Sabrina's in her hand. "There. Try again."

This time, she picked up the broccoli with no problem. "That's way better." And the smile that blossomed on her face was worth every penny in Adley's bank account. She literally had that thought: *I would hand over every cent I have to see that smile every day.* She met Sabrina's gaze with her own. Held it. The room got warm. Didn't it?

Yeah, they weren't going to be eating Chinese food anytime soon.

Adley spent the first moments of kissing Sabrina being amazed—again—by how affected she was by this one simple woman. How shocking it was—again—that she could be *so* turned-on *so* quickly. But it didn't take her long to tell that astonished voice in her head to shut the fuck up so she could concentrate. Because she wanted to concentrate. Sabrina was so achingly beautiful, and Adley wanted to memorize every single thing about her.

She set her chopsticks on the table and pushed the food away from the edge, then sat with her back against the couch as Sabrina climbed into her lap, straddled her. Their size difference made the position perfect, with Sabrina, slightly smaller, tucked up against her body. Adley ran her hands up and down Sabrina's thighs, feeling her tight muscles through her jeans as they kissed.

"Do you work out?" she asked through their kisses, digging her fingers into Sabrina's legs.

"I used to run a lot, but I've been dragging lately." Sabrina squeezed Adley's shoulders under her hands. "What about you?"

"I don't have time to work out, but my…job can be kinda physical at times." She thought about how she hauled big tubs of ice cream around the shop, how often she reached down into one of those big tubs to scoop some out, and how it did wonders for her arms and shoulders. Their gazes held, and to Adley, it was like they were both aware that their no-work-talk rule was becoming sillier the more time they spent together. Before she could comment on it, though, Sabrina was kissing her again, and all thought flew right out of her brain.

How long had it been since she'd had sex? Over a year, at least, right? Nearly two, if she was being honest about it. Jesus Christ on a cracker, how had she let that happen? How had she forgotten how amazing and wonderful sex felt? How incredible it was to have somebody want her the way Sabrina clearly did? How intensely erotic it was to run her fingers along the soft skin of another woman? God, how had she gone this long without any of that? She felt like she'd been walking in the desert, dying of thirst, and along came Sabrina and just doused her with cool water. She held on tighter, pulled Sabrina closer, pushed her tongue in harder.

Sabrina moaned into her mouth and it sent Adley into overdrive. Pulling her mouth away, she tugged on the front of Sabrina's shirt, then held eye contact as she slowly unfastened each button, both of them breathing raggedly. When she pushed the shirt open and off Sabrina's shoulders to reveal a navy-blue bra with lace trim, Adley felt another surge of wetness between her legs. Sabrina's skin was creamy and pale, and Adley wanted to taste every square inch of it. Reaching around, she surprised herself by flicking the clasp of Sabrina's bra open with one try. Sliding it off her shoulders, Adley gasped softly as Sabrina's breasts were revealed to her, pink nipples hard and begging for her mouth.

Who was she to deny them?

Hands splayed across Sabrina's back, Adley pulled her closer, took one nipple into her mouth, and sucked. Gently at first, then more firmly, feeling Sabrina's entire body moving on her lap, grinding into her. She switched from one nipple to the other and back, using her hand to occupy the one that wasn't currently in her mouth, and before long, Sabrina was nearly writhing, her breathing fast, her hands in Adley's hair, fisting it and tugging it. When Adley took a moment to look up at her, Sabrina's head was thrown back, and she reached up, then ran her hand from Sabrina's chin, down her throat, between her breasts, down her belly, and right into the apex of her still jean-clad thighs. When she pressed her palm into the denim at Sabrina's center, a small cry filled the living room, and Sabrina crushed her mouth to Adley's. Hard. Demanding.

Then Sabrina stood up before Adley even had a moment to feel the loss of her body heat. She stood in front of her, wearing jeans and nothing else, and held down her hand to Adley.

It was seriously the sexiest sight Adley had ever seen.

"Come with me," Sabrina ordered, her voice husky. "Now."

Adley was no fool. She reached up and put her hand in Sabrina's. One tug and she was on her feet, but Sabrina didn't let go. Just led her to the bedroom. They were barely through the doorway when Sabrina took Adley's face in both hands and kissed her like her life depended on it, walking her backward the whole time. And when Adley's legs hit the mattress, Sabrina gave her a little shove that sent her down on her back on the bed.

Okay, so the sexiest sight she'd ever seen—Sabrina standing above her, topless and holding out a hand?—yeah, totally overtaken by the sight of the same topless Sabrina crawling up her body as she lay back on the bed. Holy shit. It wasn't possible for Adley to become any wetter. It just wasn't.

"God, you're sexy." The words slipped out. She hadn't meant to say them out loud, but when the smile broke across Sabrina's face, she was glad she had.

"You're one to talk. You should see things from where I sit." And with that, Sabrina grasped the hem of Adley's shirt, pulled it up, and brought her mouth down on the sensitive skin of Adley's bare stomach. When she swirled her tongue, Adley felt another wave of arousal, knowing it was a preview of what was to come. She wondered if she'd survive long enough to experience it or if she'd spontaneously combust into a pile of ash just from the foreplay.

Sabrina pushed her shirt up farther, baring her bra-covered breasts. But instead of removing the bra, she reached into the top of it and pulled a breast out, and something about the pressure of the fabric combined with Sabrina's mouth doing wonderfully erotic things to her nipple made Adley whimper. Actually whimper. She slid her fingers into Sabrina's hair, cupped the back of her head, and pulled her harder against her. *More. More, more, more.* It was the only coherent word her brain could manage.

Sabrina's skin was so soft. Impossibly so. Adley ran a hand up and down her bare back, in awe of how anything could feel so silky and not be actual silk. And then Sabrina shifted so they were face-to-face, and then she kissed Adley again, and again, all thought left her brain.

Clothing was removed in some mysterious stealth fashion because the next thing Adley knew, they were both naked. And she would swear on any Bible or child or pile of money that she'd never seen anything quite as beautiful as Sabrina naked. If she could've taken a moment to just stare and not have it seem weird, she would've. But gawking wasn't smooth and it wasn't flattering, and besides, she wanted her hands all over that gorgeous naked body as soon as possible. She reached for her, and Sabrina commented on the goose bumps across Adley's arms.

"You're cold." Sabrina pulled the covers back.

"I don't care," Adley said, and it was the God's honest truth. "Come here." Working their way under the covers while their mouths were fused together was a challenge, and they ended up laughing for a moment as legs got tangled in sheets and pillows got in the way.

"I mean, I like a big bed, but this is ridiculous," Sabrina said through her laughter.

"Seriously, how thick are these pillows?" Adley laughed. "How do you not smother in your sleep?" She tossed one to the floor, then peeked over the side of the bed after it but felt a warm hand on her chin. Sabrina turned her head so she faced her, and there was no more laughing.

How did one describe actual sex with Sabrina?

Adley lay in the bed later, well into the wee hours, and took stock of her body. Sabrina was curled up against her, her head on Adley's shoulder, her arm draped across Adley's stomach, her leg tucked between Adley's. She wasn't snoring, but her breathing was deep and even. Relaxed. Adley should be asleep, too, but she was still keyed up. And if she was being honest? Still turned-on. Everything about being with Sabrina was hot and sexy and erotic. God.

She shifted slightly and felt that wonderful soreness in her lower body. In her thighs, from being held open longer than they had been in a long time. In her center, from being touched, rubbed, and stroked wet for a sustained period of time, which she hadn't been in so long. Her lips still felt swollen. A little chapped, but in the best of ways. Her brain tossed her an image from less than two hours ago—her legs splayed wide, Sabrina's beautiful hands holding them open while her tongue did unspeakably sensual things to her center. There came a point when Adley had no idea where Sabrina was touching her. Every touch blurred into one big wave of sensation until Adley's entire body seemed to pulse with color, then explode. That was orgasm number three, each one more intense than the last. Sabrina was a talented woman. She was also a bit of a control freak. Adley got to have her way with her, but she had to work for it. Sabrina definitely liked to be the alpha, which Adley didn't mind at all because it was fucking hot. And as she lay there flashing back, she felt her own body start to simmer again. To tingle. Her fingers flexed, and she ran her tongue around her mouth, over her teeth, because yeah. She wanted more.

Sabrina took that moment to shift in her sleep and roll onto her back, off Adley but still touching her. Adley pushed herself up onto an elbow and just stared. It was dark, but the moon was full and they hadn't gotten around to closing the blinds, so the room was bathed in an ethereal blue light. Sabrina slept soundly, her breathing still deep, her blond hair spread out across the pillow. One hand was on Adley's hip, the other tucked up against her chin, and Adley watched her face for a few moments, found herself missing those big blue eyes, especially when they were focused on her. Then her gaze began to move. The sheet only covered Sabrina from the waist down, so her beautiful breasts were on full sexy-lighting-and-all display. Adley couldn't help it. She reached over and brushed a fingertip across a nipple. Once, twice, until it began to harden before her eyes. She let her fingers drift along Sabrina's warm skin, her stomach, her shoulders, her sides, until Sabrina inhaled softly and turned her head, and there were those eyes, trained on her, hooded, and Adley didn't wait. She rolled herself on top of Sabrina and wasted no time sliding down her body. Opened her legs. Dipped her head. Tasted.

Sabrina whimpered, and Adley felt hands in her hair, and she sank into the warm wetness of this woman, taking her time in the dark, stroking, exploring, pressing harder then easing up, and in no time at all, Sabrina's hips rose up off the bed, her fingers tightening in Adley's hair. Ragged breaths and her name on a moan of pleasure. Adley held on to Sabrina's hips, stopped moving her tongue but kept her mouth pressed against her until Sabrina slowly came down.

"Oh my God," Sabrina whispered as Adley laid her cheek against Sabrina's thigh.

She watched as Sabrina's chest moved up and down, up and down, and she gathered herself, settled.

"Oh my God," she said again, then reached down until her fingers were under Adley's chin, and she pulled a little, a clear sign she wanted Adley up where she could see her.

Adley crawled up her body, kissing various parts as she went, lingering on a nipple that she flicked with her tongue, then bit gently. The soft gasp Sabrina made almost had her ready to go again, but the clock on the nightstand caught her eye, and she knew she needed to get at least *some* rest.

"Wasn't I sleeping about five minutes ago?" Sabrina asked as she kissed Adley's mouth.

"You were. I'm sorry. You were just so gorgeous, and I couldn't help myself." She felt slightly sheepish, but not really all that sorry.

"Please." Sabrina touched her fingertips to Adley's lips. "Don't ever apologize for that." She gave her entire body a little shake. "That was incredible. Something about it being unexpected, I think."

Adley lay down against her, and this time it was she who tucked her head under Sabrina's chin, the flat of her palm sliding across her stomach. "You're so fucking beautiful," she whispered, feeling sleep finally settling over her.

The last thing she remembered was a warm, gentle kiss being pressed to her forehead.

CHAPTER EIGHT

It was Monday morning.

That was the first bit of bad news Sabrina realized as she opened her eyes three minutes before the alarm on her phone was set to wake her. She quickly turned it off because Adley was curled up next to her and wound around her like some kind of vine, legs tangled with hers, arms around her, dark hair everywhere.

This is the best way to wake up.

Where had that thought come from? The last couple of times she'd woken up with somebody else in her bed, her first thought had been *How do I get them to leave without being an asshole?*

She didn't think that about Adley. In fact, she toyed with calling in sick. Or at least late. Because she wanted nothing more than to curl up with Adley and go back to sleep. Then make love to her when they finally woke again. Then cook her breakfast and maybe make out with her in the kitchen.

What was happening here?

She knew what was happening here. Of course she did. But that's not how it was supposed to go. This was supposed to be physical and that was it. No ties. No attachments. Just…release. Plain and simple, and Adley seemed to get that as well. So what was all this business about wanting to play hooky and spend the morning with her?

Okay. Yeah. Time to get up. The only way this was going to stay what she'd intended it to be was if she made it stay that way. She slid herself out from under Adley—no easy feat—intending to head for the shower. But she couldn't get her feet to move, so she stood there next to the bed and watched Adley sleep for another moment or two. With a final sigh, she headed into the bathroom.

Her eyes were closed and she was lathering up her hair when she felt a change in the air. And then hands slid around her from behind, caressed her stomach, and moved up until they cupped her breasts. And then her back was against Adley's front.

"Good morning," Adley said, her voice still husky with sleep. "Thought you might like a little help washing."

She turned in Adley's arms. "I'd love a little help."

Adley's mouth crushed to hers and Sabrina's back hit the cool tile of the wall and fingers were between her legs and they stayed in that shower until they ran out the hot water.

"I think every day should start with an orgasm, don't you?" Adley said as they were drying off.

"People would certainly be happier." She kissed Adley's cheek. "Coffee?"

"God, yes."

The morning routine with Adley was shockingly easy, and Sabrina didn't quite understand it. Like, how? How was she not freaking out right now with this stranger in her space? Why wasn't she ushering Adley out the door with a travel mug of coffee and a quick kiss? Why was it that, when Bryce sent her a text with notes for the morning's meeting at the new site, she was still toying with telling him she didn't feel well and was going to take an extra hour or two—which meant she'd then go back into the bathroom and remove the clothes Adley'd just put on and take her back to bed?

"Hi." Adley arrived in the kitchen in her clothes from the night before, and just like that, all Sabrina's weirdness seemed to just drift away, and she smiled and handed over a mug of coffee.

"How do you take it?"

"Just a little sugar," Adley said, then kissed her on the mouth. Nothing sensual. Just a quick kiss hello, but Sabrina felt it all the way down to her toes. And back up again.

Sabrina handed over the sugar and watched as Adley spooned some into her coffee. Watched her hands. Those hands that had done so many incredibly sexy things to her and— "Okay, that is a lot more than *just a little sugar*," she said with a laugh, making air quotes. "In fact, I'd call that a lot of sugar. Next time somebody asks how you take your coffee, tell them the truth. *I'd like a wheelbarrow of sugar in it, please.* Like that."

"I'm feeling a little judged right now," Adley said, hiding her smile behind the rim of her cup.

"That's because I'm judging you, weirdo. How do you have all your teeth still?" She grasped Adley's chin and made a show of squinting as she looked at her mouth. "Or are those fake?" Before Adley could protest, though, she kissed that mouth softly and whispered, "I'm just teasing you."

"I know," Adley whispered back and deepened the kiss just a little. Then she pulled back a touch and said, "I hate to sip coffee and go, but I'm meeting Scottie for breakfast in an hour."

"Totally okay. I have a meeting."

They stood there quietly for several moments, sipping their coffee, leaning against each other, smiling. "I had a great time last night," Adley said.

"Me, too."

Adley took one more sip and set the mug down. "Walk me out?"

Sabrina nodded and followed Adley through the house where she grabbed her purse and opened the front door. The morning was chilly, and Adley rubbed her hands up and down her arms in her short-sleeved shirt. The car chirped as Adley opened it, tossed her purse in, then reached for a pale pink zip-up hoodie that sat on her passenger side seat.

"Can we do this again?" Adley asked as she pushed her arms into the sleeves and adjusted the hood. "I really hope we can."

"I'd like that." Sabrina leaned forward and kissed Adley softly one more time. "Okay. Go, before I drag you back inside and we both miss our meetings." She took a step back so Adley could get into her car, and that's when she saw it. The logo on Adley's hoodie.

It was a purple line drawing of an ice cream cone, the words *Get the Scoop* in a circle around it.

Oh, shit.

❖

Scottie was already at a table near the window, sipping her coffee, when Adley arrived at the little diner called Sunny Side Up. It seemed busy for a Monday morning, but Adley didn't care. She hadn't driven there—she'd floated in on a cloud.

"Hi," she said as she pulled out the chair across from Scottie and sat. A robust waitress whose name tag said she was Kitty smiled at her and poured her a cup of coffee, promising to be back in a few minutes to take their orders.

"You look different," Scottie said, narrowing her eyes. "What is it?"

"What do you mean? How do I look different?" Adley added sugar, then smiled at the memory of Sabrina and the wheelbarrow. She picked up her mug and sipped, the coffee hot and strong, and waited for Scottie to answer.

"I'm not sure…You're, like, happy. Like, really happy. And I think you were humming when you came in. It's not like you—" She gasped suddenly, then covered her mouth and pointed at Adley.

"What?" Adley looked around. "What?"

Scottie leaned over the table and said in a stage whisper, "You had sex!"

"Oh my God, how could you possibly know that?" Adley whispered back, looking around the diner to make sure nobody heard them.

Scottie sat back in her chair and sipped her coffee, her grin huge, looking far too pleased with herself. Their eye contact held, as if they were in some kind of a standoff. Finally, Adley sighed, but with a big smile on her face. She couldn't help it.

"And?" Scottie asked. "How was it?"

Adley did an all-over full-body shudder, big smile still in place. "Amazing. Wonderful. Hot. Sexy. Thrilling. So many things."

Kitty returned then and took their orders. Omelets for both. When she'd turned and moved to another table, Scottie was looking at Adley. Studying her.

"What?" Adley asked. "What's that look for?"

Scottie sighed quietly and set her coffee down. Forearms on the table, she leaned forward slightly. "I'm just worried about you. That's all."

"I thought you'd be happy for me. You're the one who's always saying how I work too much, I spend too much time at the shop, I don't get out enough. Now…" Adley lifted one shoulder. "Now, I might've met somebody special."

"Who doesn't even live here," Scottie pointed out. "Who isn't staying. Who's supposed to be just a physical release. Remember?" She sat back again. "I just don't want you to get hurt is all."

Adley couldn't be mad about that, could she? Scottie was looking out for her, had only her best interests in mind. She knew that. "I get it. I hear you. I do. But for right now? I just want to ride this high a bit longer. Okay?"

Scottie looked like she wanted to protest, hesitated for a second, but ultimately nodded. "Okay. I can back off. As long as you know that I stress about this for you."

Adley grinned. "Sweetie, I've known you almost my entire life, and *I stress* is your life's motto." Scottie's childhood had been messy, and now her divorced parents were each remarried with other children, and she often found herself overlooked or even forgotten. Adley tipped her head to one side and softened. "I hear you. I promise."

"Okay. Good. That's all I ask."

When their breakfasts came, they were back to normal, chatting about Jaden, Marisa's nephew she'd been raising since the death of her brother. They chatted about Scottie's salon and how good business was, and Adley told her she had a couple ideas for new flavors. And all the while, her mind flashed back to the previous night. To that morning. To any and all the times she'd spent with Sabrina so far, and she'd get a tingle that started somewhere around her stomach and worked its way down.

"Marisa and I have been looking at houses," Scottie said, and *that* got Adley's attention.

"What? You are? Since when?"

Scottie's entire demeanor softened, the way it always did when she talked about the future with Marisa. Adley was always so happy to see her best friend so happy, but she also always felt a little pang of envy. She loved what Scottie and Marisa had. She *wanted* what Scottie and Marisa had. "We sort of danced around it for a few weeks, but I think it started—at least for me—about a month and a half ago. I mean…" Scottie looked down at her plate, pushed her eggs around for a moment, and when she looked up, her eyes were wet. "She's the one. Capital *T*, capital *O*. You know? I can't imagine my life without her. She's it. She's it for me."

Adley reached across the table and closed her hand over Scottie's forearm. She hoped her happiness was clear as she squeezed. "You deserve the best, Scooter. I'm so glad you found it. Especially after talking to my sister."

"Oh God, that's right. How did that go? What'd she say?"

Adley reiterated the story Brody had told her, talked about all the things she'd said were missing in her marriage. When she finished the story, she set down her fork. "Honestly? It kind of colored my whole view on happily ever after. I thought she and her husband were great role models. Just goes to show that none of us really knows what goes on in other people's relationships."

"Ugh. So true."

"But you and Marisa have given me hope."

Scottie laughed. "Glad to hear it." Then her expression grew serious. "Don't give up, Ads, okay? There's somebody out there for you."

Adley noticed the clarity with which she *didn't* mention that maybe it was Sabrina, and she had to consciously tell herself not to get upset about it. It likely wasn't Sabrina. How could it be? She lived in Atlanta, many states away. She traveled all over the country. She wasn't looking for a relationship. They were basically fuck buddies, to put it bluntly, a situation she'd agreed to.

So why couldn't she stop thinking about her?

❖

"Oh my God."

Sabrina sat at the dining room table, laptop open, papers scattered all over, and read the screen. It never occurred to her to find the website for Get the Scoop because she had the address and a brief synopsis of the shop, its best-selling products, hours of operations, and such from the email sent to her from the home office. She had no reason to find the website.

Until now.

"Ooh, it fucking figures," she muttered, as she sat with her head in both hands and stared at the sentence on the screen under the heading *About us*.

Get the Scoop is owned and operated by its third generation of the Purcell family, Adley Purcell. Call the number below or use the message box below to contact her with questions, party needs, or details on upcoming new and exciting flavors!

"Oh my God," Sabrina said for about the thirtieth time since seeing the logo on Adley's pink hoodie.

What the hell was she going to do?

That was the question. It stayed with her all day, reverberating through her head when she was driving. While she sat through a meeting and listened to Bryce Carter go on and on about how easy it was going to be for Sweet Heaven to take over the ice cream business in Northwood. While she went to the new site and walked around, listening to the foreman tell her what would happen there over the next two to three weeks.

And while she flashed back on the previous night. The images of a naked Adley beneath her, above her, beside her. Of her dark, hooded eyes, of the sexy sounds she made, of her sure touch and the way she could shift from letting Sabrina have control to taking it herself. Their night—and morning—had been sexier and more satisfying than any experience she'd had in a very long time. Years, even. She liked Adley. She liked her a lot. She liked her too much.

And then she heard her mother's voice. "Business is business, Sabrina. Business is not personal." She'd said that once a year or two ago when Sabrina had accused her of seeming a bit too happy to help create a Sweet Heaven monopoly in the smaller cities they'd infiltrated. Big cities were harder, but something the size of Northwood, New York? Sweet Heaven could easily run the smaller shops right out of business.

What the hell was she going to do now?

Without even thinking for longer than a second, she grabbed her phone and texted Teagan.

Not 911, but important. Call asap?

She didn't want to interrupt Teagan's entire day, but she was spiraling here and needed something to ground her.

Her phone rang less than a minute later.

"Hey, what's up? You okay?" Teagan's voice was smooth. Steady. Like a tether that suddenly had her and kept her from floating off into oblivion. Sabrina immediately felt herself relax.

"Yeah, I'm okay, but…" And then something weird happened. For the first time that she could remember since splitting up with Teagan and settling into a wonderful friendship, she lied to them. "I'm just being weird. It's okay. Never mind."

"Bri." That one syllable had always been able to force her to spill whatever it was that was bothering her. But this time? She kept her jaw clamped tight, so tight it made her face ache. "You sound weird."

She forced a light laugh. "I'm fine. Just…Mom stuff again. You know how it goes." Another light chuckle. *There you go. Make it seem silly and inconsequential.* "Ignore me."

"If you're sure…?" Teagan didn't sound convinced, but then Sabrina heard a voice in the background calling them. Kyra needing something.

"Totally sure. Go. Take care of your wife."

"Okay, but I'm calling you later."

That was fine. It would give her enough time to come up with a lie to tell Teagan that would satisfy them. Sabrina set the phone down and blew out a long, slow breath. "Business is business," she whispered. "Business is not personal."

She dropped her head into her hands. "Yeah, I bet Adley Purcell would disagree."

CHAPTER NINE

L *akeside again?*

Adley read the text over and over, not ready to hit Send. "Hmm," she said aloud to nobody. "Can't assume." She made some changes.

Thinking of sitting by the lake at dusk.

That was better. Just a statement of fact. She squinted at it. Typed some more.

If you get bored, that's where I'll be. FYI...

Yeah, that was better. Even though she wanted to assume that, now that they'd slept together, things had maybe changed a bit, she also knew assumptions could be dangerous. But it was Thursday, and she hadn't seen Sabrina since their Sunday night together and subsequent morning after, and she was having withdrawal. They'd texted some, but Sabrina had said her job had kicked into high gear, whatever that meant, and again, this not talking about their jobs was just silly. She was going to fix that tonight at the lake. She'd decided.

"You're humming." Mandy's voice startled her enough to make her flinch, and she glanced up into her employee's face.

"I'm sorry?"

"You. You're humming. It's new. It's...weird." Mandy grabbed a bunch of waffle cones Adley had made that morning, and as she was headed back to the front of the shop, she turned to regard Adley. "You're okay?"

Adley smiled. "I'm great. Thanks for asking."

With a nod, Mandy was gone.

The rest of the day went by smoothly, happily. At one point in the afternoon, she realized Mandy was right, she was humming. Some happy little made-up tune, nonlinear, nonsensical. Just humming and smiling.

Mandy was also right—it *was* weird. But in the best of ways.

When things started to die down a bit at the Scoop, around seven thirty, she grabbed the cooler, the picnic basket, and the bottle of wine she'd stashed in the refrigerator earlier. Mandy was going to lock up tonight, so she quickly changed into a T-shirt that didn't smell like waffle cones and didn't have ice cream stains on it, brushed out her hair, refreshed her mascara and lip gloss, and headed out to her car. Still humming.

The evening was a gorgeous, early-summer-in-upstate-New-York kind of night. Cool, but not cold. Still too early for tons of bugs—they'd show up in a few weeks, along with the super uncomfortable humidity that people not from the Northeast didn't think the Northeast actually got. She smiled, thinking about how Sabrina, being from Atlanta, was probably very well-acquainted with humidity. They didn't call it Hotlanta for nothing.

There were more people at the lakeshore than last time, but still not a ton. Adley found a spot in a far corner, where they were away from the other cars but could still see the lake. She backed into the spot, then hopped out and popped the trunk. In about fifteen minutes, she had two chairs set up with the cooler between them, acting as a makeshift table. On top, she spread out the mini-charcuterie board she'd made. Sharp Vermont cheddar, Manchego, and smoked Gouda sat alongside some prosciutto and spicy pepperoni. She had crackers and a red pepper tapenade, some stuffed grape leaves, and big green olives stuffed with Gorgonzola. Probably way too much, but she was going for impressive here.

The plan had been to wait until Sabrina showed up before opening the wine, but Adley felt a little bit of that sizzle of nerves, so she uncorked the buttery chardonnay and sat down to watch the water and wait for Sabrina.

People walked by from either direction, some strolling along the shore, some on the paved path that circled Black Cherry Lake. There was a picnic table about twenty-five yards from where she sat, where a woman and twin girls were hanging out, blowing and chasing bubbles.

Adley smiled as she sipped her wine, watching the girls as they squealed and jumped, clapping at the bubbles the woman—their mom?—blew for them. Then she sighed. She wanted kids. Badly. It was something she'd always wanted, to be a mother. At thirty-four, her clock wasn't exactly ticking yet, but it would be close in another year or two.

And then, of course, her mind wandered over into Sabrina Land again, and she wondered if she wanted kids, wondered what kind of mother she had, what kind she'd be, how they'd be as parents together...

"Oh my God, stop," she muttered to herself. Because she was straying into dangerous territory now. Sabrina wasn't her girlfriend. They were fuck buddies at best, and she hated the term, but it was accurate. It was what they'd agreed to.

Did she want them to be more?

A sigh, because she had to sit with that one for a bit.

She hadn't signed on for more than the physical. She had zero idea if Sabrina had any of these same thoughts. The woman wasn't from here. *For love of all that is holy, stop this train of thought. Right now*, her brain screamed at her, but hopping off said train was hard. She focused on the little girls again, who were now looking for rocks, if Adley'd heard them correctly. Their blond hair was in matching ponytails, and their little flowered shorts matched. One girl had a purple shirt and the other pink. They were probably four or five years old and had those little-girl laughs that sounded like tinkling glass. It wasn't long, though, before their grown-up was packing up their stuff and telling them they needed to get home because it was past their bedtime. That comment prompted Adley to glance at her phone.

Eight forty-five.

No texts.

Sabrina must be working late.

She'd been nursing her wine but now took a healthy gulp. The cheese was getting soft from being out in the open, and the pepperoni had gone a little shiny. She cut a piece of the cheddar and topped a cracker with it, then popped it into her mouth. Chewing slowly and watching the water was what she did for the next twenty or so minutes, trying to give Sabrina a little more time. But when her phone read nine fifteen and she still hadn't heard, she sighed and started to pack things up.

So much for a romantic evening at the lake that might lead to something else.

There was hurt. She admitted that to herself, then was immediately annoyed. Sabrina didn't owe her anything. Yes, they'd slept together, but they'd made it pretty clear what this was—physical release for two very busy people who were attracted to each other.

"How busy can I be if I found time to make a charcuterie picnic at the lake?" she muttered as she shut the trunk, then was instantly mad at herself. "Oh my God, stop it. You have no right to be mad."

And she wasn't mad. But she was stung. A little bit. With a sigh, she got into the driver's seat and started the car, then sat there for a quiet moment. It had gone fully dark and the lights from different locations around the lake twinkled happily. She picked up her phone and typed.

You missed a beautiful night on the lake...

No. She wasn't allowed to guilt Sabrina. That wasn't fair. She deleted and tried again.

Sorry to have missed you. Next time. Sweet dreams...

She read it over and over. Nine words and she went over them three times that. Finally deciding it was a good, kind, honest message, she hit Send.

She blew out a long, slow breath of disappointment and shifted the car into gear.

❖

"You are a fucking coward."

Sabrina stared at her reflection in the bathroom mirror. Glared at it. Pointed at it.

"A fucking coward."

Adley's text had come just before nine thirty. Sabrina hadn't been busy. Well, she had been—she'd had paperwork spread out all over the dining room table and her laptop open—but she wasn't doing anything that couldn't be set aside. She could've gone to the lake. Absolutely. She wanted to go to the lake. But there was no way she could be around Adley now and not tell her who she worked for, except she didn't know how to do that. It wasn't guaranteed that Sweet Heaven would put Get the Scoop out of business, but it was certainly a possibility. Especially if the public records were correct. Get the Scoop was struggling financially, its yearly profits decreasing a bit over the past three years. That made her feel worse because she wanted to help.

It was now after eleven and she hadn't texted Adley back. Such a fucking coward.

God, how did this get so complicated?

She clicked the light off and headed toward her bedroom. The day had been lovely, and the night was the same. Adley had been right—it would've been perfect for sitting by the lake. Maybe with a little wine. Some cheese or something. She slid under the covers of the bed that wasn't hers in the house that wasn't hers and sighed as she reached for the bedside lamp and clicked it off. And before she even realized it was coming, her eyes welled up.

"Oh, come *on*," she whispered to the dark of the empty room. But the feeling didn't abate, so she let it come, then lay there as hot tears slid sideways from her eyes into her hair and waited them out.

She had to tell Adley. No, they didn't owe each other anything, but she owed her that. She did.

Feeling slightly better about the decision, she rolled onto her side and waited for sleep that avoided her for pretty much the entire night.

She tossed and turned for the next six hours and logged maybe a total of two hours of sleep within them. By five thirty in the morning, she gave up and decided to do something she hadn't done in weeks: take a run. She'd chosen this particular Airbnb for its location. She could walk to the hip Jefferson Square—get a feel for the public in Northwood, what was popular and what times of the day—and the site for the new Sweet Heaven location wasn't far from there. It was a lovely sixty degrees, so she donned leggings and a closely fitting T-shirt, pulled on socks and sneakers, and grabbed her earbuds. She pulled her hair into a ponytail, did not nearly enough stretches, and headed out.

She started out slowly, knowing her body wasn't ready to do a full-out run. She used to run all the time, every morning, like clockwork, and she'd feel it—both in her body and in her head—if she missed a run. Then she got busier, and her mother promoted her to her current position that required huge amounts of travel. Still, she did her best to make time for runs. But the last couple of cities, something happened. She didn't even know what. Her attitude had shifted. She was tired. Mentally tired. Maybe that meant she should have run more, but instead, her runs went from daily to every other day to a couple times a week and continued to dwindle. She was pretty sure the last time she'd run was over a month ago.

She ran to country music. Teagan thought that was the funniest thing they'd ever heard, but something about the beat and the guitar and the occasional twang worked for Sabrina. Walker Hayes started in, singing about being fancy, and she picked up the pace, rounding the corner and watching the neighborhood morph from residential to commercial. It was a really nice transition, slow and easy. Northwood knew what it was doing when Jefferson Square was built. The sidewalk that was usually fairly populated, if not bustling, was empty now, the shops and restaurants mostly closed. There was a small coffee shop with its lights on and a few people milling about inside, but things were mostly quiet. She ran down the entire length of the block, then took a right, then a left, until she came upon the future Sweet Heaven location.

She stopped there, bent at the waist to catch her breath, and pushed her fingers into her side where a hitch had set in, reminding her that her body was annoyed at this treatment after so long sitting at a desk.

The building was nice. Not too big, not too small. Sweet Heaven, Inc., had purchased the entire building, but the actual Sweet Heaven shop would only take up half. The other half would be rented out until they got a handle on how successful the ice cream shop would be. That way, if they needed to expand, they could. Her mom was smart that way, didn't mess around with having to move in order to increase business.

The sign was obnoxious. She saw that now, but only because she was looking at it through Adley's eyes. It was huge, bright, lots of exclamation points. She wondered if Adley had seen it.

"I mean, I'd know if we hadn't instilled the stupid let's-not-talk-about-work rule." She muttered it into the quiet of the morning, knowing that if they hadn't agreed on that rule, they likely wouldn't have spent any time together at all. When she tried to imagine not having met Adley at all, not having spent time with her, not kissing her, not being with her, not making her laugh, not looking deeply into those gorgeous dark eyes, her stomach flipped in a super not-fun way that didn't help matters. At all.

The tears threatened again, and that just pissed her off. Why the hell was she crying over this? Over Adley? They didn't know each other well—*my fault*, she thought as she straightened up to standing again. But…they could. Couldn't they? Her gaze landed on the sign, on its exclamation points, and a lump took up residence in her throat.

"Probably not," she whispered.

A sound reached her ears, interrupting her pity party. She cocked her head. A small sound. Kind of high-pitched and soft…a whine? She strained to hear it, followed it around the side of the building. The sun had broken over the horizon as she'd run, and a ray of it slashed at the industrial beige cinder block wall adjacent to the parking lot, where the construction crew had piled trash. Pieces of wood, cardboard, broken drywall and such made up a pile, and there she saw the source of the sound, curled up on an old, broken-down cardboard box and shaking like the proverbial leaf.

A very tiny, super dirty, way-too-skinny puppy.

"Oh my God." The puppy looked up at her with the saddest brown eyes she'd ever seen. His little tail wagged subtly, as if he was afraid to hope that this human might help him. "What in the world are you doing here?" Sabrina squatted down and held her hand out so the puppy could sniff it. She knew enough not to make sudden moves at him or she'd terrify him even more than he already looked like he was. She moved a splintered two-by-four out of the way and sat down on the ground next to him, still holding out her hand and letting him sniff.

"How did you get out here, buddy? Did somebody dump you here?" As she sat, she scanned the area slowly. The rest of the pile, then the parking lot, looking for any other movement that might indicate another puppy or a mother dog, but she saw nothing. No stirring. No far-off whining or whimpers. Seemed the little guy was all alone.

She hadn't been sitting there long when he decided to move, that she was a safe space, and he crawled up into her lap and curled into a ball. He was filthy and smelled like it. She saw a couple of fleas right away.

"You need a bath, little man," she said quietly as she stroked his head. He was mostly white—well, dingy white—with some spots of light tan. His fur was wiry, and she surmised he was likely a terrier of some kind. Maybe. She didn't know a ton about dogs. She loved them and always wanted one, but her constant travels made it impossible. She wasn't cut out for a pet.

Which this little guy seemed to disagree with, as he sighed heavily and closed his eyes. Soon, he was twitching in his sleep. The sun came up fully and bathed them in warmth, and Sabrina let her eyes drift closed, too. She didn't sleep heavily, but she rested for a while until traffic picked up and people began to populate the street.

When she stirred, the puppy lifted his little head up and looked at her with those eyes, and she was lost.

"Goddamn it," she muttered as she stood and took him with her. In her arms, he seemed completely content, and when he swiped his little pink tongue along her chin, she couldn't help but laugh. "Listen, you've already sealed the deal. I'm taking you home. You don't have to work on my heart anymore." She didn't tell him she had no idea how she was going to do this, how she'd need to call the host of her Airbnb and beg for permission—which might include offering some extra money—but she'd deal with that later. "First things first, though. You stink, my little man. I see a bath in your very near future."

CHAPTER TEN

If Adley saw another billboard or online ad or commercial on television for that damn Sweet Heaven ice cream shop, she was going to punch someone. It was barely eleven in the morning, and she'd already heard the jingle twice on the radio she had playing in the kitchen of the Scoop, and seen an ad go by as she scrolled Instagram. It wasn't enough she was living with a constant bubbling panic that simmered in her stomach and made her worry about an impending ulcer. Now she had to be reminded that the possible nail in the proverbial coffin of her business was about to open up and wanted everybody to know it? Twenty-four hours a day?

Okay, that was an exaggeration, but still.

She was churning a new batch of Baby Bear for the day when her phone pinged in her back pocket. She didn't even want to look. She'd slept crappily, woke up with a headache that wouldn't leave her alone, and had to do books today. She sighed, fed up with the day already, and slid the phone out. A text from Sabrina.

"Oh, perfect." She knew deep down that being irritated with Sabrina made no sense. She didn't owe her anything. Her being a no-show last night was not an affront to Adley. They were not exclusive. Hell, they weren't even dating. So Adley's hurt was completely out of line, and she was well aware, but it was still there just the same. She thumbed the text and read.

Can you get away for a few minutes? I need your help.

Well. That was cryptic.

Mandy wouldn't be in for another hour and they didn't open until two, so yeah, she could get away. "Fine," she sighed, then typed.

Sure. What's up?

The gray dots bounced for what felt like a long time. Bounced. Stopped. Bounced. Stopped.

It's better to show you. Can you come by my place?

Wow. Okay. More mystery. Adley tipped her head to the left in an attempt to stretch out the tension in her neck. Maybe this was good. Maybe this was perfect. They could talk while she was there. She could tell Sabrina she wanted to change the rules they'd put in place. What would Sabrina think of that? Better yet, what would Scottie think of that?

The answer wasn't hard. Scottie would lose her mind. She'd remind Adley that this was just supposed to be physical release, two people with the same needs and obstacles. She'd remind her that Sabrina lived in another state. That she wasn't staying. That Adley would be setting herself up for heartbreak.

The worst part was that she could see all of that, every bit of it laid out before her in a neat little line. And Adley didn't care. She just didn't. She'd never felt a connection like this. Not in her entire life, and there was a voice in her head that kept telling her if she didn't act on it, didn't at least say what she was feeling, she'd regret it for the rest of her life.

"Fine," she said again with more sighing as she took off her apron and moved the Baby Bear to the freezer. She'd go. She'd talk. And if Sabrina told her to jump in the lake, she'd leave knowing she at least gave it a shot. Right? She looked down into the container of Baby Bear as she stood in the cold. "God, is this the stupidest thing I've ever done?"

The ice cream didn't answer.

❖

"Is this the stupidest thing I've ever done?" Sabrina asked the puppy as she held him up to her face so they were nose to nose. "Is it? 'Cause it just might be. What do you think?"

The puppy put his paw on her face and licked her chin in response.

"Oh, little dude, you know how to get everything you want already, don't you?" She kissed his head, which smelled kind of funky, but she wasn't sure if she should wash him with her own shampoo. Adley would know.

And why? Why would Adley know? She'd said nothing about having any pets, so why did Sabrina think she'd know anything at all to help?

She didn't. That was the answer. She just wanted to share the puppy, and Adley was the first—and only, if she was being honest—person she wanted to share him with. She hadn't even called Teagan, and that spoke volumes about where her brain was. *Volumes.*

"God, what am I doing?" she whispered to the empty living room of her rental. She was supposed to be at the construction site but had asked Bryce if he minded taking over for the day, as she wasn't feeling well. Which was sort of a lie. Her stomach had been churning unpleasantly since seeing Adley's sweatshirt on Monday. Now, it was four days later, she'd hardly eaten, she'd avoided Adley like she was contagious, and here she was, waiting for her to come to her house.

Seriously, how much could she take?

The Universe decided she didn't get an answer because her doorbell rang right then. The puppy barked in her arms. Well, bark-squeaked, which was adorable. Sabrina took a deep breath and looked at him. "Here we go," she said softly, then crossed to the door and opened it.

Adley stood there looking gorgeous, as always, despite her very casual attire. Today's outfit was a pair of well-worn jeans with holes in both knees and a white T-shirt with capped sleeves and a V-neck. Oh yeah, and a pink hat with the Get the Scoop logo because of course. Sabrina had called her away from work. Her eyes were stuck on the hat when Adley dissolved into nonsensical baby talk sounds, her eyes on the puppy.

"Oh my goodness, who is this adorable-worable wittle guy?" She put her nose right up to the puppy's, and the puppy began to writhe and wiggle in her arms, clearly excited about this new human in his life.

"I found him this morning on my run. He was curled up in some trash."

"He smells like it," Adley said, but still in the baby voice. Then she glanced up at her with those dark, dark eyes. "I didn't know you ran."

"It's been a really long time." She pointed at the puppy, now in Adley's arms and licking her face, Adley giggling like a small child. "I think God put him in my path to keep me from keeling over, which I probably would've done if I'd kept running." Watching Adley with the little fur ball, how happy it made her, did warm things to Sabrina's body, to her heart. "Anyway, I'm sorry to bother you midday, but...I don't know the first thing about what I need for this guy. He needs a bath, like, now, but I don't think you're supposed to use human shampoo on dogs. I don't know why I think that, but maybe I read it somewhere?" She was babbling now, and she knew it, but if Adley noticed, she hid it well, cooing at and nuzzling the puppy.

"No, I think you're right. Let's go to the pet store, then. Yeah?"

And just like that, they were in Adley's car. Sabrina sat in the passenger seat with the puppy in her lap, then up near her shoulder because he clearly wanted to look out the window but was too small. He watched the world go by, totally content with his tiny front paws on the ledge of the door. "I think he likes to ride."

Adley glanced over with a smile, then went back to driving, and Sabrina was just about to say something about...What? Their jobs? Not showing up the other night? How she'd missed Adley all week? But suddenly, they were in the parking lot of the pet store, and all the starts of her conversations stayed in her head. "Let's go see what we need."

The pet store wasn't a chain or a franchise. It was a locally owned small-town shop, like so many businesses in Northwood seemed to be.

"Hi there," a woman stocking shelves said to them as they entered. She wore a blue apron, her name tag said she was Beth, and her gaze immediately fell on the puppy in Sabrina's arms. "Oh my goodness, who do we have here?"

Sabrina explained the story of finding him that morning. "He needs a bath badly. And he's probably hungry. I made him some scrambled eggs, and he gobbled them right up, but I'd like to get him some dog food." She felt Adley's eyes on her and turned to meet her gaze.

"You made him scrambled eggs? How cute are you?"

And Sabrina blushed. She knew she did, could feel the heat rise up her neck and into her cheeks, as Beth stood close and petted the puppy, looking him over.

"Okay, let's get him some flea shampoo and some food," Beth said. "Follow me."

The two of them followed her down an aisle, then up another. "You gonna keep him?" Beth asked.

Sabrina hesitated. "I haven't really made a decision yet." As if understanding her words, the puppy shifted in her arms so he faced her. He swiped his tongue across her chin, and damn if he didn't look right into her eyes. "You stop that," she whispered to him, but Adley was watching, a sweet, sexy grin on her face.

"Yeah, she's keeping him," she said to Beth, then looked back at her, rubbed a hand down her arm, and said softly, "We'll figure it out."

They'd figure it out.

That was a statement that was so comforting and so frightening at the same time. Because the reality was, there were things about Sabrina that Adley didn't know yet. Once she did, she might not want to figure out anything except how to walk out the door.

They spent the next hour in the pet store, buying things for the puppy. Food, toys, a bed, a crate, a collar, a leash, a harness, more toys, some treats.

"This little boy was certainly found by the right people," Beth said as she rang up all the purchases. Sabrina handed over her credit card, not even blinking at the astronomical total. Somehow, it was totally worth it.

The puppy was tired. No looking out the window this time as they settled back into Adley's car. He nuzzled into Sabrina's neck on the ride home, and soon, tiny little snores could be heard.

"Is he the cutest thing you've ever seen?" Adley asked, whispering like she'd wake him up if she talked too loudly. She gave him a gentle pat as they sat at a red light.

"Thank you," Sabrina said, and it kind of just blurted from her mouth. "I really appreciate you dropping everything to help me."

Adley's smile was warm. Soft. God, she was beautiful. "You're welcome."

Back at Sabrina's, they unloaded their goods. The puppy was still sleepy, but Sabrina wanted to get him bathed and cleared of fleas before letting him wander around the house. The last thing she needed was a flea infestation. She filled the kitchen sink with warm water, and together, she and Adley scrubbed him clean. They used the tiny comb Beth had sold them to comb through his hair and make sure the fleas and flea dirt were washed away. By the time they were drying him in a soft, fluffy towel, he was practically falling asleep standing up.

"I'll get his bed," Adley said, left, then returned with the small circle of softness. "Where do you want it?"

"Let's just put it in the living room for now." She followed Adley there, the puppy still in the towel in her arms.

Adley set the bed down in a corner where it could be seen from the couch. "And do you have a sweatshirt or something that smells like you? It might make him feel more secure."

Sabrina loved how Adley thought of that. "I think I left one on the chair in the dining room last night." She'd been working in there and gotten chilly.

Adley nodded. "Got it." And disappeared.

She set the puppy down on the little bed. Already half asleep, he curled up in a ball and, with a big sigh, burrowed right in. He'd eaten a small amount before they bathed him but now seemed more interested in sleeping.

"I wonder if he was so stressed out from being alone and scared that, now that he feels safe, he can't keep his little eyes open." She said it as she heard Adley coming back into the room, sweatshirt in hand. "You think?" She turned to look at her, and there was something on her face. Something in her eyes. A shadow. A disappointment? "What's wrong?" she asked.

Adley walked over to the dog bed and carefully tucked the sweatshirt around the sleeping puppy. He didn't stir at all, and Sabrina found herself envying such a deep, undisturbed sleep. But her gaze moved back up to Adley's face. Adley's eyes were downcast, which was unlike her. Normally, she would look right at Sabrina.

"Adley?"

Adley sat down next to the dog bed and let out a sigh that made her sound like she hadn't sat down in days. Her brow furrowed as she studied the floor, picked at an invisible spot with her nail. Sabrina almost said her name again, but something about the way she held herself…it kept her voice quiet. She waited.

When Adley finally spoke, it was soft. Quiet. Barely above a whisper. "You have papers and your laptop and stuff on the dining room table. I wasn't snooping, but…you work for Sweet Heaven?"

Shit.

Oh, shit.

Shit, shit, shit.

She hung her head and sighed almost as heavily as Adley had.

"Yeah. I do. I was going to tell you, especially once I realized you own Get the Scoop. But I—"

"You knew?" Adley's eyes went wide. "You knew and you said nothing?"

"I mean, I didn't know, not until Monday when I saw your shirt—"

"*Oh*," Adley said, and she drew the word out so it seemed to have about fifteen syllables. "That's why you didn't have time this week to see me, and you didn't show up last night."

"Now wait. That's not fair—"

"It's not. I know. You're right. But, Sabrina..." And here, the worst thing happened. Adley's eyes welled up, and Sabrina felt it like a hand had reached in and grabbed her heart, slowly squeezing. "Your company is pretty likely gonna put my shop out of business. The shop my grandfather started. And I know that's not your problem or even your fault, but..." She threw her head back and growled. Literally growled out her anger, her hands balling into fists. When she returned her gaze to Sabrina, the tears had spilled over. "Why did it have to be you? Why?"

"I—" But what could she say? How could she make this better?

"I like you so much." Just like that, Adley's anger seemed to have vanished, replaced by sorrow and sadness, and Sabrina didn't know which was worse.

"I like you, too." Her own voice was hoarse. Scratchy.

"But...I can't." Adley pushed herself to her feet. "God, why did it have to be you? This *sucks*." Adley was at the front door before Sabrina even realized she was moving. She stopped with it open and looked back, and their gazes held. Seeing Adley about to walk out the door with tears streaming down her face was pretty much the worst sight Sabrina could remember. She pushed to her feet and followed Adley to the door, but she was already through and out. Sabrina stood in the doorway and watched as Adley opened her car door and looked back at her.

The anguish in her eyes was brutal.

A lump formed in Sabrina's throat as Adley started her car and backed out of the driveway, then drove away. She was pretty sure her heart was in that car, and it left with Adley.

"Fuck," she whispered as she stood there.

GEORGIA BEERS

The sky had darkened since the time they'd come home with the puppy, steel-gray clouds moving in, and now, and it began to rain. Big fat drops fell on the small porch, and she looked up into the sky and sighed and shook her head. "Perfect. Just fucking perfect."

CHAPTER ELEVEN

How had this happened?

Adley didn't understand it.

It was July Fourth weekend, and she'd said good-bye to Sabrina nearly three weeks ago. Not that that had stopped Sabrina from texting, because it hadn't. True, the texts had become less frequent—a skill Adley had perfected over the years was ignoring somebody who'd hurt her, just ask any of her exes...or Scottie, after that time she'd forgotten to meet Adley for dinner and left her sitting in a restaurant alone for an hour—but they were still coming. Every day, she'd get at least one. At first, they were all apologetic. Sabrina was sorry about not telling Adley the second she realized where she worked, she was sorry for suggesting the no-work-talk rule in the first place, could they please talk, she missed her, etc., etc., etc. After the first week, the texts began to slow. Adley was pretty sure Sabrina wouldn't be ballsy enough to show up at Get the Scoop, but the texts kept coming, and now, they were mostly photos and updates about the puppy. Sprinkles, she'd named him, which Adley thought was the stupidest name possible... and also the cutest.

Speaking of texts, her phone pinged as she was mixing flavors, and she sighed. Sometimes, she didn't look for hours, and other times, she glanced right away, just to get it over with. This was one of those moments, so she slid the phone out, but it wasn't Sabrina. It was Scottie.

Meet you on the hill by 8.

Another sigh. Adley was doing a lot of sighing these days, as everything seemed to take energy out of her. She was meeting Scottie, Marisa, and Jaden tonight for fireworks, and she was not feeling it.

At all. Before she had a chance to come up with some kind of excuse, another text came.

Don't you flake on me either...

Damn it. Why did Scottie have to know her so well? She'd promised, that had been her first mistake. She'd never gone back on a promise. Not to Scottie.

"Fine," she said out loud to the ice cream and texted back, *I'll be there*, then sent it and repocketed her phone. It pinged again, and she sighed again. Probably some cute emoji from Scottie in celebration of having browbeaten her into going to the fireworks. "I'm going for about twenty minutes and that's it," she muttered as she opened her screen again.

But this time, it wasn't Scottie. It was Sabrina.

Literally Sabrina. A photo of her and stupid Sprinkles, quite possibly the cutest puppy there ever was. It was a close-up. Sabrina's blue eyes aimed right into the camera. Sprinkles snuggled up under her chin, his orange collar the perfect accent to his rusty spots. Adley felt so many different things looking at that photo. Irritation. Longing. Sadness. Happiness. More longing.

The back door opening startled her so that she flinched and dropped the phone to the floor.

"Hey, Smudge," Brody said as she came in, using the nickname she'd given her sister after seeing her mother's ultrasound and announcing the baby looked like nothing more than a smudge in the photo. She picked the phone up before Adley could and glanced at it, because of course she did. "She's still texting, huh?"

Adley nodded and took the phone back.

"You're still not answering, huh?"

Adley shook her head and returned her focus to the bowl in front of her.

Brody took a seat on a nearby stool. "I don't have a ton of time, but I wanted to come by and see that you're living and breathing. Mom and Dad are starting to wonder."

"I am. Living and breathing. No worries."

"Why are you working on a holiday?"

Adley lifted one shoulder.

"If you don't mind my saying so, you look like shit."

Adley met her gaze and wanted to lash out. To be angry. But she also knew her sister was right. She wasn't eating much. She was hardly sleeping, which the dark circles under her eyes announced to the world. And she was sad. Sadder than she'd expected to be.

Brody reached a hand out and closed it over Adley's, stopping her movements. "Are you sure you don't want to talk to her?"

"There's no point," Adley said, and she meant it. She'd been over and over it all in her head. "She's not even staying, so why should I bother? It's probably better it ended the way it did, just"—she made a chopping motion with her hand—"done."

"Yeah, 'cause you're handling that so well."

"You know what, Brody? What do you know? You're cheating on your husband." As soon as the words were out, Adley regretted them and clamped a hand over her mouth. "I'm sorry. I'm so sorry. That was mean. Ignore me."

But Brody shrugged. "Don't apologize. You're not wrong. I am cheating on my husband. But it's because I'm tired of putting my needs off to the side so they're never met, never even addressed. No, I'm not doing things the right way, and it's probably going to bite me in the ass at some point if I don't figure out a plan of action." She shook Adley's arm until they made eye contact again. "I don't want you to settle for something less and then spend the rest of your life wondering what would've happened if you'd given Sabrina a real shot. That's all."

This wasn't news. Scottie had said the same thing, which was interesting to her, as they'd both changed their tunes from *Please be careful* to *At least hear her out*. What neither of them seemed to remember was that, whether she meant to or not, Sabrina James pretty much held the fate of Get the Scoop in the palm of her Sweet Heaven–employed hands. Adley'd spent far too much time on the Sweet Heaven website, growling low in her throat when she realized that guy who'd been in last month and wanted to sample every fucking flavor actually worked for them. Probably there to steal her ideas. If Adley could get some kind of investor, an influx of money to help update some equipment and maybe come up with a marketing campaign, that might help. But her parents weren't interested, and she'd already used up all her good graces at the bank. The reality was that Get the Scoop likely wouldn't survive a conglomerate like Sweet Heaven so close, even if its ice cream was chemical-laden and cheap. And while she'd told Scottie this and she'd told Brody this, she didn't think they actually *got* it. Because there was no way she could go back to seeing Sabrina, knowing that Sabrina's ice cream shop was going to cannibalize hers.

Brody seemed to understand that Adley was in no mood to go down this road yet again. Not today. She was barely hanging on right now. "You'll be at the fireworks tonight, yeah?" Complete change of subject, for which Adley was thankful.

She nodded. "Scottie will have my head if I don't show." She looked up at her sister and pointed a spoon at her. "But I am *not* staying long."

Brody saluted. "Yes, ma'am." She slid off the stool and kissed Adley on the cheek. "Love you, Smudge."

"Love you, too."

And then she was gone, and Adley was alone in her ice cream kitchen once again.

Happy to be alone.

Sad to be alone.

❖

The shop was coming along nicely. Sabrina was pleased. The counter was in, and the freezers were being delivered later in the week. Next week would be the tables and chairs and dishes and utensils. The painters were hard at work yesterday, but it was a holiday today and everybody was off. Sabrina was there alone. Well, Sprinkles was with her. Thank goodness. She didn't know what she'd do without the little guy. Teagan had said that the Universe knew she was going to need him, and maybe they were right. He'd certainly kept her on her toes. Kept her busy. Kept her occupied. She'd taken him to a local vet, gotten him checked out. A little malnourished, but otherwise, in perfect health. Her Airbnb host was surprisingly amenable to having a puppy in her place, so Sabrina had promised up and down and sideways that she'd clean up any messes. They did everything together now, which was new for her. He'd kept her steady.

He hadn't stopped her from thinking about Adley, though. Or from texting her. Or from sending photos of him to her.

She'd gotten exactly zero responses, which was hard. And which hurt. And she'd thought about driving her ass over to Get the Scoop, knowing if Adley was going to be anywhere, it was there. But she also knew what a huge line she'd be crossing if she did that. So she stayed away.

She missed Adley. God, how she missed her. And that made her angry. How had this happened? How had she allowed it to happen? This was exactly why she didn't date when she was on the road. Too many entanglements. Too complicated. Too...

She sighed and leaned against a counter, suddenly feeling too tired to even stand up straight.

How did I get here?

That was the question that echoed through her head more often than any other thought. She considered herself a highly intelligent woman, and how the hell she'd ended up in this space, she had no idea. It just made her mad.

And *that* didn't stop her from thinking about Adley.

Giving herself a mental shake, she finished checking out the shop, pleased with the progress. They'd be ready to open in about three weeks or so. August first was the grand opening. They had a booth at the July Fourth festival tonight, and while she'd make an appearance just to be sure things were running smoothly, she was relieved she no longer had to do things like actually man the booth. She'd done enough of that in her early years with Sweet Heaven—didn't matter that her mom was the CEO. She still had to earn her way up the corporate ladder. And now?

"Now, I make lots of money, have no roots and nobody to put them down with. Go, me."

Sprinkles whined at her and pawed her leg as if he took offense to that remark. She bent down and scooped him into her arms.

"I'm sorry. Of course, I have you now, don't I? Don't I?" She caught a glimpse of her reflection in the glass door of a cabinet and stared in wonder. Dressed in joggers and a T-shirt, no makeup, hair up in a messy bun, wiggling puppy in her arms. Not at all the image she was used to seeing of herself. She was used to being all business. Power suits. Heels. Perfect hair. Makeup on point. It's who she was. It was how she was most comfortable. But this? This new, casual, more relaxed version of her? Where had she come from? And more importantly, why did Sabrina like her so much?

She set Sprinkles down on the floor and walked him toward the back door. "Come on, little man. Let's take a walk and then we have to go home. I need to change and get ready for tonight. Wanna be my date?"

❖

Adley wanted to be somewhere else.

Anywhere else, really.

But the Fourth of July Festival was a big deal in Northwood, and everybody went. To mingle. To eat awesome things like cotton candy and fried dough and candy apples and kettle corn. To sip beer and wine and ooh and aah over fireworks. She'd gone every year, as far back as she could remember, and she knew there was no way the one-two punch of her sister and Scottie would let her get away with not being there tonight. Toss in her parents, and she was doomed.

So here she was, wandering across the grass of the park that was tamped down by hundreds of feet tromping over it. She always felt bad for the groundskeeping crew that had to clean up after something like this. Pick up all the litter. Coax the grass back to life. She carried a beer but took only small sips, as it felt like acid in her stomach, her own fault for not eating more than half a peanut butter sandwich today.

"There you are!"

She heard Jaden's little boy voice before she saw him, and then a little rocket blasted at her and hit her around the waist, and she looked down at his mop of dark hair. Jaden was going on six and just an adorable kid.

"There's ice cream over there!" Everything Jaden said seemed to have an exclamation point after it, and he pointed past her.

Marisa was suddenly there, and she grabbed his hand and tried to stop him from pointing, even though she surely knew it was too late. Adley looked over her shoulder at the big Sweet Heaven booth about twenty-five yards behind her and sighed. Of course. Of course they had a booth. She'd thought about having one, but it wasn't cheap, and she couldn't justify the cost this year. They even had a couple teenagers barking for them, each one several feet away from the booth, talking loudly about *ice cream* and *come get your sample tasting*.

They were doing sample tastings?

Adley sighed. That was smart marketing. She hated it.

"I guess there was no way to keep you from seeing that, huh?"

Scottie had appeared out of the crowd, and Adley turned to look at the cute little family of three.

"It's fine," she said with a shrug. "What am I gonna do, burst into tears in the middle of the festival? It is what it is." Scottie didn't look convinced, but Adley turned her attention to Jaden. "And what have you been doing with your summer, sir? Have you picked a college yet? Did you get your driver's license?"

Jaden pushed at her playfully. "You're funny, Ad."

"I try."

"Wanna walk?" Scottie asked. "Your parents are that way." She pointed in the opposite direction of the Sweet Heaven booth, thankfully.

"Sure."

"But…ice cream," Jaden said in a voice that was both little-kid whiny and kind of sad.

"You know what?" Adley said. "Let's get him some ice cream."

"I can get it," Marisa said, her dark eyes shifting from Adley to Scottie and back. "You guys go on ahead."

"No. I actually would like to see their setup here." Adley held her hand out to Jaden. "Coming?"

"Yes!"

And then his little hand was in hers and they were walking with purpose toward the Sweet Heaven booth for ice cream.

Sabrina was nowhere in sight, and that was a bigger relief than Adley had expected. Ordering was much easier without those blue eyes studying her, without her searching for the blond head. Jaden wanted a chocolate cone with sprinkles, and Adley went ahead and ordered their chocolate almond just because she couldn't fight her own curiosity. Scottie and Marisa had hung back, maybe wanting to give Adley space, let her decide how she wanted to handle things. When she glanced at them, they both looked worried.

That guy was in the booth, though. Not scooping, just watching, and Adley squinted at him, the guy who'd come into her shop and sampled almost everything. Bastard. Probably stealing her flavors. She threw some dagger eyes his way as she was handed her order, but he was scrolling on his phone and didn't notice. Damn it.

With a sigh, she and Jaden turned and headed back to Scottie and Marisa, who both still had those concerned expressions on their faces.

"Oh my God, stop it." Adley shook her head. "It's fine. I'm fine." Jaden seemed very happy with his cone, and he stood licking it and taking in all the people around them.

Adley tasted her own cone, let the ice cream sit on her tongue for a moment. It had a pretty good mouthfeel. Creamy, not grainy. The ice cream itself wasn't bad. It wasn't amazing, but it wasn't bad. The almonds were too small, though. And not enough salt. The whole point of chocolate almond ice cream was the salty-sweet combination, and this didn't have it in the right balance.

"What's the verdict?" Scottie asked, watching her face.

She lifted a shoulder. "Meh. It's fine. Not great." She held the cone out to Scottie, who tasted it and nodded.

"Agreed. It's fine, but it doesn't blow me away." She handed the cone to Marisa.

"Yours is way better. And I'd say that even if you weren't my favorite ice cream maker." She smiled gently, and Adley was reminded why Scottie had fallen in love with her. She was one of the kindest, sweetest people Adley had ever met.

The four of them strolled along through the festival, in an unhurried hunt for Adley's parents. The weather was good for fireworks, a relief as it had been gloomy and gray earlier. The crowd was gradually growing in size as the evening wore on, and they shouldered their way through a clot of young women, giggling and cheersing with their plastic cups of wine. Adley pointed to one of them as they walked by.

"I want one of those," she said to Scottie.

"Same," Marisa added, and their search subject flipped from Adley's parents to the wine booth. During their search, they happened upon the poutine food truck and all progress came to a grinding halt.

"I need poutine," Scottie said. "I just realized it this minute."

"Same," Adley said, and they all laughed and got in line.

Maybe this night wasn't going to be so bad. Maybe coming out and being around people was exactly what she needed.

Adley was gazing around the park while Scottie and Marisa chatted about Jaden's hair, and he stood impressively still while Scottie examined it. She had barely finished her thought about this all being a good idea when she felt eyes on her. It was a weird sensation when you knew somebody was looking at you but couldn't find who right away. She spun in a slow circle and...there. Blue eyes.

Her heart began to hammer. Her stomach flip-flopped. Her palms began to sweat. And she couldn't look away.

Sabrina looked different, though. She had Sprinkles in her arms, leash gathered up in one hand, and she looked...nervous? Uncertain? Worried? The puppy wiggled and squirmed in her arms as she stood still.

"What are you looking at?" Scottie asked, following her gaze. "Oh, she's pretty. Wait. That's her. Right? Is that her?"

And then Marisa was looking and made a small *oh* sound and then Jaden wanted to know what they were all looking at.

"Something's wrong," Adley said.

"What do you mean?" asked Scottie.

"I know her face. She's worried."

Scottie snorted. "*Psh*yeah. She's homing in on your turf. She *should* feel weird."

Adley shook her head. "No, that's not it. I'll be right back." And before she could think about it and before Scottie could talk her out of it, she was walking across the grass, sidling between people, bumping shoulders, and then she was there. Standing next to Sabrina, gazing down at her.

Before she could say a thing, Sabrina said in a flurry of words, "I shouldn't have brought him, I thought it would be good for him, socialization, the vet said to socialize him, but I think this is too much, he's just shaking like crazy, and the fireworks haven't even started yet, I'm a terrible dog mom, oh my God, what was I thinking?"

The first thing she wanted to do was make Sabrina feel better, and that annoyed the crap out of her, but she couldn't help it. "It's fine. Don't worry. Here, give him to me." She took the dog out of Sabrina's arms. He was definitely shaking, but also, the prospect of a new human to sniff seemed to distract him a bit, and he licked her face as if he remembered her. "Hi, buddy. How are you?" she said softly to him as she petted his small head. "Is this too much for you? Too many people? I know. I get it. It's too many people for me, too." She continued to stroke him and talk quietly to him, and before long, his shivering stopped.

Sabrina ran a hand down his back, and it was all Adley could do not to stare at it, at that beautiful hand with the long fingers that did crazy intimate erotic things to her body once upon a time.

"How'd you do that?" Sabrina asked, yanking Adley's attention away from her hand and back to the current state of things.

"Dogs feel what you feel. He was probably sensing your nervousness, and that made him nervous. If you stay calm, chances are, he will, too."

"You know a lot about dogs."

"I had one up until about a year and a half ago."

"You did? I didn't know that."

"Well, there's a lot you don't know about me."

Before Sabrina could respond to that or the snark it was coated in, Scottie appeared with wine, God bless her.

"You guys looked like you could use this." She handed them each a plastic cup of white wine that Adley was pretty sure would be mediocre at best. "Hi, I'm Scottie Templeton." She held out a hand to Sabrina.

"Sabrina James. Nice to meet you. And thank you so much for this." She shook Scottie's hand, then held up the cup. "I can definitely use it."

"I can always tell when a customer is freaking out about something," Scottie said.

"You a bartender?" Sabrina asked.

"Hairstylist. Same thing, really." And Scottie laughed and so did Sabrina, and Adley didn't know whether to relax and laugh along with them or throw her wine in Sabrina's face and stomp off with Sprinkles. She opted for Door Number Three—she smiled politely and sipped and said nothing as Scottie talked about how Jaden had wanted to go on a couple more rides and while Marisa was great on them, Scottie always bowed out because nobody wanted some strange woman throwing up on them.

Dusk was sliding slowly into actual dark as Scottie chatted up Sabrina, and Adley stood with Sprinkles now sleeping in her arms, watching the crowd, glaring at couples holding hands because how dare they be happy? Not fair. Her wine almost gone, she caught Sabrina's eye by accident and looked away quickly. She had to or she'd fall into them. Get lost in them. She couldn't do that. She wouldn't.

"I guess I should take this guy home before the fireworks start." And then Sabrina was petting Sprinkles again, so there was her hand again.

Adley was surprised to find herself reluctant to give up the puppy. When she'd lost Ty nearly two years ago, she forced herself to accept that she was at the shop way too much to have time for a dog. If she'd run an office, she could've brought it in with her, but she couldn't have a dog in the ice cream shop. Laws and health codes and shit. And she'd resigned herself to probably not getting another one for a long time.

And now she was yearning.

Was she yearning for Sprinkles or for his mommy? That really was the question, wasn't it?

She let Sabrina take the puppy out of her arms, trying hard not to touch her without looking like she was trying not to touch her. Of course, she failed, and Sabrina's warm hands touched hers, brushed against them, and they were soft and yeah, more yearning. How could she hate somebody and want them so badly at the same time?

"It was so nice to meet you, Scottie, and thank you for the wine." Sabrina's voice held sincerity, which impressed Adley, since she knew Scottie was Adley's bestie. And then those eyes locked on hers and Adley wanted so much to look away. And she couldn't. She was a prisoner. "It was really good to see you, Adley. Thanks for the help. Come visit him anytime you want, okay? You know where we are." There was a beat and their gazes held and then Sabrina turned and walked away and Adley let go of a lungful of air.

"Jesus Christ, I hate her." She shook her head, then turned to meet Scottie's gaze.

"Yeah, I can tell by all the hand touching and eye sex."

"What?"

Scottie snorted. Actually *snorted*. "Ad. I love you. I love you more than life, you know that. But you have it bad for that woman. And what's more, she has it bad for you."

"You think?"

Scottie gave her a look that said *duh*. Then she actually said, "Duh."

Adley sighed. Long and deep. Because none of this was news. "I know. It's just, the situation is so…icky."

"I know." By unspoken agreement, they began to walk toward the fairway where the rides were set up, eyes scanning for Marisa and Jaden. Scottie texted them to ask where they were, then glanced sideways at Adley.

"What can I do for you, sweetie? How can I help?" She ran a hand down Adley's arm.

"If you could fix it so she's, I don't know, a doctor or a teacher or something, that'd be really great."

"Lemme see what I can do."

Chapter Twelve

*H*onestly, it could be better.

Adley stared at the words from her CPA on the screen of her laptop. They didn't come as a surprise, not really. Couldn't anybody's bottom line be better? Isn't that what business owners strove for? A better bottom line? No, it wasn't a surprise. But damn, it was no fun seeing it typed out like that, words staring at her in all their computerized glory, telling her she was failing miserably.

Scrolling on her phone, she stopped on the calendar where an entry for tonight had a question mark next to it. Netwerx. God, couldn't people just spell things correctly? Did it always have to be some fun phonetic spelling?

"Wow, I'm a barrel of laughs lately, aren't I?" She said the words quietly to the empty kitchen of the Scoop.

It was a networking meeting that occurred once a month at rotating locations for women who owned businesses. It was informal and often held at a bar or restaurant, and women would grab a cocktail or coffee and mingle with other like-minded women. Casual. Informal. Sometimes, there was a presentation, sometimes not. Adley had always thought such things were a waste of time and just excuses for socializing, but as she sat there and reread the email from her CPA, she sighed heavily, knowing she had to do whatever she could to save her floundering business.

"Hey, boss." Mandy came in through the back door, chipper as always. "What's new in ice cream world?"

Adley absently closed the laptop. No reason to get her best employee worried about the state of the business. "Not much at all.

What's new in Mandy world? How's Terra?" Asking her about her daughter was likely a good way to derail any curiosity, and she was right. The rest of the morning and into the early afternoon was spent listening to Mandy talk about Terra's various summer activities, everything from day camp to piano lessons to horseback riding. The kid was barely seven and Adley wondered if she ever had a chance to sleep.

Business wasn't terrible that day. Not busy, but fairly steady. Not bad for a Wednesday. At one point around three in the afternoon, a bus pulled up and emptied out about twenty-five kids from a summer camp, so that was nice. Adley jumped into the fray and helped scoop, swirl, and sprinkle for nearly ninety minutes. A rush like that always lifted her spirits, and she was in a good enough mood after that to make the decision to attend the networking meeting that evening.

"You think it's a good idea?" she asked later, on the phone with Brody, as she changed clothes.

"Absolutely." Adley could hear the sound of pots and pans in the background as her sister made dinner. "I've gone to several of those meetings. Even if you meet only one person, chances are you can pick each other's brains for marketing ideas, sales, customer relations, all kinds of stuff. And the presentations are always informative."

"I do like that." Chatting with like-minded women and sharing ideas for business success sounded like a worthwhile evening. "I don't love walking into a room of strangers, though."

"Bet you ten bucks you see at least two people you know there."

Her mood lifted slightly, and she signed off with Brody and gave herself a last once-over in the mirror. Not one to dress up very often, especially for work where, more often than not, she'd end up with some kind of flavoring on her pants, she'd done her best—dark jeans, a cute pair of strappy sandals, and an ivory tank top under a black blazer with the sleeves rolled up. She also didn't wear a lot of jewelry but put on some large, thin silver hoop earrings and a long necklace with a heart on it to top off the outfit. She turned one way in the mirror, then the other, studying her reflection.

"Not bad," she whispered to the empty room, "if I say so myself." Neat and casual with a touch of professional, just the look she was going for. She was ready for this. Tonight's meeting took place in the private back room of a local restaurant and would feature a presentation on marketing followed by time to mingle and chat with the other attendees. Grabbing her purse, she headed out to her car and pointed it in the right direction, feeling a bit more hopeful than she had in a while.

❖

"Sprinkles!" Sabrina shouted the puppy's name louder than she'd intended. His ears went back, he tucked his tail, and he cowered in the corner, which made her feel instantly terrible. With a sigh, she picked him up and cuddled him close, smelling his puppy breath—seriously, why didn't somebody capture, bottle, and sell that smell as a relaxing elixir of some sort?—and kissed his furry head. "Buddy," she said, her voice much calmer, "do you have any idea how much these shoes cost me?" She picked up one of her black leather heels and examined the tiny tooth marks where part of the seam was missing. "I can't wear these now, and my outfit hinged on them," she explained. "I can wear these other ones, but they're not as comfortable." She slipped her feet into her extra pair, knowing in three seconds that she'd end up with a blister by the end of the night. "You, sir, are going to owe me a foot massage later." She took one of his adorable tiny paws in her hand. "Though I'm not sure this thing is gonna cut it."

With a quiet sigh, she kissed his head one more time, then put him in his crate and shut the door. She hoped not to have to crate him forever, but she'd been lucky so far that all he'd chewed up had belonged to her. The last thing she wanted was to come home and find he'd unstuffed all the throw pillows or eaten the couch. Pretty sure her Airbnb host wouldn't be thrilled about that.

"All right, I'm off." She tucked a treat through the crate and Sprinkles took it from her, then curled himself into a ball in his blankets to munch. "Be a good boy, okay? No parties, no strippers."

She was running late, which she hated. Northwood had not been the location of her best business performance, that was for sure, and she thought about that as she drove. She wasn't herself here. Of course, she knew the exact reason, and it started with an *A*. For the past couple of weeks, she'd struggled to get herself back on track. Both her mind and her heart felt…just *off*. She didn't know how else to explain it—that was the only word she could find that even remotely fit. Sometimes, she felt like the Universe was trying to tell her something. Other times, she thought it was punishing her.

She gave her head a little shake and tried to focus as she pulled into the parking lot of the restaurant. Running a good fifteen minutes behind, she headed in, was directed to a back room, and quietly slipped in and took a seat in the back, not wanting to disrupt the flow of the woman speaking. She had a PowerPoint presentation, so some of the lights were off, casting the room in a soft yellow glow.

Sabrina wasn't really here to learn about marketing, though any and all tips were welcome. Yes, she'd been doing this job long enough not to need a marketing education. Plus, marketing wasn't her job. Sweet Heaven had an entire marketing department for that. She was more the local face for the moment, and she wanted to meet some of the women business owners who surrounded her shop. After all, Sweet Heaven was woman-owned, and she liked to make sure whatever new city they were opening in knew that.

Her gaze slid around the room, taking in the different women sitting enraptured by the presentation. Probably close to a hundred people, a diverse palette of ages and races represented, which Sabrina was happy to see, and then her gaze halted. Just stopped dead on the back of a head of dark hair. Thick, beautiful waves of it. Hair that Sabrina knew well, that she'd run her fingers through and buried her nose in. *Of course* Adley was here. *Of course* she was. Why wouldn't she be? Why had Sabrina not even thought of that?

Goddamn it.

Nobody in her world had ever caused such dichotomies in Sabrina's thinking. Happy and sad. Excited and fearful. Drawn toward and pushed away. How was that possible? How could one woman confuse her on so many levels?

She should leave. She'd slipped in unnoticed—she could slip back out the same way, right? She should go. On the one hand, she knew she was only doing her job, but on the other, she worried that she was stepping on Adley's toes. Her business toes. And that actually made her angry because she *was* only doing her job. There were no laws or rules that said Adley had to have the only ice cream shop in town. Jesus. But just as quickly as the anger had bubbled up, it simmered back down, and Sabrina hung her head and stared at her own hands for several moments, just trying to steady herself and her racing train of thought.

The presentation ended then, and the applause yanked Sabrina's gaze back up, and *bam!* her eyes met Adley's. She didn't have to try in order to read all the emotions that marched across Adley's face—surprise, happiness, confusion, irritation, annoyance, anger, disgust—before she looked away.

But yeah, happiness was there. It was just a flash and it was gone quickly, but Sabrina had seen it.

The audience members were instructed to stretch their legs, use the restrooms, and grab cocktails and appetizers from the bar on the left-hand side of the room and the tables placed in various locations. Sabrina stayed in her seat for a moment, watching the room, watching Adley as she headed for the bar. She couldn't just ignore her. She'd seen her. Ignoring her now would just be rude, and Sabrina was not going to be pushed into being rude. She remembered her mother's voice, which seemed to be making a habit of appearing unsolicited. *Business is business, Sabrina. Business isn't personal.* She hated everything about those words, no matter how true they might be. "Pretty sure Adley would think it's personal," she whispered.

"I'm sorry?" The woman standing next to her chair bent down as if trying to hear her better.

Sabrina shook her head and waved a dismissive hand. "Oh, nothing. Just me talking to myself again." She forced a chuckle.

"That doesn't happen any less as we get older," the woman—she was probably in her early fifties—said with a smile. "Hate to break it to you." She stuck out her hand. "Hi. Shelly Ingram. I own a payroll company called PayDay."

"Oh, I've heard of them. You've done a nice job growing your business." Sabrina shook her hand. "Sabrina James. VP of new markets for Sweet Heaven."

"The new dessert shop going in over on Fox, right? It's starting to look almost ready. I drive by there every morning on my way to work." Shelly was taller than Sabrina—though most people were—and impeccably dressed. Where it seemed several attendees leaned a bit toward the more casual side, Shelly Ingram did the opposite. Full dark blue power suit, complete with skirt and heels. Her hair was pulled into a neat twist, and her makeup was on point. Sabrina knew instantly that this kind of gathering was no-nonsense for Shelly. She was here to network in every sense of the word. As if to put a period at the end of Sabrina's thoughts, Shelly handed her a card. "I know your company is national, but if you ever want to explore your payroll, give me a shout."

Sabrina nodded, glanced dutifully at the card, then slipped it into her pocket. "I'll do that. Thank you."

With a nod and a smile, Shelly headed toward the bar. Exactly where Sabrina'd like to go right then…except Adley was also standing there. Looking her way again. Their gazes held, a moment passed, and then Adley rolled her eyes, shook her head, and grabbed the two glasses of white wine the bartender gave her.

And then she was walking toward Sabrina.

Sabrina almost ran. Literally thought about turning on her heel and fleeing the room like her ass was on fire. But she forced herself to stand still, and then, there was Adley. Standing in front of her, beautiful dark eyes boring into her, holding out a glass of wine.

"Here," was all she said.

Sabrina swallowed and took the glass. "Thanks."

They stood quietly and each sipped from her glass. Then Adley said without looking at her, "Are you here to see who else you can put out of business?" The edge on her words stung, it did. "Sadly, Earl's is owned by Earl, not a woman, so he's not here."

"No," Sabrina answered quietly.

"I'm not going down without a fight, you know." The fire in Adley's voice was surprising. Energetic. And yes, sexy. "The Scoop has been in my family for three generations."

Sabrina nodded, took another sip. She was incredibly uncomfortable, torn between wanting to run away from the sharpness of Adley's words as if they were physically slicing at her skin, and just being so fucking happy to be standing next to her. God, she smelled good, like cinnamon and waffle cones. She looked great. Dark circles under her eyes, yes, but that spark was so sexy. Seeing her so passionate was a beautiful thing. And the blazer over the tank? A gorgeous look on her.

Jesus, get ahold of yourself, Bri, her brain screamed at her. *She hates you now. Keep that in mind.*

It was true that she'd not so much forgotten that little tidbit as set it aside. She glanced down at her wine, then raised her eyes to meet Adley's, whose were flashing. "I know. I'm sorry."

"That's it? You're sorry?" Adley gaped at her like she'd grown a third eye on her forehead. A few people near them had started to glance over.

"I don't…" Sabrina cleared her throat. She was a businesswoman, damn it. A VP. Yes, her mother owned the company, but her mother had also made her work her ass off to get where she was, and she hadn't done that by cowering in the face of an angry small business owner. "I don't know what you want me to say." Ugh. That was it? That was all she could manage to come up with? She should've told Adley to suck it up or to work harder or that maybe her shop had run its course. But she said none of those things. All she did was shake her head again and apologize. Again. God, she was pathetic.

Her plan had been to mingle. To network. That's what networking meetings were for, weren't they? To meet new people and see if you could help each other out in any kind of business sense. All her intentions were shot to hell, however, when she felt her eyes well up, which horrified her because what the actual fuck? She was a businesswoman. She was tough as nails. How the hell did people think she'd gotten here? She was a badass. A firecracker, her father had called her, because she was small and explosive. Nobody messed with her. Nobody made her feel less than. Nobody.

Except for this gorgeous brunette she'd slept with and couldn't get out of her mind. Yeah, this woman clearly had the ability to get to her, and Sabrina had to get the hell out of the room before her tears spilled over. She handed her wine to Adley, who took it with clear surprise on her face, and she bolted. Out of the back room, out of the restaurant, into the parking lot and her car, and she started it up and drove home. The whole time, tears rolled down her cheeks, making her equal parts heartbroken and angry.

What the fuck was wrong with her?

CHAPTER THIRTEEN

Wow, I can't believe you made her cry."

The words Annie from the massage place in Jefferson Square had said to her last night as Sabrina had fled the networking meeting had stuck with Adley all night and into the morning. She was meeting Scottie for coffee before the salon opened, and Annie's voice still echoed through her head as she opened the door to Starbucks and was greeted by the hum of morning conversation, a soundtrack of emo music coming from the speakers in the ceiling, and the wonderful smell of freshly brewed coffee. She found Scottie in line already.

"Morning," she said and cleared her scratchy throat, as that was the first word she'd spoken aloud since last night.

"Hey, badass," Scottie said by way of greeting. At Adley's odd look, she explained. "Demi was at the networking meeting last night. She said you made Sabrina cry and run away."

Demi was one of Scottie's two business partners. "I didn't see her there."

"She came in late and had to leave early. Typical Demi." The line moved forward a couple steps. "Is it true, though? You made her cry?" Scottie's expression was hard to read, and Adley knew her well, so it felt weird not to be able to tell what she was thinking.

A shrug. "I didn't intend to," she said, and that was the truth. "I hadn't set out to be an asshole. But the Scoop needs some help, and I thought the meeting was a good place to look for some and then *she* showed up and..." She shook her head. "I think it was just the last straw for me yesterday. I kinda let her take the brunt of my frustrations."

She shrugged again, working really hard to make it all look nonchalant when the truth was, the unshed tears in Sabrina's eyes had stabbed at her like little knives, right into her soul, and she'd had no idea what to do with that.

Instead of prying further, asking exactly what had been said, Scottie nodded, said, "Huh," and moved up in the line again. After a moment, she added, "That doesn't sound like you."

"I know." Scottie wasn't wrong. Adley wasn't a person who ever actively tried to hurt another. Sure, she'd gossip behind the back of somebody who'd pissed her off, but she never strove for somebody else's pain. That's not who she was. "I'm not proud of it, you know."

Scottie turned to meet her gaze and ran a hand down her arm. "Oh, sweetie, I know. It's not that you told her what you thought that's odd to me. It's how much that *wasn't* you. You know?"

The barista looked at them expectantly, and they placed their orders—a flat white for Scottie and a blond vanilla latte for Adley... which, of course, made her think about Sabrina. Again. "I should apologize," she said, not really directing the words toward Scottie, just saying them out loud.

"What?" Scottie treated and they moved down the line to wait for their drinks. "Seriously?"

Adley tipped her head. "I made the woman cry, Scooter. In public."

Scottie said nothing for what felt like a long time and just held Adley's gaze. Finally, she blew out a long, slow breath. "This chick has got you all discombobulated, doesn't she?"

"Discombobulated? Do you have a vocabulary calendar or something?"

That got a smile. "I'm serious, Ad. I feel like you're...going through something."

Adley took that in and was rolling it around in her head when the barista called out, "Cappuccino for Lousey!" She met Scottie's eyes and mouthed *Lousey?*

"Oh my God," a woman next to Adley muttered as she made her way forward. "It's Lucy." She made eye contact with Adley and rolled her eyes, and Adley smiled at her.

A few minutes later, they had their coffees—for *Scootey* and *Hadley*—and were seated at a small table for two by the window. The sunny morning had clouded over, and the clouds seemed to be getting darker by the minute. Rain was definitely coming.

"How's my friend Jaden doing?" she asked, then took a sip of her way too hot latte.

"No-no." Scottie held up a finger. "Don't think you're getting away with changing the subject on me."

Damn it. She looked down at her cup and took the top off. Scottie grasped her wrist gently.

"Ad. Talk to me."

Adley sighed, then turned her gaze to the window. "I don't know what to say." It wasn't lost on her that she'd just uttered the same words Sabrina had the previous night. She shook her head. "I honestly don't know what's wrong with me."

"Sweetie, nothing's wrong with you. But I do think, like I said earlier, that you're going through something."

"Yeah, but what does that mean? I'm going through something. What? What am I going through?" She was edgy now. Again. Edginess was starting to feel regular. Normal. She didn't like it.

If Scottie was surprised by that edge, she didn't show it. She just shook her head and then sipped her coffee. "I think this woman has affected you more than you expected. I think…" She looked like she was thinking about her words, rolling them around before deciding to say them out loud.

"Just say it," Adley said. "Say what you're thinking."

"Don't get mad at me."

"I won't. Scootey."

Scottie grinned, but it didn't stay. She took a deep breath and looked at her hands as she spoke. "I think, for all your *this is casual, this is just physical, just a release* talk, you ended up developing feelings for her. And that makes who she actually is much more painful for you than if she *had* only been casual."

The assessment wasn't surprising. At all. Adley'd had the same thoughts bouncing around in her own head. But hearing them spoken aloud felt like a whole different plane. Like they were no longer in her head, but out in the Universe. Solid.

Real.

To her horror, she felt her own eyes well up. Damn it. A lump formed in her throat and she stared out the window, not trusting herself to look Scottie in the eye and be able to hold it together. Keeping her gaze on the window, she whispered, "I hate her."

"Mm-hmm."

A swallow around the lump. "I also think I might be in love with her."

"I know, sweetie."

"What do I do?"

❖

The grand opening of the new Sweet Heaven was two weeks from tomorrow. Exactly fifteen days away.

And Sabrina couldn't care less.

Normally, she was fully submerged. Normally, by this point, she was spending twelve to fourteen hours a day on a new location, supervising the finishing touches on the store, doing marketing, introducing herself around town, building up excitement, getting everybody psyched up to hit the new shop on opening day. Normally.

Here? In Northwood? Nothing felt normal. Nothing. She wanted to go back to her Airbnb and cuddle with her dog and order pizza and shut out the world. The business world, at least. She wanted nothing to do with work or the grand opening or Sweet Heaven. Nothing. At all.

When had that happened?

That was the stupidest of all questions, though, wasn't it? She knew exactly when it had happened—the night she'd spent with Adley Purcell. That's when. That's when all this had happened.

Adley.

God, how could she miss somebody who so clearly hated her? How could she want nothing more than to spend time with her? Why did she want to apologize over and over when she was simply doing her job? Adley, of all people, should understand that, shouldn't she?

Currently, she sat at a table in a small conference room in the hotel where Bryce Carter was staying. Rather than renting an Airbnb like she did, Bryce preferred a hotel room. Sabrina was sure it was because he liked having his room cleaned for him, his bed made for him, and food delivered to him. It didn't matter to him that it was likely more expensive for the corporation to put him up there than have him rent a condo and have him take care of himself. No. He liked being catered to.

Tilda James was on the large computer screen in front of them. Joining her and Bryce around the table were Matt, the head of construction, Grayson, the guy in charge of getting equipment delivered, and Maggie, Sweet Heaven's interior designer. Matt had been in Northwood all along. Grayson and Maggie had only arrived in the past week or two.

"Well," Tilda was saying now as Sabrina did her best to return her focus to the meeting at hand, "everything looks to be on schedule. I'm very pleased." Not that you could see the difference with her mother. *Very pleased* looked pretty much the same as *very unhappy*, as far as Sabrina could ever tell.

Bryce's grin grew large at her mother's words, and Sabrina had to force herself not to roll her eyes. "What about the new flavors?" he asked before Sabrina's mom could end the meeting.

"When is inventory coming?" Sabrina asked, feeling suddenly out of the loop and hating it, even though it was likely her own fault.

"Bryce gave us some ideas for a few new ice cream flavors," Tilda said. "We're still working on a couple, but the test kitchen sent an email yesterday saying…" She squinted at her screen. "Ah, yes. Honey Bear and Island Dream are good to go. We should have some available a week or two after opening, so have them put on the menu. Good work, Bryce."

Sabrina blinked as the meeting came to a close and her mother signed off, and the screen went black. She could hardly believe what she'd just heard, those new flavors sounding *way* too familiar. She turned to Bryce.

"You barely even changed the names."

Bryce looked confused. "I beg your pardon?"

"The flavors you stole from Get the Scoop. Honey Bear? Really? Lemme guess. Honey ice cream with doughnut pieces, right? Could Island Dream possibly be mango-pineapple with coconut?"

Only the red spots on Bryce's cheeks gave him away. His expression stayed calm. Steely. "I didn't *steal* anything. Nobody owns flavors, Sabrina. Taste combinations don't belong to anybody." And with that, he gathered his things and left the room behind Matt. Maggie and Grayson watched him go, then turned their gazes toward Sabrina in tandem, like they were one person. It would've been funny if Sabrina wasn't so angry.

"Son of a bitch," she muttered, gathering up her own things as Grayson and Maggie talked about what was being delivered that day.

"Um, Sabrina," Maggie said, "Gray and I are headed back to the shop. Do you need a lift?"

She took a moment and pulled herself together, then smiled at Maggie. "I actually need to run back to my place for a few. I left something there I need to take care of. But thank you." She didn't add that the something she needed to take care of was her puppy. She hadn't told anybody at Sweet Heaven about him, and she actually wasn't quite sure why. Sprinkles was just something she'd decided to keep to herself for the time being, and in the next fifteen minutes, she was in her rental car and headed back to the house.

As soon as she slid her key into the lock, Sprinkles began to bark his high-pitched, adorable—and super piercing—puppy bark. Had anybody ever been as happy to see her as her dog? Like, ever? It was almost impossible to be sad when that little nugget of love was bouncing around in his crate, waiting to lick her face off.

"Well, hi there," she said as she let him out of his crate and he jumped at her leg like it was his job. "Hi. Hi. Hi. How are you? Ready to go potty?" She slipped his harness over his little body, clipped his leash on, and out they went. The backyard of the house was actually fenced in, but she was in the mood for a walk. Between the disaster of running into Adley last night and Bryce's stolen flavors—she didn't care what he said, he had stolen them—her emotions were all over the place. It shouldn't matter that Adley had been angry with her last night—she wasn't doing anything wrong by showing up to a networking function. She shouldn't care that Bryce had suggested new flavors to corporate—that's how business was done.

But it *did* matter. And she *did* care, goddamn it.

The day was stupid hot already, and her suit jacket didn't help. She took it off and draped it over her arm as she walked Sprinkles. Well, an acceptable facsimile of walking. It was more a series of stutter starts and stops, as he was still learning the leash. He'd pull out way ahead of her, and then she'd have to tug him. But they'd get it. She was actually surprised by the amount of patience she had with him. She'd never had a dog before, so she was getting as much of an education as Sprinkles was.

Her phone rang in the pocket of her dress pants, and she considered letting it go to voice mail. It was likely Bryce. Or her mother. Or somebody at the shop calling with a problem. She didn't have to respond right this second. But responsibility won out as she heard her mother's voice in her head saying, "Yes, you actually do need to answer *right this second* because that's your job." And the voice wasn't wrong.

With a sigh, she slid the phone out, surprised to see Teagan's face on the screen.

"Hey, bitch. What are you doing calling instead of texting? Everything okay?" She was stopped at a tree that Sprinkles found especially interesting.

"I don't know. Woke up with an odd feeling, so decided I needed to hear your voice. Everything okay with you?" Teagan got what they called their *pokes*, feelings that woke them up or interrupted their day and made them feel like they needed to touch base with a certain loved one for whatever reason. On occasion, their pokes had been alarmingly accurate. Once, their dad had just been in a car accident and suffered a broken arm. Another time, their sister had an allergic reaction to a bee sting. And they always seemed to know when Sabrina was struggling in some way.

"Yeah." Then she made the mistake of letting a quiet sigh slip out, and Teagan was on it like a cat on a plate of tuna.

"I knew it. I knew something didn't feel right. What's going on?"

"I honestly don't even know how to explain it, T." And she didn't. How did she put into words what she'd been feeling lately? How strangely her mindset had shifted? "I'm feeling really unbalanced. If that makes sense."

"How so? Can you pinpoint it for me?"

Talking to Teagan had always made Sabrina feel better. Nobody got her like Teagan did. Even after they'd broken up. Even after Teagan had met and married Kyra. Sabrina would be lying if she didn't say that there'd been some jealousy—or maybe envy was the better word. Teagan had found someone, settled down, and was now about to become a parent, while Sabrina did the same thing she'd always done. Alone. But still, they had a connection that would never be severed. When Teagan was hurting, Sabrina always knew it. And when Sabrina was floundering, Teagan could feel it.

She spent the next twenty minutes strolling with Sprinkles, letting him sniff and pee and pee and sniff to his little heart's content while she tried to explain to Teagan everything that had happened and everything she'd felt about it over the past couple of weeks. Concluding with, "I feel like I've lost my passion for so much," she felt her eyes well up, and she made a frustrated sound. "And I'm on the verge of fucking tears half the time."

"Holy shit, this is serious." Teagan was only half joking, and Sabrina knew it. "You are so not a crier."

"Apparently, I am now." She told Teagan about the night before at the networking meeting, when Adley had almost made her cry. "What is happening to me? Why am I struggling so much here? And honestly, T, why has it been so easy for me to just machete through all the competition for Sweet Heaven up until now? What kind of person is okay doing that?" She practically wailed the question, then nodded at the woman walking by who looked at her questioningly and put a couple extra steps between them. "Sorry," she muttered to her. "I'm fine."

"Babe, you are clearly not fine, and you need to figure this out."

"That's your sage advice? I need to figure this out? Listen, don't bother sending me a bill for this session. I'm not paying it."

Teagan's laugh was husky. "Sorry about that. You know what I mean, though. None of this is like you. None of it. The Universe is talking to you. That's what I think." Never one for religion, Teagan preferred to think of their hunches and feelings and pokes as signs from the Universe. They didn't believe in God per se, but they believed there was *something* guiding them.

"Yeah? Well, I'd like to request that it speak a little more clearly because I have no idea what the fuck is going on with me, and I don't like it. Not one bit."

"Okay, okay, I can see that. Just…don't panic."

"Might be a little late for that." She scoffed as she turned a corner and headed back toward the house, noting that Sprinkles was slowing down, his little legs probably tiring. "I accused Bryce of stealing Adley's flavors this morning."

"Oh, wow."

"Yeah." She cleared her throat. "I mean, he did steal them. But as he pointed out, nobody owns taste combinations."

"He's such a dick." Teagan had heard many, many stories from Sabrina. Enough so they'd formed their own opinion about the asshole that was Bryce Carter.

"Truth." She walked on, and the conversation stopped for a moment or two. There was always something comforting about just being on the line with Teagan, even if they weren't talking.

"You okay, kiddo?" Teagan asked as Sabrina and Sprinkles turned onto their street again.

She sighed. "I guess. I just...I don't like not understanding what's going on with me. I'm usually very routine when I do a new opening. Come into town, scope out the area, the competition, do some marketing, meet local businesses, get things set up, do the grand opening, head home for a week or two until the next. I do it in the same order every time. I've done it—what?—ten times now? Fifteen? I have it down to a normal, repetitive routine."

"You've never hooked up with a girl before while you're away." Teagan said it quietly. Gently. It was the elephant in the room, the thing Sabrina had been purposely not factoring in. "That's not part of the normal, repetitive routine. Have you thought about that?"

"Of course I've thought about that. I also have tried really, really hard *not* to think about that." They'd arrived home, and Sabrina pushed through the front door and unclipped Sprinkles, who rushed to his water bowl and gulped down almost the entire thing, then flopped on his side like he'd run a marathon. "She hates me now, T. I could see it on her face last night. She hates me, so why can't I just let go of it all and move on?"

"Not sure you're ready for the answer to that one yet, babe." Teagan added a chuckle, probably so they didn't sound too serious. "I think, just do your best to breathe. Focus on your work. How much longer until the grand opening?"

"Fifteen days."

"There you go. See? Fifteen days. You can manage that, can't you?"

Could she?

"I'll do my best." She thanked Teagan for listening and hung up, bummed to realize she didn't really feel all that much better. She needed to get her ass over to the new location, had things that needed to be dealt with, and for the first time since landing in Northwood more than a month ago, she was glad for Bryce's presence because she knew he'd be all over it. How unlike her to suddenly be grateful for the guy who wanted her job so badly, he could probably taste it.

She sat down on the floor next to Sprinkles and stroked him as he panted, feeling more confused and unlike herself than she could remember. Like, ever.

"I don't know what to do," she whispered into the air.

CHAPTER FOURTEEN

Ⅰt's just not something we want to spend our money on, honey. You understand."

Those words, spoken by Adley's mother exactly three hours and seventeen minutes ago, continued to reverberate through Adley's head. Echoing, like they were shouted from the top of a mountain. And they might as well have been, given how loud they were in her brain.

She sipped her pinot grigio as she sat at the bar in Martini's. She'd been there for an hour now, and this was her third glass. Yes, she was overdoing it. No, she didn't care.

"You understand." She said it softly to herself, but in a mocking tone. Sneery. Raised lip and everything. Which was not how her mother had said it, but that was exactly how it had felt. Did her parents have any idea how hard it had been for her to ask them for financial help? Any idea at all? She had never, not once, asked for money from them. Not for college. Not for her first car. Not when she'd purchased the Scoop from her grandfather. Not ever. She hinted that she could use it and they'd hinted back that they weren't interested in helping, but didn't they know how hard it had been for her to approach them today? To beg? With tears in her eyes because she was facing the reality of losing the Scoop altogether?

She finished her glass and signaled the bartender with the pink streak in her hair for another. She should probably ease up, but for the first time in years and years, all she wanted was to get drunk and forget about the entire day. Or, honestly, the entire summer so far. Yeah, that'd be better. She'd like to rewind back to April, before things started on a downhill trajectory. Or wait. Maybe she'd rather fast-forward. To winter. Ice cream would be gone. The Scoop would probably be gone. Sabrina would definitely be gone...

Ugh.

Her eyes found the doorway that led to the ladies' room and she stared. Remembered.

Sabrina.

Goddamn her.

Why? Why did it have to be this way? Why did the one person she'd connected with in longer than she cared to remember have to end up being the enemy? Why couldn't she be traveling to set up a mall? Or an office building? Or because she was selling flooring? Why did she have to be competition?

The fourth glass of wine went down too smoothly. And way too fast. And now she was a little blurry. Her vision. Her thoughts. Her emotions. All of it was...blurry.

She needed to see Sabrina. Yes. That was the best idea right now. She would see her and tell her what she thought of her. Perfect. *Let's do that.*

She paid her bill and slid off the stool. Not completely trashed, but very, very tipsy. Too tipsy to drive, which was fine because she knew where Sabrina lived and she could walk there. Too tipsy to make rational choices regarding life, and she knew that, too, but didn't give a crap.

So she walked. Muttered a little bit as she did. In less than a few minutes, she was away from the bustle of Jefferson Square on a Saturday night and turning the corner onto Sabrina's street. And then she was in front of her house without a whole lot of recollection of actually walking down the street. Okay, maybe she was a little drunker than she'd thought. And now she was up the front steps and standing at the door with her hand up, fist closed, ready to knock, and all right, maybe this wasn't the best idea. Like, maybe Sabrina wasn't even home. Sure, her car was in the driveway, but that didn't mean she was here. Then another thought hit her. Hit her hard, like a Mack track coming out of nowhere at full speed. What if Sabrina had company? What if there was somebody else in there with her?

Her brain screamed at her that this was a terrible idea and she should turn around and go. And she was just about to do that because oh God, what if Sabrina had somebody else in there with her, when the door opened, surprising her so much that her entire body flinched. She let out a tiny squeak and blurted, "But what if you have somebody else in there with you?"

Sabrina stood there, one hand on the doorknob, blinking in obvious confusion for just a second or two before her entire expression softened, and was that a smile? A gentle turning up of the corners of her mouth? "There's nobody else in here with me," she said quietly. "It's just me and Sprinkles." As if hearing his name gave him permission, the puppy started to bark, a tiny, high-pitched sound that made Adley grin. But only for a second. Then she remembered why she was here.

"I am here to tell you what I think of you." She made sure to furrow her brow so she looked angry and intimidating. She also shook a finger in Sabrina's direction.

"Again? *Okay*," Sabrina said, drawing the word out.

And wait—Sabrina was smiling at her, wasn't she?

"No. No smiling. There is to be...no smiling. Stop it."

Sabrina rolled her lips in and bit down on them for a minute before saying, "Oh, okay. No smiling. Sorry. Are you drunk?"

"I..." The world tilted a bit, and Adley grabbed the doorframe for balance. "I have had some wine. That's all you need to know." She pointed again. "'Cause I'm so mad at you."

Sabrina nodded, and the shadow of a smile was back, and it made Adley growl in her throat. Sabrina held out a hand. "How about you come in? Okay? You can say hi to Sprinkles so he'll stop making so much noise, and I'll get you some water, and you can tell me how mad you are at me. Yeah?"

"Fine," Adley said, because a glass of water actually sounded really good right about now.

Sabrina stuck her head out and looked up and down the street. "You didn't drive like this, did you?"

Adley snorted her insult. "I'm drunk. I'm not a fool."

"Well, thank God for that. Come in." She ushered Adley inside with a warm hand on her elbow. Adley wanted to shake it off, but it felt so nice. Warm. Solid. Once inside, the door shut behind her, and Sabrina held up a finger. "Let me get Sprinkles out of his crate. I put him in there when I saw a shadow on the front porch. Didn't want him scooting out."

Adley followed Sabrina into the living room and watched as she opened the door to the small crate in the corner. Sprinkles shot out of it like he was launched, running headlong into Adley's legs, then jumping, jumping, jumping, until she really had no choice but to sit on the floor with him. He jumped right into her lap and began to kiss her face off, clearly so excited to see her. "Well, hello there, handsome," she said. "Hello. Hello. Hello. How are you?" The puppy answered her by continuing to jump and lick and bounce and wiggle and waggle and do all the things that made puppies irresistible. Plus, sitting on the floor felt a lot safer than standing. Less precarious.

A glass of water appeared in front of her face, and she realized she hadn't even noticed Sabrina leave the room and come back. She took the water from Sabrina's hand, when the other appeared and handed her four small, orange tablets. She looked up into those gorgeous blue eyes.

"Motrin. You're gonna need it, trust me." Sabrina pointed at the glass. "Drink all of that, and I'll get you some more."

She did as she was told, popped the Motrin into her mouth, and downed the entire glass in one go. She handed it back to Sabrina and went back to her puppy lovin'.

"I'll set this right here." Sabrina put a second glass of water on the coffee table, then sat on the couch and simply watched as Adley and Sprinkles played and played.

The puppy made everything better. It was true and she hadn't expected it. It was like he bounced in and stole all the angry wind from her pissed-off sails. Now she was just floating, still sad, but not nearly as furious as before. Still a little inebriated, though. She sighed loudly.

"I'm sorry I showed up out of the blue like this."

"I'm not." Sabrina's gaze was intense. She sat on the couch, her legs crossed, just watching. For the first time since she got there, Adley took stock of what she looked like tonight. Blond hair in a messy bun, escapee strands brushing her face. Denim blue joggers, a white V-neck T-shirt that looked like it was loved—worn and soft and stretched out. Nearly see-through, which was probably why there was a tank on underneath it. No bra. Adley could see that easily, Sabrina's nipples greeting her happily.

Fuck.

Adley hadn't accounted for how good Casual-at-Home Sabrina would look. How tempting. Her throat went dry in a split second, and she reached for the water glass, nearly spilling it before she managed a good grip. She drank half of it, forcing herself to look anywhere but at Sabrina. Oh God, what was she doing there? Her head still swam a bit, and she knew she was moving through the stages of being drunk. She was about to leave the bravado stage, where things that are terrible ideas seem to be fantastic ideas, and on to the stage where you regret everything you've done so far.

"I shouldn't be here," she said, only realizing belatedly that she'd actually said it out loud. Okay, maybe she was a little drunker than she'd thought. "I should go." Sabrina stood and was next to her in what seemed like a flash. Was she The Flash? "How'd you get next to me so quick?"

Sabrina's grin was back as she held a hand down to her. "These things called feet. You have them, too."

"Ha ha. Hilarious. You shouldn't be joking with me." She poked Sabrina in the shin. "I'm mad at you."

"So you keep saying." Sabrina wiggled her fingers. "Come on, let's get you settled."

"I can settle myself, thank you very much." She put her hand in Sabrina's and needed three tries before she was able to stand up.

"I see that."

"Shut up," she said, but there was no venom in it. Her body leaned into Sabrina's all on its own. She wasn't trying to do that. Didn't want to. But Sabrina was right there in all her warm, see-through-T-shirt-wearing glory, and Adley's body clearly wanted to be next to her.

"Let's get you into bed, okay?"

Adley didn't argue. She wanted to. She really, really did. But then they were in Sabrina's bedroom, and it smelled like her, and instead of shouting her anger, she just wanted to cry. Her eyes welled up, and she clenched her jaw so hard to keep from crying that it started to ache. She felt hands at the hem of her shirt.

"Here. Take this off. I'll give you something to wear." And like a little kid, Adley lifted her arms up, and Sabrina pulled her shirt over her head so she stood there in her bra and jeans. Warm fingers were suddenly at the fly of her pants, unfastening, then pushing them off. Adley put her hands on Sabrina's shoulders for balance as Sabrina pushed the jeans to the floor and told Adley to step out of them. "I'll get you a shirt," Sabrina said and turned to the nearby dresser. Adley unfastened her own bra and let it drop to the floor. When Sabrina turned back, she stopped in her tracks, eyes wide. Adley heard her swallow, and then she handed her an old Atlanta Falcons T-shirt. It was black and soft and worn almost as thoroughly as the shirt Sabrina was wearing, and it smelled like her. Adley put it over her head, pushed her arms in, and inhaled deeply.

Sabrina pushed back the covers so Adley could climb into the bed that also smelled like Sabrina, damn it. Hunkered down, she let herself revel in the softness, the warmth, as Sabrina pulled the covers up over her. "I have the AC set at seventy-two, but if you're too hot or too cold, just let me know, okay?"

Adley nodded, feeling her eyes get heavy almost immediately. Sabrina stroked her forehead, and it felt...*divine*. That was the word. Sabrina stroking her, touching her in any way, just felt divine. She closed her eyes. She was going to regret all of this in the morning. Somewhere in the back of her mind, she knew that. But she was too sleepy to grab on to the thought.

Sabrina bent forward, clearly to kiss her on the forehead, but Adley lifted her chin and caught Sabrina's lips with hers. The kiss was soft. Tender. It sent little sparks zipping through Adley's body, but she was too inebriated to do much about them. She sighed instead.

"I'm so mad at you," she said, her voice sleepy and quiet.

"I know," Sabrina said back, just as quietly.

❖

What the actual fuck?

That was the main thought in Sabrina's head, and it ran through on a loop. What was the Universe trying to do to her, sending a drunk and adorable Adley right to her front door? What the hell?

She flopped onto the couch and blew out a breath, then immediately noticed the absence of a particular little being with four paws. With a soft groan, she pushed herself back to her feet and headed back toward the bedroom. She slowly pushed the door open and peeked in, and there was Sprinkles, all curled up in the crook of Adley's arm, his chin on her shoulder. Both of them were sound asleep.

"Traitor," she murmured but couldn't stop the smile.

Back in the kitchen, she poured herself the glass of wine she'd been about to have when she glanced toward the front of the house and saw Adley's silhouette on the front porch. She leaned the small of her back against the counter and took a sip of the merlot, then shook her head.

What the actual fuck?

Heading back into the living room, she bypassed the work she had spread out on the dining room table and went right back to the couch. Adley showing up at her house was completely unexpected. And surprising. And not at all unwelcome. And super confusing. And now she was asleep—well, passed out, really—in Sabrina's bed, and what was she supposed to do now?

Her phone was sitting on the coffee table, and it pinged a text notification before she could answer her own question. She glanced at the screen and felt relief flood through her. Teagan. She began typing without even looking at their greeting.

Guess who showed up at my house drunk and is now passed out in my bed.

The little gray dots that told her Teagan was typing bounced and bounced and bounced. They must not have been able to decide what to say because the message that finally came was short and simple: *You're shitting me.*

Sabrina chuckled and shook her head as she typed back. *I shit you not. Showed up on my porch about a half hour ago looking adorable. And a little tipsy.*

She sipped her wine while the dots bounced some more. The next text popped through. *What did she say?*

A snort because Adley had really had only one thing to say. *She said she came to tell me how mad at me she was.*

Teagan's answer came quick. *And?*

And nothing. That's as far as she got.

The phone rang in her hand, and she laughed quietly as she answered.

Teagan didn't even wait for her to say hello. "What happened? Where is she now?"

"She's in my bed with my puppy, sleeping it off."

"Wow," Teagan said, and there was a beat before they said again, "Wow."

"Yeah."

"What are you gonna do now?"

Sabrina sighed. "I don't know. Sleep on the couch."

"That's not what I mean, and you know it."

Yeah, she did know it. She just didn't have an answer.

"She's clearly not done with you," Teagan went on. "I mean, she has too much to drink and instead of bitching with her friends, she goes right to your house? Alone?"

That had crossed her mind as well. Adley wasn't out drinking with Scottie or with her sister—if she had been, Sabrina was reasonably sure neither of them would've let her come to her house—but she was alone, and the first place her intoxicated brain took her was right to Sabrina.

"That says something, don't you think?" Teagan asked, their voice a bit less edgy than when they'd started.

"I don't know what to do with any of it, T. I'm only here temporarily. What happens after I'm done?"

"Well, that's really up to you, isn't it?"

Goddamn it. She hated when Teagan got all philosophical and threw things out there that made Sabrina think. "I hate when you give me non-answers, you know."

"I do know." There was a grin in Teagan's voice. She could hear it on the fringes. "But this is something you need to figure out."

Sabrina groaned. "Just *tell me* what to do."

"Oh no. This is all you, babe."

"I hate you."

"Lies."

They stayed on the phone in silence for a moment before Sabrina growled quietly.

"Maybe sleep on it," Teagan suggested before they hung up.

Sleep. Sabrina laughed through her nose because it was funny. Sleep. She didn't sleep well in general, but now? Yeah, she wasn't gonna sleep at all, and she knew it already. With resignation, she tiptoed into the bedroom and got her pajamas, then scooped up Sprinkles to take him outside one more time. He did his business like a good boy, and when they were back in the house, instead of heading to his crate where he usually slept, he went right back to the bedroom and put his front paws up on the bed where Adley snored quietly.

Sabrina shook her head but boosted him up anyway, then whispered, "If you pee on my bed, we're gonna have a problem, sir."

Sprinkles ignored her and curled himself up in a ball next to Adley's head, then laid his chin across her throat.

"Traitor," Sabrina whispered again, then took her pajamas and phone charger out to the living room. Grabbing an extra pillow and blanket from the hall linen closet, she made herself a cozy little bed on the couch, refilled her wineglass, and clicked on the television, hoping she could find something to watch, the whole time painfully aware of Adley's adorable little snuffles coming from her bed and wishing she was lying next to her in there, curled up with her, their puppy in between them.

"What the actual fuck?" she said to the empty living room.

CHAPTER FIFTEEN

Where the hell was she?

That was the first question that popped into Adley's head when she opened her eyes. That was not her ceiling. This was not her bedding. That wasn't her dresser across the room. And where was the hot breath on her neck coming from?

Slowly, a little at a time, facts became clear, like a fog was lifting and making the world it had obscured visible again. She turned her head—ow—and there on the nightstand was a half-full glass of water and a clock that said it was six fifteen. The hot breath on her neck smelled good. Smelled familiar. She turned her head and saw big brown eyes, a furry brown and white head, and then a pink tongue unfurled like a New Year's Eve party horn as Sprinkles yawned, a soft squeak coming from his throat.

Sprinkles.

Oh God.

She knew exactly where she was, and as she concentrated, little bits and pieces of the previous night came floating into her mind. She was at Sabrina's house. She'd walked here. Oh, dear sweet Lord, she'd had too much wine and she'd walked here to Sabrina's house to give her a talking-to.

"Oh my God." She covered her eyes with one hand, wishing she could crawl all the way under the covers and not come out. Like, ever. But Sprinkles wasn't allowing that. Nope. He was awake with a capital *A* and he wanted to play. He hopped around her, making little puppy squeals, and it occurred to her that he probably needed to go out before he wet the bed. The bed that wasn't hers.

She pushed herself to a sitting position and swung her feet over the side, and yeah, she was in her underpants and an unfamiliar T-shirt. In the name of all that was holy, did she take her clothes off while she was drunk? She glanced around the room, wondering if there was anything she could use to kill herself but then realized that as soon as she saw Sabrina, she would die of embarrassment anyway. She covered her face with both hands and let out a low, soft moan of shame. Sprinkles thought that meant she definitely wanted to play and began jumping and barking at her.

"Shh," she said as she petted him and tried to calm him down. "Let me find my pants and I'll take you out, okay?"

"No need," came Sabrina's voice, and then there she was, standing in the doorway, a mug in each hand. "He's already been out." She held out a mug, and Adley could smell the freshly brewed coffee.

She took it with both hands, held it under her nose, and inhaled deeply. What was it about the aroma of coffee in the morning that seemed to make everything better again?

Not that it was because Adley was still pantsless, and she didn't even want to think about looking in a mirror. Her mouth tasted like something had crawled into it in the night and died. She could actually feel the mess that her hair surely was, a true rat's nest on her head, she was certain. And she likely didn't smell great, wine seemingly leaking from her pores even hours after she'd drunk the last glass. She took a sip of the coffee, feeling it all the way down, into her stomach, her limbs, her veins. It gave her enough strength to say a few words.

"I'm really sorry," she said quietly, not meeting Sabrina's eyes. "Just give me a second and I'll get out of your hair."

Instead of agreeing, Sabrina came into the room and sat next to her on the bed. "There's nothing to apologize for. Listen, you don't have to hurry. It's Sunday morning. Relax for a bit. Take some more Motrin. Drink your coffee. You're welcome to the bathroom and shower if you want."

She was mortified. Truly mortified. The longer she was awake, the more she remembered about the night before—though some of it was just blank—and the worse she felt. She'd just shown up. Drunk. Just shown up at Sabrina's home to tell her off. What the hell was wrong with her? Was this what it meant to be spiraling?

"I'm also happy to talk. If you want." Sabrina's voice was gentle. She didn't seem the least bit angry. In fact, she was almost inviting.

"I'm so sorry," Adley said again, because seriously, what else was there to say? "I just…" She sighed as more pieces clicked into her memory. "I'd spoken to my parents about a loan for the Scoop and they turned me down and…" Too late, she remembered who she was talking to, and a little spark of anger flickered inside her. She finally looked at Sabrina—goddamn it, why did she have to look so pretty in her casual Sunday morning clothes? "Yeah, that's right. I need an influx of cash to keep my ice cream shop alive." She waved a dismissive hand at her. "Take that info back to your mother ship. Doesn't matter anymore."

The look on Sabrina's face just then…like Adley had slapped her. She blinked rapidly and gave her head a subtle shake. "I wouldn't do that," she said quietly, and somehow, that took the fight right out of Adley.

They sat in silence while Sprinkles jumped around and tried his best to get them to laugh. And he succeeded in coaxing smiles here and there as he tugged on the bedding and Adley's shirt, which reminded her that she was still minus bottoms. She glanced around the room to locate her clothes and was suddenly hit with another memory piece.

"Oh God." She covered her mouth with her hand and could not bring herself to make eye contact with Sabrina as she spoke in barely a whisper. "Did I kiss you last night?"

Sabrina took a beat or two before nodding. "Just a small one." She lifted a shoulder and smiled, like she was trying to downplay the fact that Adley had shown up at her house drunk, kissed her, and then passed out in her bed.

"Oh God." She stood up, searching frantically for her pants—for any pants, really. Mortified. That was the only word to describe how she was feeling. Absolutely mortified. Sprinkles, of course, took her jumping up from the bed and scurrying around the room as a sign she wanted to play and followed her around, bouncing next to her, his little yips the only sound in the house.

Sabrina tried to wrangle him, finally succeeding in swooping him up into her arms. "Chill, little dude," she said quietly to him, and when Adley managed a glance at them, he was licking Sabrina's chin with the kind of adoration in his eyes that only a puppy could display. The image was adorable, and in another life, Adley might've stopped to take it in for longer than the two-point-five seconds she allowed herself. Because *mortified*.

"I have to get out of here," she muttered as she finally located her pants and shirt and bra neatly folded in a pile on a chair in the corner. She stepped into her pants, fastened them, and was too much of a mess to whip off her shirt in front of Sabrina, even though they'd seen each other naked not all that long ago. She grabbed up her shirt and bra and stuffed them into her bag that was sitting right there on the floor. "I'll get your shirt back to you later," she said quietly as she pushed past Sabrina, found her shoes, and stepped into them.

"It's no problem," Sabrina said, following her around the house.

At the front door, her hand on the knob, she turned to look at Sabrina, standing there all gorgeous with a puppy in her arms— *Seriously, Universe? You've gotta hit me with both barrels like this?*— and sighed, her shoulders dropping in embarrassed defeat. "I'm really sorry I showed up here on you the way I did."

"I'm not." Sabrina's words were soft, and were her eyes a little wet?

Adley chose not to examine that any farther and shifted her focus to the dog. She reached out, gave his head a scratch, and tried to ignore how close she had to be to Sabrina to do so. "Bye, little guy. Be good."

She turned and fled.

And remembered that she'd walked there and now had to walk back to the bar where she'd left her car.

"Son of a bitch," she muttered but forced herself to keep walking and not look back. She hadn't heard the door shut so assumed Sabrina was still standing there.

Watching her walk away.

❖

She should've offered to drive Adley back to her car.

That was the first thought Sabrina had as she stood in the doorway, wiggling puppy in her arms, and watched as Adley hurried away from her as quickly as she possibly could without actually sprinting. But that thought was quickly followed by another one—that Adley would never have accepted it. She couldn't get away from Sabrina fast enough.

Being shut in a car with her would've been torture. And the last thing Sabrina wanted to do was make Adley feel any worse than she already did.

She waited until Adley had turned a corner and hurried out of sight before she finally shut the door and set Sprinkles down on the floor. She expected him to run off and find a toy, but instead, he sat next to the door and looked up at her with his sad puppy-dog eyes and whined softly.

"I know, buddy, I didn't want her to leave either." She sighed and headed into the kitchen for some breakfast. What was she expecting? That Adley would wake up and actually be happy to be there? That she'd laugh off the night before, sip coffee, and lean on the counter while Sabrina made her some eggs? "You're living in a fucking romance novel, Bri," she said out loud as she pulled out ingredients to scramble some eggs and try to shift her train of thought.

Her brain was having none of that, though. Nope. It forced her to relive the previous night as she cracked eggs into a bowl. How happy she'd been—no, she'd been downright giddy to have Adley appear on her doorstep. Even in her drunken and angry state, Sabrina wanted to grab her up and kiss her all over her scowling face. But she'd stuffed all of that down because…why? Why had she? Yeah, Adley was pissed. And drunk. And kinda looking for a fight. But what if Sabrina had just grabbed her and kissed her? What would've happened then?

She added a little milk and used a fork to scramble the eggs as she remembered how much she'd wavered, back and forth, between sleeping on the couch and crawling in bed with Adley. God, it had been so tempting. She poured the eggs into the hot frying pan and moved them around with the rubber spatula as she remembered peeking in on Adley around two in the morning, because of course, Sabrina couldn't sleep. She'd wandered the house like a ghost…a creepy ghost, given how many times she stopped in the doorway of the bedroom just to listen to Adley breathe.

The eggs finished cooking, and she tipped them onto a plate, taking a small scoop and dropping it in Sprinkles's bowl to cool. She salted and peppered her own, refilled her coffee, and took it out to the dining room table. She set Sprinkles's bowl in its usual spot in the kitchen, then sat at the table with her breakfast, her work, and her very jumbled thoughts.

She opened her laptop and tried her best to focus. The soft opening of the new Sweet Heaven was in nine days, the grand opening four days after that. Everything was on track to make the deadlines. The painters would finish up the interior this week, and after that, they were just waiting on the ice cream shipment to arrive. That reminded her of stupid Bryce and his stupidly unoriginal flavor suggestions, and that yanked her mind right back to Adley.

Her phone rang and saved her, thank Christ, and it was Teagan on FaceTime. Relief and happiness flooded through her, emotions always triggered by her best friend.

"Hey," she said as she answered on her laptop instead of her phone, since she was already sitting right in front of it.

"Hi, cutie," Teagan said with their trademark smile. "Just popping in to do a drive-by. How's things?"

"Where are you driving by to?" Sabrina used the fact that her hands were free to eat her eggs as they talked.

"Target," Teagan said, coupling it with an eye roll. "The place that has more of my money than my bank."

"Buying more baby stuff?"

"I can't remember the last time I bought something that *wasn't* baby stuff." They shook their head, but Sabrina could tell by their expression that they were far from annoyed.

"Get used to it," she said with a laugh, then realized that she actually did need to talk about the previous night.

As if reading her mind, Teagan addressed it first, asking, "I take it your surprise houseguest is gone?"

Sabrina didn't mean to sigh, but she did. "Yeah. Not long ago."

"And what happened when she woke up this morning?"

"She was horrified, of course. Couldn't get out of here fast enough. Apologized all over the place but ran out like her ass was on fire." She tried to make it sound light but knew she just sounded sad about it.

"Babe," Teagan said, then their gaze went beyond the camera, probably to their wife. A nod, then, "Okay, I've gotta run, but listen to me. You've got to figure this out because I think this chick means something to you. You know?"

Another sigh. "Yeah."

"Talk later?"

They signed off, and Sabrina sat there for a long moment. For the first time since they'd broken up so many years ago, Sabrina longed for the simple complexity of Teagan's life. Or was it the complex simplicity? Either one. The domesticity of having a home and a partner and shopping for a crib for the impending arrival of your first child sounded like heaven compared to her own life. Flying from city to city. Rarely sleeping in her own bed. No roots, no home really. Finally meeting somebody who might matter, only to find out your company might blow up her livelihood. She dropped her head into her hands and just sat there. She had so much to do, so much to go over, but she couldn't move. All she could do was sit there, hold her own head, and think about Adley.

And for the first time in a very, very long time, she had absolutely no idea what to do next.

❖

While she'd managed a shower and clean clothes, that was about all Adley could manage that morning. Rattling around her house just made her feel jittery, so she headed to the one place she felt most comfortable.

The blessed cool of the stainless steel counter was the only good thing in her life right now. Adley sat there in the back kitchen of the Scoop, her forehead directly on the counter, and contemplated—or rather tried not to contemplate—her horrific choices from the night before.

Seriously, how stupid was she?

Her head was pounding. Of course it was, she'd had three—four? five?—glasses of white wine last night. Everybody knew white was much more apt to give you a headache than red. She knew that. She also hadn't eaten, so all that wine on an empty stomach…How in the world did she not expect to end up hammered?

What she had done was a clear testament to how she'd been feeling lately—largely confused and angry. About her business. About her abilities. About her feelings for Sabrina—

Snapping her head up wasn't the greatest of ideas, but she did it at that last thought, and everything swam in her vision for a second.

Her feelings for Sabrina.

Yeah. She put her head back down.

The back door opened and startled her enough to make her jump, but not enough to make her lift her head again. She only needed to learn that lesson once.

"Happy Sunday, brought you Starbucks." Scottie was her normal cheerful self, the way she'd been since Marisa entered the picture, and Adley was jealous.

"You have an amazing life, and I hate you," she muttered, her mouth leaving a vapor film on the stainless steel under her face. "Shut up."

She heard Scottie pull up a seat and sit next to her. Heard the Starbucks cup slide across the counter so it was near her head. Heard Scottie peel the lid off her own cup and sip it, an extra loud slurp she was sure was for her benefit. Scottie sat. Sipped. Waited.

Adley sighed finally and lifted her head—slowly this time—until she was upright and in a human position again. She reached for her cup, opened the lid, and smelled the caramel pump that Scottie always got for her in her mocha latte. "I'm sorry," she said quietly. "I didn't mean that." She sipped, felt the path the warm coffee took down her throat, into her stomach, into her veins.

"I know," Scottie said, not the least bit annoyed or hurt. She sipped, her eyes on Adley the whole time. "Wanna talk about it?"

Adley grimaced. "Not really, but I probably should."

Scottie leaned on her forearms, made a show of getting comfortable. "It's my day off, and Marisa and Jaden are at a birthday party. I have all the time in the world."

She was going to need more caffeine for this. She sipped, bolstered herself. Scottie waited patiently, something she'd always been very good at. When she started to feel slightly better than roadkill, Adley took a deep breath and spilled the whole story of the night before. All of it. Going to see her parents and their refusal to help her financially, heading to the bar on her own—her first mistake, they both agreed, drinking too much wine on an empty stomach, being smart enough not to drive but too dumb to realize that walking to Sabrina's house just to pick a fight was not the most terrific of ideas, to seeing her and Sprinkles, to the very foggy memory remnants of snuggling up in Sabrina's bed.

"I kissed her," she said on a groan. "I only remembered that this morning when I was sitting next to her."

"Oh, wow." It was the only comment Scottie made, but her eyes were slightly wider than normal, a clear indication of her astonishment.

"I fell all over myself apologizing. It was horrible. I wanted to crawl in a hole." She gazed into her coffee, turned the cup slowly in her hands.

"What did she do when you said you were sorry?"

Oh, she remember that *very* clearly. "She said she wasn't."

"Huh." Scottie sipped her coffee. Nibbled at the inside of her cheek. Looked like she wanted to say something.

"What?" Adley asked her. "Please, tell me what you're thinking. I'm a mess over here. I don't know what to do. My parents were my last resort. I'm probably going to lose the one place I feel like myself, and it's breaking my heart. And in the midst of the whole thing is this woman...this woman who's indirectly responsible for what is likely the demise of my business and I like her so much...but I also hate her. What am I supposed to do with that?" Not for the first time that morning, her eyes filled with tears. Not being able to control things wasn't something Adley Purcell was used to, and it was clearly freaking her out. She held her hands up, fingers splayed, and indicated her own face. "Look at me! This isn't me. I don't cry. I'm not a crier." She shook her head and took a large gulp of her coffee, hoping it would wash the lump out of her throat. "I don't know what to do," she said softly, words that she'd rarely uttered in her life. Glistening eyes focused on Scottie, she asked on a whisper, "What do I do?"

CHAPTER SIXTEEN

Friday was hot and humid, topping ninety degrees, which surprised Sabrina. Not because she wasn't used to the heat and humidity— she was from Atlanta, for God's sake—but because she somehow didn't expect it this far north. She'd taken Sprinkles for a walk earlier, and even he tapped out in the heat, preferring to be in the house, his belly flat on the cool hardwood, and he dozed in front of the vent blowing cool conditioned air on him. Part of her wanted to lie there next to him and nap the day away. Responsibilities be damned.

She was restless, though, filled with a weird nervous energy she couldn't seem to channel. She always got a little bit like this before a big opening, so it wasn't all that surprising. She paced around the little house, hitting her laptop when she walked by to make sure there was no new email or message she needed to deal with. To be honest, pretty much everything was set. A few minor details that Maggie was taking care of with regard to the interior design of the Sweet Heaven, but nothing Sabrina needed to worry about. Normally, this was the time that she'd chill. Normally, she'd have spent the past month or two working long hours and ironing out unforeseen wrinkles and making calls and answering questions and placing orders and learning the city and its residents, so that now, she was allowed a couple days of rest before the soft and grand openings. She could sit, watch a movie, read a book. God, sleep. Relax. Breathe.

None of those things seemed at all appealing right now. Not one. She had extra energy and she needed to burn it off. If she tried to run in this heat, she'd dehydrate and pass out in a matter of minutes. So she did the next best thing.

She put Sprinkles in his crate, moving it a little closer to the air-conditioning vent, got in her car, and drove to Get the Scoop.

She paid more attention this time than the last, noticing things like how the sign could use updating. Something being artisan was trendy, and you needed to capitalize on that. The Get the Scoop sign was likely the original, and it looked it, like it had been designed in the eighties or close to it. The font was old-school and the paint was faded, chipped in places, and just generally lent a dated look to a shop that should really be celebrating its timelessness. But the building itself seemed solid. Could use a fresh coat of paint, maybe something a little brighter than the beige it currently was.

She hadn't really planned out this visit, not a hundred percent sure why she was even here. But still, she pulled the door open and went inside, and two facts hit her instantly. First, there was nothing quite as warm and inviting as the smell of fresh waffle cones. The scent of sugar and vanilla and warmth grabbed her by the nose and led her to the counter. And two, she wished it was busier. There were a handful of customers, three sharing a table and a big sundae of some kind, two in line. But it was a sweltering hot summer afternoon. The place should be packed.

She scanned the menu board, noticing a few flavors that hadn't been there the last time she'd stopped by. Campfire S'mores, Ube, and Apple Crisp. All sounded fabulous. The fact that Adley made them in small batches guaranteed freshness, something a bit lower on Sweet Heaven's list, simply because they did large batches. Factory-made batches. Which didn't mean it was bad—it was actually quite good. But she remembered the dense creaminess of the ice cream last time she'd been here, and her mouth watered in anticipation.

As if they were in a movie and Adley's cue was to walk in exactly when Sabrina stepped up to the counter, that's exactly what happened. Adley was carrying a tub of ice cream, and she did a little stutter step when she saw Sabrina but managed to catch herself and continue to the display where she deposited the tub. According to the sign, it was Baby Bear, which made Sabrina remember how Bryce had copied it.

Adley sighed. She looked exhausted. Sad. Frustrated. That flash of anger she'd had in her eyes when she'd shown up on Sabrina's doorstep—that spark?—was nowhere to be found. She just looked... defeated. Sabrina wanted to take her in her arms. Wrap her up. Rock her. Tell her everything would be okay, that she'd take care of all of it. She'd much rather deal with pissed-off Adley than sad, giving-up Adley, which was who she was worried was in front of her now.

"How can I help you?" Adley asked quietly. The redheaded employee was there, too, ringing up the other customer, and Sabrina saw her glance over at Adley with what looked like concern on her face.

Sabrina hadn't planned this far ahead, and she realized it in that exact moment. With a clear of her throat, she said, "I guess…some ice cream?"

A nod. "Sure. What kind?"

"I know it's about a hundred and twenty degrees outside, but I think I'd like to try the Apple Crisp. Please. In one of your waffle cones. Please." And before Adley could walk away, Sabrina added softly, "And I wanted to see you."

Adley turned and met her gaze. She looked tired. Exhausted, really. Embarrassed. Her cheeks blazed red. And sad. She looked so sad, and that was hard to see. She wore no makeup. And she was beautiful. So gorgeous, it made Sabrina's chest ache. Adley was still for a moment, like she wanted to say something. Then she gave her head a quick shake and muttered, "Be right back with your cone."

Sabrina stifled a sigh and watched as Adley got a waffle cone— man, they were big!—and scooped ice cream into it. She handed it over to Sabrina without making eye contact.

"On the house," Adley said softly, then walked away before Sabrina could protest. Though, what was she going to say? She didn't think telling Adley she couldn't afford to be giving away her product would go over so well. Part of her really wanted to follow Adley into the back, into the kitchen, but the last thing she wanted to do was cause a scene or make Adley feel worse than she already clearly did. Resigned, she left a twenty in the tip jar and headed outside.

The ice cream, though? Holy deliciousness, Batman. It was unlike any ice cream she'd ever tasted, and she'd been here before, so her expectations were kind of high. Despite how incredible the flavors had been during her last visit, this one blew them out of the water. The sweetness of the apple, the dense creaminess of the vanilla, the warmth of the cinnamon, nutmeg, and other spices she couldn't quite put a finger on…it all mixed and mingled and made for an absolute taste experience. Add to that the depth of flavor in something as simple as a waffle cone, and the whole thing was absolutely beyond impressive. She had no words. She simply stood there, humming in delight and eating what was truly *artisan* ice cream. Adley was an artist, that much was clear.

I should march right back in there and tell her.

That thought zipped through her head so quickly, she almost didn't register it before she started moving, her feet carrying her quickly back toward the door.

But she stopped.

She remembered the look on Adley's face. The sadness. The defeat. The anger she had last night that she simply hadn't been able to hit Sabrina with. Oh, she'd wanted to, Sabrina knew that. But she hadn't been able to. And that said so much about who she was.

The lump in her throat was hard to swallow down, but she managed, then turned back to her car and headed home.

Where she ate every last bite of her ice cream cone.

❖

Whenever Adley felt like shit—or, let's be honest, whenever she was happy or sad or alarmed or worried—the thing she wanted to do most was create. Tastes. Colors. Textures. And right now, that's what she wanted to do. It's what she needed to do. Because Sabrina James was standing in her parking lot eating the Apple Crisp ice cream cone she'd made her and looking like she was in absolute heaven doing it.

Adley could see her through the window. She'd gone to the back because standing in front of Sabrina, looking at her, had been just too much to bear. If she'd been stronger, maybe. If she'd felt less beaten down, less defeated, less depressed about the state of her business, her life, maybe she'd have been braver. Maybe she'd have gone outside, followed Sabrina into the parking lot, to her car, shared her cone, talked about it, kissed her.

Kissed her.

Yeah.

None of that was going to happen. None of it could happen. The Sweet Heaven grand opening was coming up. There'd be lots of glitz and celebration. Customers would flock. They'd make a bunch of money, and Sabrina would leave. And Adley would likely watch her own business get slowly flattened.

She couldn't blame it all on Sweet Heaven. Or on Sabrina. That wasn't fair, no matter how much of her anger she aimed at them. Get the Scoop had been having difficulty for a while now, long before Sweet Heaven showed up on the scene. No, if she wanted to place blame, she'd have to look in a mirror.

❖

Saturday night, Adley sat at Scottie and Marisa's dining room table and held her glass while Scottie poured her a second serving of wine, a pretty good indicator of how she was feeling. Sad. In a funk.

"You're staying here tonight, by the way," Scottie said, shifting her eyes to Marisa, who sat across from her and nodded. "We know what happened the last time you had wine. Jaden's at his grandparents' tonight. You can sleep in his bed."

Adley didn't even fight it. She knew better. "Fine."

Scottie set the bottle down, sat, and closed a hand over Adley's forearm. "I'm worried about you, sweetie." Marisa nodded again, and Adley loved how she was there and present, showing her support but letting Scottie take the lead.

A sigh. "I know. But you don't have to be." She took a sip, then set the glass down and turned it slowly with her fingers. "I think I just have to accept what is, you know?"

Scottie propped her chin in her hand. "Explain."

Adley had been thinking about this since the visit from Sabrina yesterday. Truly, it had been rolling around in her head for two days. "I have to accept the facts of my situation. That's all." She ticked off a finger as she spoke. "My business is in trouble, and the reality is, I can't keep going on like this with it."

Scottie frowned. "I hope you know I'd help you if I could." A glance at Marisa. "But we sank everything we had into the new salon."

Adley shook her head and smiled at her best friend. "I know. I know you would. Please, don't feel guilty about that. I should've hired a business manager from the start. But I was too stubborn, too singularly focused, thinking I could do everything by myself. I just wanted to make ice cream."

"There's nothing that can help?"

"I mean, I could win the lottery, I suppose." Her small smile was an attempt at levity, but fell short. She ticked another finger. "Sabrina doesn't live here. Her store is going to open next week and then she'll head home to Atlanta until she has her next trip. Which I think she said will be Denver."

"I'm sorry, sweetie," Scottie said, her expression sad.

"Ugh." Adley dropped her forehead to the table. "Why did you let me think I could do a casual thing?" She wailed it almost comically so Scottie wouldn't think she was actually blaming her. She wasn't. She blamed only herself.

"You had to try, right?" Marisa finally spoke up, her voice soft but much huskier than Scottie's. "I don't think there's anything wrong with that."

"There's not. You're right." Adley reached for a cracker from the plate in the middle of the table, topped it with a slice of cheese, and popped it into her mouth. She chewed thoughtfully for a moment, then said, "Why couldn't she have been less...amazing? Less...beautiful? Less...sexy? Less...from the company that'll put the final nail in the coffin of my business?" The wine was making her feel warm and pliable. The love and care of her friends was making her feel safe.

If only there was something to help her feel less sad.

CHAPTER SEVENTEEN

Northwood really was the cutest little city.

Sabrina loved it. She hadn't expected to, but she did. And it said a lot because she'd been all over the damn country, to cities big and small. There were some she very much liked: Savannah, Georgia; Asheville, North Carolina; Cleveland, Ohio, surprisingly. But Northwood had something special. Something...extra. She didn't know what it was. It was more of a feeling than something tangible. All she knew was that she felt content there, more so than she had in a long time, anywhere.

She tried to pretend it had nothing to do with her time with Adley, and it was probably a good thing she'd be leaving in a couple days. She'd texted Adley once or twice, and at first, she'd gotten no response. Then, last night, Adley had texted back. Finally.

Good luck with the opening. I hope you and Sprinkles get home safe.

That was it. No *Hey, stay in touch.* No *I really enjoyed our time together.* And could she blame her? No. Of course not. But it didn't sit well. None of it did. More than once, she'd found herself wishing she'd never met Adley, had never bought that first pinot grigio, had never walked over to her table and sat down, had never led her into the ladies' room, had never kissed her, touched her, spent the night with her. And almost immediately, she'd shake those thoughts away. Because the last thing in the world she wanted was to have her time with Adley scrubbed from her life.

Staying busy was the key. She'd spent the week of the soft opening wandering Northwood, introducing herself and her company to people and places. She passed out coupons. She handed out invitations to the grand opening. She visited parks and the zoo and two bowling alleys and several soccer fields and baseball diamonds, and after four days of doing all that, she knew Northwood like the back of her hand.

And today was the grand opening.

She was in the midst of it, and it always energized her. It was her favorite part of her job. All the hard work and the long hours led up to this day. Sweet Heaven was packed, and it looked fantastic. Maggie had outdone herself with some extra color on the walls, bright pinks and purples and blues. All Sweet Heavens followed the same general design, but Maggie had put a little zing into this one, and it had Sabrina wondering if maybe Maggie felt the magic of Northwood, too.

The din of many, many children filled the shop, and Sabrina kind of loved it. Watching them running around, playing in the play corner that every Sweet Heaven had. Or with noses pressed against the glass of the display case, trying to decide which flavor they wanted. Or looking up at their parents with sprinkles stuck to their faces and ice cream on their cheeks. It really was sweet heaven to Sabrina. She couldn't wait to have kids of her own. And that made her wonder if Adley wanted kids, and then she started back down the Adley path all over again and had to consciously tug herself back to the present, force herself to enjoy the moment. She and Sprinkles would head back to Atlanta on Monday. In two days.

She stood behind the counter and watched as all the new employees worked their asses off. There were ten of them working today, ranging in age from forty down to seventeen, all dressed in the bright purple T-shirts and white hats of the Sweet Heaven uniform. They scrambled around, filling cones and dishes, swirling from the soft-serve machine, adding toppings. There was some bumping into each other and a few dropped scoops, but those things happened. They'd get the hang of it.

"Hey, Sabrina?" It was Jennifer Fisher, the manager they'd hired. "Can we go over a couple of final things?"

"Sure." With a last glance around, she indicated the rear of the shop and followed Jennifer back there.

❖

Adley had expected the new Sweet Heaven to be busy on its grand opening day, but it was beyond that. It was a zoo. No less than a hundred people filled the shop and spilled out onto the sidewalk out front. There were balloons and giveaways and fun music playing and a goddamn clown making balloon animals. She wandered, moving through and around families and couples, soaking up the colors and the brightness. The sheer brightness. Everything was happy and sparkling. It was celebratory and wonderful.

Adley hated it.

Scanning the flavors in the display case as she moved up in line, her gaze landed on Honey Bear. The description said it was honey-flavored ice cream with a doughnut swirl. Seriously? Not that she had the market on ice cream flavors, but that was suspiciously familiar, and she knew both Sabrina and that guy from Sweet Heaven had been in her shop. She sighed quietly. It was business, she knew, but still. And now she had to order it, damn it.

When it was her turn, she ordered the Sweet Heaven waffle cone with one scoop of Honey Bear ice cream. The kid behind the counter was no older than high school age and was extra cheerful, clearly happy to be doing this job. Her smile was wide as she asked Adley if she wanted any toppings. Sprinkles? Walnuts? Chocolate chips? Adley shook her head and paid.

The waffle cone was smaller than the ones she made, factory processed and then shipped here, most likely. Her first bite of it left her less than impressed. It was fine. It wasn't terrible. But it was apparent that it hadn't been freshly made and hand-rolled that day. And the ice cream? Oh, the ice cream. Yeah. She got now why the description said it was honey-*flavored* ice cream. Because that's exactly what it was. Very obviously not made with real honey like hers was. And the *doughnut swirl* really just seemed to be some overly sweet brown sugar syrup ribbon running through the ice cream. Again, it wasn't terrible, but the only way she could describe the taste was to call it manufactured. She did her conscious best to give it a fair shot. She tasted, let it coat her tongue, and really focused on the flavor. But it was very sweet, a bit airy, and just plain artificial-tasting.

She didn't know how to feel, whether to be happy or sad that the ice cream was meh. She didn't want Sweet Heaven to fail, did she? Well, she did, of course she did, but not at the expense of Sabrina's job.

Sabrina.

Adley had seen her briefly, standing behind the counter with her arms folded across her chest. Rather than her business attire, she'd been dressed in jeans and a Sweet Heaven T-shirt in bright purple that actually looked great on her—a little snug with capped sleeves—and before Adley could stop it, an image of her grasping the hem of that shirt and pulling it over Sabrina's head filled her mind, so much so that she had to squeeze her eyes shut and will it away. With force.

Sabrina hadn't seen her, and then she'd been pulled away by another person, and Adley had watched her walk into the back room. Her heart had squeezed in her chest a little bit, she was sure, and she rubbed at the spot with her fingertips.

Part of her wanted to see Sabrina, wanted to talk with her, touch her face, hug her good-bye, because she was leaving soon. And while that was mostly a big relief—wasn't it?—it also made Adley sad. She was sad about so many things right now—from the way things had gone with Sabrina, to the fate of her own business, to her future. Not to mention the fact that standing in this ice cream shop surrounded by a million kids had somehow started her biological clock ticking very loudly in her head. How much more was she supposed to take?

It was suddenly too much. Too hot. Too crowded. Too stressful. She took her mediocre cone and felt like a salmon swimming upstream as she pushed her way through the crowd until she finally made it to the front door and pushed herself out into the fresh air. On the sidewalk, she stood and inhaled slowly, in and out, in and out, until she felt herself calm down. She absently took another bite of the cone in her hand, and nope, it hadn't magically become delicious. With a shake of her head, she tossed it into a nearby trash can. One more look at the front of the shop. The brightly colored sign, the posters in the windows featuring cones and sundaes and ice cream sandwiches, she looked at them all. And through the window, her gaze landed on Sabrina, apparently returned from the back. Their eyes locked. Adley took in that face, the perfect smoothness of it, noted the slight sadness in Sabrina's eyes. Regret? Who knew? Maybe? Adley made herself smile, just once.

"Enough," she whispered to herself. "Enough now."

She turned and headed for her car.

❖

Sabrina's entire body gave a slight jerk, as if it wanted to run and the only thing preventing it from doing so was her feet, glued to the ground. Everything within her wanted to chase Adley, wanted to vault over the counter and sprint through the front door and run down the street after her, shouting her name. *Everything* within her.

But what if she did that? What would she say when she caught up? What would have changed once she caught up? How would their situation be any different than it had been from the beginning once she caught up?

The answer was clear. Loud. In neon in her head.

It wouldn't.

She wanted to cry, right there in her place of business, among new employees looking to her as the boss of their boss. Right in front of small children and ice cream and balloons. She wanted to burst into tears and scream about how unfair things were. The distance and the business and the deception. It was too much to come back from. She knew that. It broke her heart, but she knew it.

"You okay?" Jennifer Fisher asked as she sidled up next to her.

"Me? Sure. Why?"

A half shrug. "You just looked sad and far away for a minute there."

Good to know her exact emotions were written all over her face. She fixed her expression and nodded. "Just thinking about going home is all."

"Oh, gotcha. I bet you can't wait." They watched the customers for a moment before Jennifer added, "Well, we hope you'll miss Northwood just a little bit."

"You have no idea," Sabrina said softly. "No idea at all."

Chapter Eighteen

Seven months later...

"You're sure this is what you want to do?" Brody asked, both hands wrapped around her mug.

Adley sat next to her sister in Starbucks on a snowy Sunday morning in March on a small, worn love seat near the gas fireplace in the corner. Winter was still hanging on in Northwood, by its fingernails, letting all its snow melt and allowing one fifty-degree day before plunging temps back down below freezing and dropping another three inches on the city. March was the worst, as far as Adley was concerned.

It was fairly busy for a Sunday, the quiet hum of conversation all around them. Adley took a sip of her caramel mocha latte and gazed into the fire for a long moment before nodding. "It is. I mean, it's *not*, but I think it's for the best. I've barely made payroll for the past month and a half, and it's offseason. I haven't taken a paycheck yet this year. The bank won't extend me another loan, and honestly, I don't want to dig myself into a deeper financial hole. No." She blew out a breath and said sadly, "I have to close."

Brody's hand was warm as it closed over hers. "I'm really sorry, Ad."

"Thanks."

"When, do you think?"

"Couple weeks."

"Ugh. I'm sorry," Brody said again.

"Yeah." She took a deep breath, lifting her shoulders with it, and let it out. "Hey, you remember Josh Greenfield from school?" When Brody squinted at her, she added, "Tall, big teeth, kinda gangly?"

"Oh! Yeah. Yeah, I remember him."

"He runs a restaurant on the west side and told me he's looking for a hostess-slash-assistant manager, so I'm going to go talk with him in a week or two about it."

"That's great." Brody was being extra cheerful, and Adley both loved her for it and wanted to roll her eyes. She didn't need coddling. She was way over coddling. Way over it. But she knew Brody meant well, was just being supportive, so she thanked her.

Desperate to change the subject, she asked, "How are things at home?"

Brody lifted one shoulder in a clear attempt to be nonchalant. She'd stopped seeing the redheaded guy a couple months ago, vowing to work harder on her marriage. "I don't know, Ad. I know I promised Mom that I'd do my best, but I just think sometimes people grow apart. Even if they're married." She sipped her coffee and gazed into the flames, and Adley could see the sadness on her face as if it was written there with a Sharpie. That happy spark, that joy of life Brody'd had when she'd been seeing Paul was gone, all but extinguished, and now her sister just...was. It only added to Adley's sadness.

"Hey." It was her turn to close a hand over her sister's forearm. When Brody's eyes met hers, she said, "You deserve to be happy, you know. No matter what Mom says."

"I know. You're right." Brody let go of a long slow breath while Adley waited her out. "And I think Nathan really did try for a while. He really made an effort..."

"And then?"

Brody smiled sadly, and it broke Adley's heart to see her big sister seem so defeated. "And then we ended up right back where we were before Paul."

"I'm sorry," Adley said, because what else could she say? They sat quietly for a while, just sipping and looking into the fire.

"Anything from Atlanta?" Brody asked after many minutes had gone by.

"Sporadically. I just..." Adley shook her head. "I never know what to say. It all just ended so weirdly." What she didn't say was that she missed Sabrina. Even after all this time. Even after not having seen her for half a year. She missed her. How was that even possible? What did that say about her?

"But you miss her," Brody said, as if reading her mind, and Adley's gaze snapped to hers so quickly that Brody snorted a laugh. "Don't look so surprised. You're my little sister. I've known you your entire life. Think I can't read your face?"

Adley groaned. "But it's so stupid. How can I miss her? She was here for three months. I spent exactly one night with her. What is wrong with me?"

Brody's dark brows met above her nose. "Why does something have to be wrong with you because you fell for somebody quickly? Why is that a bad thing?"

Because you fell for somebody...

Was that what had happened? Seriously?

"Please don't tell me you didn't realize that's what had happened," Brody said, a grin in her voice. "Adley Helene Purcell, what am I going to do with you?" She laughed softly, her affection clear in her eyes. "So, I taught you all about sex, but I clearly fell down on the job when it came to matters of the heart."

Why did Adley feel floored? Why was this surprising to her? How could she not have even thought maybe she'd fallen in love with Sabrina? How stupid could she be?

Another shake of her head, this one a little harder. It didn't matter. Sabrina was gone. Nine hundred sixty-one miles away, to be exact— she'd googled it. And that was to Atlanta. Who knew where she was now, in which city she was setting up the next shop in the Sweet Heaven empire? Los Angeles? Seattle? Honolulu? Tokyo? Could she be farther away?

"Doesn't matter," she finally said and shrugged to make sure it was super clear to Brody that it didn't. "Wasn't meant to be, obviously."

"Yes, because you've always been such a believer in things like fate and destiny." Brody punctuated her statement with an eye roll. Then she pressed her lips together for a moment and studied Adley's face. "But I get it," she said finally. "I do. Too many obstacles in the way."

Indeed. Too many obstacles. That was a good way to put it. Too many potholes in the road to happiness. Too many loop-de-loops in the roller coaster track to keep her from throwing up. Too much quicksand on their path through the jungle— *Oh my God, stop it*, she screamed at her brain. *Enough with the metaphors. She's gone. That's it. End of story.*

"Anyway," Brody said, changing the subject, thank fucking God, "dinner at Mom and Dad's Tuesday night. Don't forget."

"I won't."

"Do they know yet? That you're gonna close the shop?"

Adley shook her head.

"Might be a good time to tell them. I'll be there for moral support."

"Yeah, okay." She dreaded telling her parents. She already felt like such a failure, and she could picture the disappointment in their eyes. After all, the shop had been in the family for three generations. Not that they'd offered to help her, but still. A family tradition was dying.

Because she'd killed it.

❖

"Hello there, Peaches. How's Albuquerque?" Sabrina's father had the smoothest, richest voice, like it was coated in honey. Talking on the phone to him never failed to bring a calm to her world.

"It's actually really nice," she told him. "Pretty."

"Setup going okay?"

She heard the soft tinkle of his spoon against his mug, and she could picture him slowly stirring cream into his coffee. The time difference didn't matter. Sabrina wasn't sleeping much these days. "Yeah, it's fine."

"That Bryce guy there again?"

Sabrina snorted a laugh. "Yep. It's pretty clear Mom doesn't think I can handle this on my own." What she didn't say was that Bryce had been encroaching on her duties, taking care of little things that she normally would before she even realized they were done. He was honestly the biggest sycophant she'd ever met in her life. And the surprising part? She didn't care. She let him slowly creep in, knowing full well he wanted her job. She was this close to simply handing it to him.

"Oh, I don't think that's it," her father said, coming to her mother's defense, no surprise there.

"No, it is, but you know what? That's okay."

The tinkling sound stopped abruptly. "It is?"

"Yup." She didn't elaborate, and he didn't ask her to, which was unlike him. She was pretty sure he would have a talk with her mother soon. Maybe later today. But that was okay. She was figuring out her path in life, and for the first time in a decade, she let herself think outside of Sweet Heaven. It was a little scary, but not so scary that it felt wrong. In fact, it felt very, very right. "Dad?"

"Mm-hmm?"

"How did you know Mom was the one?" She felt like a kid in a sitcom—it was such a clichéd question. Also, she was a grown-ass woman asking a childlike inquiry. "I mean, you guys are so different, but you make it work. How did you know?"

He didn't seem surprised by her curiosity, and she figured that was because she'd been asking him similar questions lately. Things about life and love and matters of the heart. She'd never been able to talk to her mom about such things, but her father was a softie, a romantic at heart. He still sent flowers to her mother every month. He still sent sweet texts and left her love notes in her laptop bag. Sabrina could admit to having a hard time seeing the softer side of her mother much of the time, but her father had no such issue. He was head over heels, just as he'd been the day they'd gotten married.

"That's a complicated question, Peaches," he said. His soft exhale told her he'd sat down in his recliner to watch *Today* like he did every morning. "I'm not sure there's a foolproof sign. You just kind of... know."

"Super helpful, Dad," she said with a soft laugh.

He laughed back. "I know. Sorry about that. Why are you asking? Is this still about the girl in New York?" Man, he was astute. She had told him all about Adley but hadn't mentioned her to him again in months. She was shocked he still remembered her.

She shrugged even though he couldn't see it. "Nah. I was just wondering." She didn't think he bought her deflection, but he let it go anyway, and she was grateful. She had really hoped, after all this time, Adley would've left her head, her heart.

She had not.

The call with her father over, she sat at the small table in her current rental in New Mexico and watched out the window as the sun began to peek over the horizon, as if checking to see if the coast was clear. It really was a beautiful sight, and she found herself wishing she could share it with someone.

No.

Not just someone.

A very specific someone.

She let go of a little groan of frustration, and Sprinkles lifted his head from where he was sleeping at her feet. She reached down and gave him a scratch on his little head. "I'm fine, buddy. Just trying to figure out what the hell is wrong with me."

She didn't fly anymore. She refused to put Sprinkles in the cargo hold of an airplane. No way. She'd read way too many horror stories. Plus, she couldn't imagine how scared he'd be, piled in with suitcases in a section of the plane that was bound to be loud. And his poor ears. No. Nope. When she returned to Atlanta from Northwood, she'd purchased a new car, one with plenty of room for her luggage and her dog, and she now drove to whatever city she needed to be in for her job.

It wasn't even that she minded that. She didn't mind the driving. She played music or listened to audiobooks. It was good thinking time. Good bonding time with Sprinks, as she'd taken to calling him. He'd become a terrific traveling companion. No, it wasn't the traveling that was making her feel restless in her job. It was other things. It was one other person.

How had this happened? Seriously, how? She was a grown woman with all her faculties. Why couldn't she get Adley Purcell out of her head? It had been seven months. Two full seasons had gone by. She'd texted Adley, and at first, there had been a couple lukewarm responses, but they'd stopped.

That was a pretty big hint, wasn't it?

And she was a reasonably intelligent woman, so what was the problem exactly?

This line of thinking had been hers for more than half a year now. Every waking moment, Adley was hanging out somewhere in the back of her mind. And when she wasn't awake? She dreamed. About Adley. And her and Adley. About Adley walking Sprinks, talking about new ice cream ideas, looking down at her with a glimmer in her eye and love on her face.

It was brutal. It was brutal, and Sabrina didn't understand it. But she couldn't let it go, either. It was, quite simply, driving her mad.

With a loud sigh, she opened her laptop, as she did every morning, and did a search. Zillow. Realtor.com. She looked at single family homes. She scanned the condos. She looked at commercial property. She wasn't sure why, but she did it daily. Something compelled her to. It was silly. It was stupid. She had no idea what she was looking for.

But she looked.

CHAPTER NINETEEN

Mid-April had mellowed from the confused and indecisive March, and the day was almost warm. High fifties, sunny, gorgeous blue sky. Spring was on its way. Adley had even seen a few pops of yellow here and there where the daffodils were starting to poke their heads through the soil, the first colorful sign that winter was definitely gone.

She'd asked her friends and family to stay away today. They'd struggled with that, she knew, especially Scottie. She wanted to be there for Adley on such an emotional day, but Adley didn't think she could take the pity. No. She would do this on her own.

Doing her best not to look at the For Sale sign on the front window, she slid the key into the door and entered Get the Scoop for the last time. Her landlord had decided to sell the entire building. His family had owned it for nearly forty years, and he no longer wanted the hassle, just the money. Adley couldn't blame him, really.

It wasn't a surprise that it felt different inside, but the stab of pain was. She pushed her fingertips against her chest and rubbed as she closed the door behind her and stepped all the way in.

It felt almost foreign now. The emptiness was palpable. She'd sold the furnishings, with the exception of one of the stools near the window, which was now in her own kitchen at home. She sold off the equipment, the utensils and bowls and coolers and scoops. She'd taken home everything she wanted to keep, things that reminded her of her grandfather. In addition to the stool, she'd kept a set of spoons, a couple scoops, and some of the ice cream art on the walls—not because it was good, but because it represented a time in her life that meant more to her than she could put into words.

She wandered through the front dining area and into the back to the kitchen. God, how many ice cream flavors had she created back here? Dozens? She'd spent so many nights, especially in the beginning, just experimenting. Mixing fruits and syrups and chocolate and candy, sometimes making a mess, sometimes coming up with gold.

"We're so sorry to see this place go," one woman had said to her on the last day she'd been open. "My grandma brought me here when I was a kid, and now I bring my granddaughter. It's been a family tradition for us." The woman had honest-to-God tears in her eyes when she'd said it, and Adley had barely held it together in front of her, thanking her for her business for so long, her jaw aching from clenching it to keep her own emotion at bay.

Another customer, a man in his forties, had scoffed. "The folks that run Sweet Heaven wouldn't know decent ice cream if it walked up and slapped them in the face." No, it made zero sense, but she appreciated his sentiment and his anger for her. And she quietly admitted to herself that she loved the dig at Sweet Heaven's subpar product.

"I agree," said the woman behind him in line. "It's so...bland. Artificial. You can tell it's mass-produced."

Adley knew all of this but had to admit it was nice to hear it from her customers. Too bad it didn't do any good.

She'd spent her entire last day kicking herself, wondering what she could've done differently, sooner, that might have saved the place. Lower prices wouldn't help the bottom line. Newer equipment would've been nice, but with what money would she have purchased it? Maybe asking for help sooner? A better business plan was probably the key. Damn her and her stupid pride that let her believe she knew what she was doing just because she'd watched her grandpa for years. A business manager would've been smart. Somebody who knew how to manage the money better, how to plan so they could afford newer, better equipment when the time came. How to market and advertise.

"Coulda-shoulda-woulda," she muttered now into the empty space. That's what her dad would say when she was a kid and expressed some kind of regret. "Coulda-shoulda-woulda, Adley. You've got to let it go. The past is the past."

The past is the past.

Well, no shit.

The past is the past was the easy part. The letting go? Not so much.

She dragged her fingers across the smooth surface of the counter where she'd been her most creative. It was so weird to see it empty. No bowls, spoons, ingredients. She moved so her back was against the wall, and she stood there, just staring. At the kitchen. At the emptiness. She slid down the wall until she was sitting on the floor.

She pictured her grandpa at the counter, like he always was when she was a kid. He was a small man, only about five foot five and thin. Ironic for a guy who ate more ice cream than anybody she'd ever met. He was cheerful. Always smiling. He would pull a step stool close so Adley could stand on it and see what he was doing, help if she wanted to. And she did want to. She was helping him make ice cream from the time she understood what ice cream was. His *'sistant*, she called herself until she was a teenager.

"Maybe love of ice cream making skips a generation," her grandmother had said one day, her smile soft and tender, like it always was when she watched Adley and her grandpa working together. Adley's mother had never had any interest in the art of making ice cream, and Adley had always been a little sad for her because of it. There was nothing more in the world that Adley wanted to do.

And here it came, the emotion, just like she knew it would. It was the very reason she didn't want anybody here with her. Her eyes welled up and a lump lodged itself solidly in her throat. Her chest ached as her memories played in front of her like a movie. She literally watched herself grow up in her mind as she sat there, envisioning her younger self and her grandpa, heads together, both in their white ice cream clothes, as she'd called them when she was little, creating the most amazingly rich and creamy vanilla ice cream she'd ever tasted. Crushing mint leaves to make peppermint syrup that had just the right zing for their mint chip. When they decided to make their own birthday cake ice cream, how they'd spent an entire Sunday, from sunrise to sunset, getting it exactly right. When he'd finally rewarded her for her efforts by showing her how to make the most perfect waffle cones on the planet, how to mix the batter, when to roll them so they'd harden up just right. She could see his smile, his soft and gentle brown eyes. She could hear his soft voice as he coached her in making her first solo batch of chocolate almond. She had hoped to pass down the recipes, the skills, to her own children one day. Now, she never would, and she was pretty sure she could hear her own heart cracking in her chest.

She cried then. Quiet sobs that echoed off the ivory walls of the empty kitchen, bounced off the stainless steel counter. Time passed. She might have been there for hours, she wasn't sure. But she let herself sit on the floor against the wall for as long as she needed to, and to cry as much as she needed to, as she watched memories play out in front of her like movies. Laughter and concentration and *love*. So much love. That was the hardest part. It wasn't like she didn't know in her heart that her memories would stay with her, that she didn't need the Scoop to call them up. It was only a building. Only a shop. But still. She felt like she was losing a part of her, and it hurt. It hurt more than she could put into words.

And so she sat.

It was only when she blinked and realized she was having a little trouble seeing that she knew it was time. She inhaled slowly, filling her lungs with her last big breath of Get the Scoop air. It wasn't quite the same, not having the scents of chocolate or peppermint or roasted nuts hanging in the atmosphere, but it was still her place. It was still her identity. Exhaling, she finally pushed herself to her feet and stood in her kitchen one last time.

Hands on the counter, fingertips sliding subtly back and forth on the smoothness of it, she whispered into the emptiness. "Good-bye, Grandpa." She pictured him smiling at her, could swear she felt him laying his cool hand against her cheek. She closed her eyes and soaked it in. Then she left her keys on the counter, as the Realtor had asked her to, locked the doorknob lock on the back door, and left Get the Scoop for the final time, tears coursing silently down her cheeks.

When she turned away from the building to go to her car, she was surprised—and also not surprised at all—to see Scottie standing there, leaning against her own car, arms folded, waiting for her. She didn't say a word. She simply walked to Adley, opened her arms, and wrapped her in a gentle hug.

Adley thought she'd cried it all out inside the Scoop.

She was wrong.

She felt Scottie press a kiss to her temple.
And she cried.

❖

"Close the door."

The tone of Sabrina's mother's voice was stern, but it was always stern, so it was hard to gauge what was up. She did as she was told and shut the door of the office behind her. When her mother indicated the maroon velvet chairs in front of her desk, Sabrina took a seat. She hadn't been there in several months, as she was usually in some other city, but currently, she was in the midst of three weeks at home in Atlanta. And she was honestly feeling a little bit stir-crazy. She tried to seem relaxed in the chair but knew her foot was moving back and forth in a constant rhythm. She hoped her mom didn't notice.

Tilda James was no-nonsense. That was the best way to describe her. Sabrina had lots of other adjectives as well, but that one fit best. She didn't mince words. She didn't suffer fools. She didn't waste time. She said what was on her mind and got to it. No pussyfooting around, as her father would sometimes say. And even though this was her mom, and this was her mom's office, Sabrina was still nervous. Like being called to the principal, but not knowing why.

Her mother's chair was, unsurprisingly, large and leather. Black. Soft. Sabrina knew this from sitting in it as a kid and spinning it with her feet. No, this wasn't the exact same chair from twenty years ago, but her mother always replaced it with an exact replica. She'd told a young Sabrina that when something worked, you stuck with it.

She didn't know if she bought that, but she'd always nodded like a good daughter.

"What's going on with you, Sabrina? I'm concerned." No-nonsense. Cut to the chase.

Sabrina fixed her face to be carefully blank. "What do you mean?"

Her mother's slight head tilt was pretty clear. It said *Who do you think you're talking to? I know you.* When Sabrina said nothing more, her mother sighed quietly. "Your job performance is slipping. Bryce is picking up all your slack. You seem less than interested." Of course Bryce had ratted her out, the little prick. Sabrina wasn't surprised by that. "I think you're unhappy." That was a surprise, though. And her mother's voice became uncharacteristically tender when she asked, "Are you unhappy?"

Just like that, Sabrina found herself in unfamiliar territory. This was the kind of conversation she'd have with her father, not her mother. It was pretty clear he'd talked to her, but she usually dismissed such emotional issues with the irritated wave of a hand. But now? Her mother's blue eyes were trained on hers, and what Sabrina saw in them was nothing short of shocking. Worry. Concern. Love. And the combination brought tears to Sabrina's eyes. Actual, honest-to-God tears. From her mother. What the hell was happening? She swallowed several times, hoping to clear away the emotion that was stealing her ability to speak, but it wasn't working, so she nodded instead.

Her mother breathed in slowly, a big breath, and Sabrina knew from experience that she used that time to think, to plan out her words. A slow exhale, and then her mom folded her hands on her desk and the eye contact was laser focused. "What do you need? Less travel? Different responsibilities?"

To say the direction of this meeting—barely five minutes in— was wildly different than Sabrina had expected would be a colossal understatement. She had no idea what had happened—if her father had had a heart-to-heart with her mother, if her mother actually was more astute emotionally than Sabrina had given her credit for. She'd come in wearing her suit of armor and now felt like she'd overdressed.

Deciding she owed her mother honesty, she wet her lips. "I don't know, Mom. I really don't. I've been struggling, yeah. I just…I'm not sure what I need." She shook her head and shrugged at the same time, unable to articulate exactly how she was feeling.

To her mother's credit, she seemed to accept this weak explanation with a nod. Her intercom buzzed, and she gave a clipped, "Not now," to her secretary through it. Turning back to Sabrina, she said, "Well, you're scheduled to head to Ohio next week. Would you prefer to sit that one out?"

Sabrina blinked. Once. Twice. Three times. Because what? Her mom was actually…cutting her some slack? Offering to take some of the pressure off? Giving her some downtime if she needed it? She frowned for a moment before saying, "I'm sorry, what is happening?"

Was that a flash of a smile on her mom's face, just for, like, a split second? "Well. It's possible it's been brought to my attention that I haven't…" Her mom stopped and seemed to gather her thoughts again before continuing. "That I haven't paid attention to you lately beyond your"—a clear of her throat—"employment."

It was Sabrina's turn to hide a smile. Her dad at work. Definitely.

"And I would like to apologize for that and do better."

"*Okay.*" She drew the word out, not trying to be sarcastic, but really just completely thrown by this new path her mother was choosing.

"Do you"—more hesitation—"want to talk about it? About what's been on your mind?"

Sabrina wanted to be horrified by this, by her mother walking very clearly unfamiliar emotional territory for her, but she couldn't be because her mom was actually trying. Like, making what seemed to be an honest effort to connect with her daughter, and how could Sabrina brush that off? It was new, and it was surprising, and she was absolutely not ready to talk about what had been on her mind.

"You know what, Mom? I do. I do want to talk about it. But maybe not yet?" It came out as a question because she was going for gentle, wanting her mom to know she could see her effort, that she appreciated it. She tried to read her mom's face. Disappointment or relief? A little of both, maybe?

Her mom seemed to take a moment, as if this hadn't been the answer she'd prepped for. She smoothed her hands over the surface of her desk and seemed to gather her thoughts. "All right. Here's what we're going to do. How about you skip Ohio? Stay home. Take a few weeks to just relax. Spend some time with your dog. See your friends. Have dinner with your parents." She smiled at that last one. "We'll revisit things after that."

More blinking from Sabrina because…what the actual fuck was going on? This was so not her mother. This gentleness? This soft, kind demeanor? She made a mental note to call her father and ask him just exactly what he'd said to his wife.

Managing to pull herself out of her shock, she nodded. She should be concerned about her job. Bryce would take over the opening of the new store in Ohio, and he'd be thrilled about it, and Sabrina didn't care. It was fine. Let him do it. She didn't like him but knew he'd do a good job. He was a dick, but he loved the company. "Okay. That sounds good." She pushed herself to her feet, needing this meeting to be over because the weirdness was almost too much. She met her mother's eyes across the desk. "Thanks, Mom. I'll call later."

Her mother smiled but also looked as happy to have this meeting come to an end as Sabrina did.

Sabrina left the office feeling a mix of joy, relief, and utter confusion. That conversation had not been even remotely close to emotional—not in the actual sense of the definition of the word. But it had been *very* emotional for a conversation between her and her mother, and that was just mind-boggling. She got in her car to head back to her place but, instead, just sat there in the driver's seat, staring out the windshield at nothing. Because seriously, what the hell was going on with her life right now?

❖

"Sprinkles, sit."

The dog dropped his butt to the floor and looked up at her with those big brown eyes that Sabrina had grown to love more than just about anything.

"Good boy." She handed over the tiny piece of bacon. She'd made extra with breakfast specifically to have something he loved for when they worked on his training.

She'd never had a dog before, still wasn't sure what had made her decide in a split second that she was keeping Sprinkles rather than dropping him off at a shelter. There had never been a question, and sometimes, she lay awake at night and marveled over that decision.

"Down." She made the hand gesture the trainer had shown her, and Sprinkles stretched his front paws out until his belly was on the kitchen floor. "Good boy." More bacon.

Clearly, she was changing. Or something within her was changing. She no longer felt like herself. Well, no, that wasn't quite accurate. She was still her, but things within her were shifting. Interests. Priorities. What she saw for her future. What she *wanted* for her future. She didn't really understand it. Any of it. Something she'd read a while back said that your thirties are the Age of Enlightenment. She'd had no idea what that meant at the time she'd read it, but she was wondering about it now. Was this it? Was that what was happening? Was there enlightenment now?

A snort. Because no, she didn't feel enlightened. If anything, she felt like she was in the dark about what was going on with her. It wasn't a comfortable place to be.

She squatted. "Up." Sprinkles sat up again. "High-five." It took a couple tries, but he got it, put his paw against her raised palm. She gave him the last of the bacon. "You are the best boy. Should we go for a walk? Wanna go to the dog park?"

At the mention of the *W* word, Sprinkles's ears perked up as he popped to his feet.

"Let's get you hooked up," she told him, grabbing his leash and harness out of the front closet. He loved walks, and he loved sniffing the perimeter of her fenced-in backyard, but nothing gave him more exercise than running with another dog or two around the dog park. She tried to take him a couple times a week if it wasn't too hot. They were just about to head out the front door when her phone pinged from her back pocket, and she pulled it out, gave it a quick glance. A text from the Realtor she'd spoken to.

Got a couple properties that tick most of your boxes. Attached.

Slipping the phone back in her pocket, she saved the text to look at once she was at the dog park with time to kill.

April was probably Sabrina's favorite month when it came to weather. It was warm, usually in the low seventies, but not hot. Not humid. She didn't mind the humidity—she'd lived in Atlanta for most of her life and she was used to it—but she didn't love it either. Being outside was something that made her feel calm and centered, and sweating like a farm animal did not lend itself to calm and centered. Today was gorgeous, though. Sunny with an occasional puffy cloud floating in the electric-blue sky. Seventy-two degrees. The dog park was within walking distance of her house, a perk she hadn't realized she'd had until Sprinkles had come into her life, and she'd done some googling. In true terrier fashion, he sniffed pretty much every blade of grass along the way. She didn't so much have walks with Sprinkles as she had slow strolls. Moseys. Saunters. She didn't mind. These walks with him over the past few months had given her more time to think than she'd ever allowed herself in the past. Yes, she'd scroll on her phone while they walked or read email or research. But for the most part, their walks had become her peace, her respite from the relentlessness of her work life, which had very nearly become all-consuming without her even realizing it.

In about thirty minutes, they arrived at the dog park, a small fenced-in area divided into two large sections, one for dogs twenty-five pounds or less and one for bigger dogs. Currently, there were five dogs running around in the big dog section and only one in the little dog section, a Westie, standing at the fence and watching the big dogs with what could only be described as envy. Sabrina was familiar with her—Bella—and she was relieved because she knew Bella would run Sprinkles ragged, and once they got home, he'd collapse and sleep like a baby, happy and exhausted.

She unclipped Sprinkles's leash, and he flew toward Bella like she'd shot him out of a cannon. The endless sprints began. With a nod to Bella's mom, Sabrina headed to her usual bench. It was another thing she liked about Bella being at the park—her mom wasn't terribly social, which was totally fine with Sabrina. She wasn't up for inane small talk normally, but especially lately. She'd been so solitary, so in her own head, that it had freaked Teagan the hell out and they'd said as much.

"You're a social butterfly," they had said during their last conversation. "You go out to bars by yourself in unfamiliar cities and strike up conversations with strangers. This *I vant to be alone*"—they'd used a terrible Swedish accent there—"thing is so not you. It worries me. It's not like you to be stuck in your own head like this. What can I do?"

Sabrina had laughed it off, promised them she was fine, that she'd tell them if she needed something, some kind of help. Teagan had balked a little, hadn't quite believed her, but had finally relented, promising to check in on her even more than usual.

The truth was, she felt fine, but more pensive. Teagan wasn't wrong—Sabrina *was* in her own head a lot, like, most of the time, and it wasn't her usual thing. She was a stand-up-and-do-it kind of person, not a sit-down-and-think-about-it one. But she'd definitely been overthinking since…well, yeah. Since Adley.

With a sigh—she'd been doing that a lot lately, sighing like she was an old woman who needed to sit down every few minutes—she sat down on her usual bench under the enormous oak tree that grew in the middle of the park and pulled out her phone to take a closer look at the links her Realtor had sent. She wasn't even sure what she was doing.

Exploring her options? Living out a fantasy? Dreaming of a different life? She tried not to dwell on it because if she did, she'd feel terribly guilty for what was likely a waste of her Realtor's time. But for now, it was fine.

She clicked on each link. A cute shop in Vermont. She'd have to get used to snow. Scroll. Another in Seattle. She loved how gorgeous the Pacific Northwest was but didn't think she could take that much rain and gray. Scroll. A storefront—currently a gift shop, by the looks of it—with an apartment up above at the base of the Adirondacks. If only she skied or something. Scroll. Wait.

"What?" She said it aloud and sat forward on the bench, any tiny smidgeon of relaxation she might've felt vanishing in a heartbeat. She sat there, staring at the phone in her hand, at the real estate listing for the building that housed Get the Scoop in Northwood. "Oh God. Poor Adley," she whispered into the park air. Her heart squeezed in her chest, and she closed out of her Realtor's text and scrolled down until she got to Adley. So long ago, it seemed like. She'd thought many times of just deleting the entire thread, but she couldn't. It included Adley's cool, detached texts, yes, but it also included the ones before. Way before. When they were…God, what had they been? A fling? Fuck buddies? Convenient? She opened a new text message, but her thumbs hovered over the keys because what the hell was she supposed to say? *Gee, sorry my company drove yours out of business?* The reality was, there had been other issues. Get the Scoop had been floundering already, she knew that. But Sweet Heaven certainly hadn't helped.

Business is not personal.

She heard the voice in her head, and it made her close out of the open text box.

"I bet it felt pretty personal to Adley," she said quietly, sadly, repeating the same thought she'd had every time the business-versus-personal line ran through her head.

Bella and Sprinkles flew past her, running full speed like dogs tended to do. Sprinkles was slightly smaller, but a titch faster, and they ran the entire perimeter of the park over and over until they both collapsed in the grass, doggy lungs heaving, tongues lolling.

To be that carefree… Sabrina smiled sadly and shook her head as she looked at her exhausted dog. Wouldn't that be nice? To not have to worry about anything except food and play and sleep? To never be concerned about love, to know without a doubt somebody adored you?

She looked down at the phone again. Called up the Scoop's listing again.

Bookmarked it.

CHAPTER TWENTY

It had been an extra rainy May in Northwood. Normally, Adley would be bummed about that because May signaled the beginning of ice cream season in the Northeast. Rain and gloom didn't make people think they might like a cone or a sundae. But now that she had no ice cream to worry about, she found herself embracing the rain. The gray. The damp chill in the air. It all matched her inner mood. She didn't tell anybody that she worried this might be who she was now, that this gloom might be permanent.

That was her inner mood. Her outer mood was a different story. She put on a happy face. After all, she was the hostess and assistant manager at Chumby's, a nice midscale restaurant on the outskirts of the city. It wasn't ever ridiculously busy, but it was never empty, and she began to appreciate the benefit of good, steady business. It could be counted on, which meant bills could be paid.

"Hi there. Reservation for three under Nichols." The man in front of her was in his forties and had two women with him. Adley guessed from their ages they were his wife and his mother.

"Of course," she said with a smile. She had to force herself to inject it with warmth. Smiling was easy, but making it look and sound genuine was harder, and that was something she was working on. She checked his party off on her computer, grabbed three menus from under her desk. "Right this way," she said and led the trio to their table.

She didn't hate the job here, and that was a good thing. It wasn't hard. She took care of reservations and made the schedule for the staff each week. Took care of payroll and placed orders for supplies. She really liked the beginning of a shift because she got to sample the day's specials along with the waitstaff. She enjoyed savoring the different flavors as the chef explained how something was made and offered up little details that the waitstaff might enjoy passing on to customers. It was also a job that was easily left behind when she headed home, and that was new. She didn't spend her evenings thinking up new flavor combinations or playing switcheroo games on her accounting software so she could make sure everybody got paid that week. This job didn't stress her out.

She could admit that last part was a relief.

But her days were free now. She didn't have to be at work until four o'clock. Chumby's opened at five. So she had her mornings and early afternoons free, and oddly, that was the biggest struggle she had now—what to do with those open hours.

She saw her parents now, more than she used to, but it felt weird to her. They were fine. Their normal selves. They talked about the usual things. But they didn't seem to see her sadness, which made her wonder if she was hiding it better than she thought. But then she'd catch a worried glance from Brody. Her sister saw it. Her sister was worried about her. She knew that.

So was Scottie. She called Adley every day. Every single day, and Adley had started doing something she'd never, ever done with Scottie in their whole lives. She'd started not answering her calls. Not all of them. She didn't ignore every call—that was a surefire way to get Scottie to hunt her down wherever she was just to make sure she was still breathing. But every third or fourth call she'd let go to voice mail. She just got so tired of reassuring everybody that she was fine.

And she *was* fine. For a person with no path in life, she really was. She had a job. She had a house. She wasn't wealthy by any stretch of the imagination, but she was able to pay her bills on time. That was new. She kinda liked it.

Fine and floundering, that's what she was. Or floundering, but fine. Either description was accurate. And she wouldn't flounder forever. She knew that, even if the people who loved her weren't so sure. But she was allowing herself time. To mourn. To grieve. She'd lost something very important to her, both tangibly and emotionally. She'd lost her identity. It sounded dramatic, yes, but it was true. She'd been involved in ice cream for pretty much her entire adult life, and now that part of her was gone, and she felt like she was missing a limb. Some of her friends and family thought she was overreacting—her mother had actually used the word *silly*, which had sent Adley directly out the door, into her car, and home. She'd ignored her mother's calls and texts for nearly a week. She would recover. She knew she would. But for her own sanity, she had to be able to grieve the loss of her business, so she gave herself permission to be miserable, at least for a while.

The night ended a little early. Cassandra, the manager, would often close things early if there were no new customers. She'd release people one or two at a time until there was a skeleton crew left to finish up with whatever customers were left at their tables. Then she'd lock the front door behind them, and cleanup would begin. Adley was out by nine thirty, a good hour or two earlier than normal, and she was grateful. Her feet hurt from standing for five solid hours, and she was tired. Still, she took the detour route home like she did a good three or four nights a week.

It was hard to see Get the Scoop dark, the windows blacked out from the inside to prevent burglars from peeking in and deciding to steal what was left, which wasn't much. The day the For Sale sign had gone up, she'd cried all the way home, then cried herself to sleep, then called in sick the next day and didn't leave her bed for more than twenty-four hours. She turned the corner now that would drive her past the building, and she literally gasped out loud in the car.

SOLD.

The huge red sign plastered over the For Sale sign was a shock. Almost literally. Her entire body jerked as if she'd touched a live electrical wire. She pulled to a stop in front of the place, shifted into park, and just sat. Just stared. Her building was not just up for grabs now. It had been grabbed. Snapped up by some unknown entity. She wasn't quite sure how to feel about that. It hurt, of course, but it wasn't her building to begin with. Which had been too bad, really, because maybe if she'd owned it instead of renting, she'd have found a way to keep the business alive.

"Stop it," she said into the emptiness of the car, her voice firm. She refused to jump onto that train of thought. It took her nowhere good.

She slowly began to nod. The building had been sold. It was done now. Soon it would be something new. A diner or a shoe store or a card shop. Who knew? But it was done now.

Shifting her car back into drive, Adley inhaled a slow, deep breath and let it out. She didn't have to drive by here anymore. "Enough," she said and headed home.

❖

Hi there. I know I'm probs the last person you want to see, but I'd really like to talk to you about something specific. Would you have time to meet with me?

Sabrina stared at the text. Read it. Reread it. And reread it. And reread it. Driving herself mad looking at the same words, the same letters, over and over and over as if they were going to change.

"Fuck it," she finally said and hit Send.

The storm door banged, and Teagan came in carrying three boxes in a stack, completely blocking their face. And their ability to see where they were going. "Help," they said, and Sabrina reached for the top box.

"I already know what a badass you are," she said with a laugh. "You don't have to prove it by carrying all the boxes at once."

"You think I'm going to let you move a thousand miles away and not make sure you're okay?" Teagan set down the boxes, then straightened up and looked Sabrina in the eye. "You're sure you know what you're doing, yeah?"

"I do. I have a plan."

Teagan nodded, likely because they'd heard that before, but Sabrina hadn't shared said plan with them. "So you've said." Their tone held clear skepticism laced with worry, and Sabrina loved them for it. She gave their shoulder a squeeze.

"I promise." Teagan stared at her for a full five or six seconds before giving one nod.

"All right. Just a few more boxes." They dodged a large guy coming in the front door carrying an ottoman.

"You know I hired movers, right?" Sabrina called after them with a laugh.

Teagan waved over their shoulder as they headed up into the back of the moving truck.

This was over the top. Wasn't it? She glanced at her phone. Nothing back from Adley. Yet. Would she answer? Or would she ignore the text? It really could go either way, and Sabrina knew that. After a good fifteen minutes of doing things with her phone in her hand, she sighed, realized what she was doing, and slid it into the back pocket of her jeans. She needed to push it out of her mind and focus on her current situation.

Problem was, it had been nearly nine months, and she had yet to push Adley Purcell out of her mind.

Nine. Months.

It defied explanation as far as she was concerned. Teagan had wondered if maybe Sabrina was making everything bigger in her memory, the way humans did sometimes, making normal times seem happier, more important, playing things up in her mind. But Sabrina didn't think that was the case. She'd done everything she could to stop thinking about Adley, including going on a couple dates while home in Atlanta. But nobody interested her the way Adley had. Nobody had turned her on physically the way Adley had. Nobody had touched her heart the way Adley had.

It was very possible that Adley would ignore her text completely. Or worse, tell her to fuck off. But something in the back of her brain told her to hold tight. To be patient. That little voice that all the gurus tell you to always listen to, that gut instinct. So, that was her plan. She would wait and see, and in the meantime, she'd move forward with her plans.

"I like this little place," Teagan said later, after the movers had gone and the two of them sat on Sabrina's navy-blue couch with bottles of beer and sore muscles. Sprinkles was wandering around his new house, sniffing every corner, exploring.

"Me, too," Sabrina said, and it was the truth. It was a small bungalow, two bedrooms and a bathroom upstairs, a small office along with a cute living room, cozy gas fireplace, surprisingly updated kitchen, and powder room on the first floor, and a small, fenced-in, square backyard for Sprinkles. She'd purchased it, rather than renting, and realized that might bite her in the ass if her plans ended up in the toilet. "Do you realize that this is the first time in my life I went with my gut?"

Teagan turned to look at her. "Yeah?"

A nod. "I always, always second-guess myself. I always play it safe. This time? My gut said to do this, and my brain screamed that it was stupid and reckless and did I know how badly it could all blow up in my face?"

Teagan chuckled. "Yeah, that sounds like your brain."

"But my gut said it was the right thing to do and…I just went with it."

"And now?"

"Not gonna lie, I'm a little bit terrified."

"A little terror is good for the soul."

"Is that a quote? Who said that?"

"I believe the credit for that one goes to Teagan Rosecki from the couch of one Sabrina James sometime in the spring of 2023, Northwood, New York."

She laughed and bumped Teagan with a shoulder. "I hate that I took you away from your wife and baby, but I'm really glad you're here."

"You think I was about to let you drive from Atlanta to here all by yourself?" Teagan grinned at her. "I'm glad I'm here, too."

They were interrupted by the buzzing of Sabrina's phone from her back pocket. She lifted her hips so she could reach it, and surprise swamped her when she saw the screen. "It's Adley," she whispered.

"What does it say?" Teagan whispered back. "And why are we whispering?"

Meet with you? Are you here in Northwood?

"I kinda left that part out, didn't I?" she said after she read it aloud to Teagan.

"I mean, it's a pretty important fact."

"Valid." She typed back, *Yes, I'm in town.*

Teagan leaned toward her, and they both watched the little gray dots bouncing and bouncing and bouncing. Then they disappeared completely, and Sabrina held her breath. Then they came back, bounced some more, left again.

"She's not sure what to say," Teagan said.

"Or she's trying to figure out the nicest way to tell me to go fuck myself."

"Oh, I think she'd just come right out and say that if that's what she was thinking."

"Thanks, you're a huge help."

They watched the dots for another moment or two that felt like years, and then the text finally came through: *Where and when?*

"All those bouncing dots for three words?" Teagan asked.

Sabrina didn't even snark back because she was too happy about the fact that Adley had actually agreed to meet with her. No, there'd been nothing personal in her words. Nothing happy, nothing that said Adley was happy to hear from her. Nothing even asking why she was in town again. Just the facts, ma'am, as her dad would say.

"Where and when?" she asked quietly because, honestly, she hadn't even thought that far ahead. She looked at Teagan. "Where and when?"

Teagan's eyes widened. "You're asking me?" At Sabrina's frantic nod, they said, "Um…what about the dog park?"

Sabrina blinked at them. "Actually, that's not a bad idea. We've met there before. It's pretty. Fairly quiet. If we can go at the right time, there probably won't be many other people."

"Better for her to kill you and hide the body."

Sabrina nodded. "There is that." She typed in her response. *Dog park? Tomorrow morning at ten?* She sent it, realizing too late that maybe Adley had a nine-to-five job now, but she didn't worry for long because her response came right back.

OK.

"Yeah, she hates you," Teagan said, her tone only partially teasing.

"Maybe," Sabrina said with a sigh. "But also, maybe not. If she hated me, I think she'd have just ignored me."

"You make a good point, despite the fact that a simple *OK*, just letters and not the word, usually also stands for *fuck you very much*." Teagan said. The doorbell rang and they jumped up and bolted toward the door, Sprinkles barking and jumping at Teagan's leg. "Pizza's here!" And their mutual excitement had Sabrina laughing.

"I'm gonna miss you, weirdo," she said in the kitchen a few minutes later as they dished out their pizza and got more beer from the fridge. Teagan had a flight back home booked in the early morning. They'd taken two days to drive, met the movers and unloaded, and she felt guilty she'd kept Teagan from her wife and newborn for so long.

"Stop feeling guilty," Teagan said as if reading her mind. They sucked tomato sauce off their thumb. "I came to help because I wanted to. Kyra is fine. My baby boy is fine. I'll be home tomorrow." They took a bite of pizza, chewed, and looked Sabrina in the eye. "I'm gonna miss you, too." And the two of them stood there, gazes held, eyes welling up. Teagan was the first to break eye contact, clearing their throat and looking around the kitchen. "You sure you don't want me to stay and help you unpack?"

Sabrina shook her head. "No. You've helped me more than I ever could have asked for. I hope you know how much I appreciate it."

More nodding. More eyes filling with tears.

Finally, Sabrina laughed. "Look at us. A couple of blubbering babies." Teagan laughed too for a moment, and then they put down their paper plates and fell into each other's arms, hugging tight. Sprinkles barked and jumped at their legs, clearly wanting in on the hugging action.

"I'm worried about you," Teagan said against Sabrina's ear. "I don't like worrying about you."

"I know. I'm okay," Sabrina whispered back. "I promise. I'd tell you if I wasn't."

Teagan pushed back and held Sabrina by the shoulders as they stared at her face. "You would? You swear it?"

"I swear it." She narrowed her gaze and said firmly, "I'm okay." She scooped up Sprinkles and cuddled him as she said, "I'm nervous, yeah, of course I am. I don't know what will happen with Adley, true, and I'm nervous about that. But I feel okay. Whatever happens, I'll be okay."

Teagan studied her face, as if looking for a clue that she was lying. Apparently satisfied, they gave one nod, ruffled the wiry hair on Sprinkles's head, and picked their pizza back up. "Okay. But if you need me, you call me. I can be back up here by plane in two hours."

"I know."

"Good. Now let's go sit back down with our pizza and our beer because my feet are fucking killing me."

Sabrina laughed and nodded. "Deal." She set her dog down and grabbed her dinner. Following Teagan back to the couch and looking around her new place as she did, she felt...settled. It was the only way to describe the sudden feeling that came over her without warning. Settled. Like she was exactly where she was supposed to be.

She'd never felt that before. Ever.

Maybe it was a good sign? It sure felt like one.

Time will tell, she thought and flopped down next to her best friend in her new living room to enjoy a dinner of pizza and beer. Not a bad day. Not a bad day at all.

Chapter Twenty-one

What the hell was she doing?

Adley sat in her car, inhaled a big breath, let it out very slowly, and tried to center herself. She was beyond nervous. Like, way beyond. She was confused. She was angry. She was curious. Yeah, that last one was the main reason she was in the car at all and driving to the dog park to meet Sabrina.

God. Sabrina.

She hadn't seen her in nearly a year. Nine months, to be exact. The time it took to grow a whole baby. She shook her head and made a left. She hadn't told anybody about the meeting. She didn't want to be talked out of it. She didn't want to be talked into it. It had to be her own decision, with no influence from anybody else. God, Scottie was going to kill her when she found out.

What could Sabrina possibly want?

That was the question that had been on her mind since they'd texted yesterday. The question that had her stuck in her own head during her shift, had her dropping menus and bumping into chairs, had Cassandra shooting her glances of concern. The question that had kept her from getting any meaningful sleep at all.

And she was feeling that now. As if on cue, a yawn cranked her mouth open as she steered her car into the parking lot at the park, the dog park tucked in toward the back. She'd have to walk a bit. She turned off the ignition and noticed her hand shaking. Not a lot, just a slight tremor, and she made a fist, squeezed it shut, and willed the nerves to go away. Then she took a deep breath in the hopes of bolstering her confidence, and she pushed herself out of the car.

She could see the edge of the dog park as she walked. It was midmorning, so not at all crowded. As she got closer, she could see two golden retrievers in the large dog section. Then she rounded a corner, and there was the little dog section. There was Sprinkles, running around with a black dog about his size.

And there, on a bench, watching her approach, sat Sabrina.

Adley's heart felt like it did a complete somersault in her chest, and she had to stop for a second and force it to calm down. And in that second, all the anger and hurt and confusion vanished. Just evaporated because there was Sabrina, an uncertain smile on her face, and Jesus Christ on a barstool, had she ever looked more beautiful? Simple jeans and a black T-shirt, Converse on her feet, she looked casual, comfortable, and gorgeous. Adley pulled herself together and kept walking until she reached the entry gate and slipped in.

Sprinkles saw her then and sprinted to her like he'd been launched from a slingshot. Suddenly, he was jumping at her legs and bark-squealing with happiness, and honest to God, Adley had never been happier to see a living thing than she was in that moment to see Sprinkles. She squatted down and gave him all the love and hugs and kisses he needed, telling him how much she'd missed him and asking him if he'd been a good boy. Finally, after much, much love, he decided it was time to resume his game of chase with the black dog, which Adley now saw was a poodle. They took off at full speed, and she watched for a moment while she worked up her nerve. After a long moment, she turned to the bench where Sabrina sat, still watching her.

Here we go.

As she approached, Sabrina stood, and Adley was reminded of all that beauty and fire that was crammed into a small body. Determined not to let the tornado of emotions that was in her heart and head show on her face, she made sure her expression was neutral.

"Adley," Sabrina said. And was there relief in her voice? "It's so good to see you." She made a move but stopped herself quickly, and Adley wondered if she'd been about to hug her but thought better of it.

"Hi," Adley said and took a seat on the bench without waiting. She heard Sabrina exhale as she sat next to her. "Sprinkles has gotten so big," she said before she could stop herself.

"He's a good boy," Sabrina said. "A really good dog. I got lucky with him."

Silence reigned for what felt like a ridiculously long period of time until Adley thought she might explode. "What's this about?" she finally asked. "What are you doing here?" And she actually looked at Sabrina for the first time since they'd sat. Her blond hair was loose, the gentle breeze lifting strands up and blowing them away from her face. She noticed something she hadn't at first—Sabrina had lost a little weight, it seemed, her face thinner, her cheeks a bit hollow. Slight half-circles of shadow underlined her eyes. She was still achingly beautiful, but it was clear to Adley that she'd been battling something. "Are you sick?" she blurted before she could stop herself, and she wondered if the fear in her voice was as obvious to Sabrina as it was to her.

Sabrina turned to her in surprise. "Am I…what?" And then it seemed to hit her, to become clear, and she smiled sadly. "No. No, I'm not sick. I've just…had a lot on my mind these past months."

"Oh. Well. That's good." Adley cleared her throat. "That you're not sick, I mean."

"Yeah." Sabrina gave a soft chuckle. "So…I'm actually here because I have a proposition for you."

Of all the things Adley thought Sabrina might have said to her in this moment, that was not even close to the top of the list. She frowned. "A proposition? What does that even mean?"

Sprinkles zipped up to them then, jumped right onto the bench, pink tongue lolling as he panted and hopped into Sabrina's lap. "Are you checking in?" Sabrina asked him with a laugh, and Adley found herself immersed in simply watching the two of them, their bond clear. Sabrina grabbed his head in both hands and kissed the top of it—three loud smacks—and he jumped off and was back to running with the poodle. Adley realized then that another woman sat across the park on her own bench. The poodle's mom, must be.

"Yes. So." Sabrina cleared her throat and clasped her hands together, and it occurred to Adley then that she was nervous. "I want to hire you."

Adley blinked at her, wondering if she'd heard her right. "I'm sorry?"

"I want to hire you."

Adley swallowed and tried to choose her words carefully, to keep her voice steady. "Sweet Heaven put me out of business. What the hell makes you think I want to work for them?"

Sabrina met her gaze then. "I don't work for Sweet Heaven any longer."

"I'm…" Adley narrowed her eyes, her thoughts jumbled. "Wait, what?"

Sabrina inhaled slowly and took her time letting it out. It was clear she was gathering her thoughts, maybe trying to figure out how to say what she wanted to say. Adley waited her out because what the hell? What was she talking about?

"I've made some changes since I left Northwood last year." She cleared her throat again and adjusted her posture so she was sitting up straighter. Adley watched with interest. "I left my job. I bought some property. I moved."

"You moved?"

Sabrina nodded. "Yeah. When I was back in Atlanta for a couple weeks, I felt restless. Like I couldn't relax. I had no idea why at first, but then I realized that the most relaxed I've ever been, the most content I've ever been in my entire life, was here."

Adley watched her, unsure what to say or where this was going.

"I tried to ignore it. I figured I just needed time to settle back into being home. And I waited for months. Six, to be exact. And I still felt restless." She rubbed her hands on her thighs, smoothing them over the denim of her jeans. "I talked to my dad about it. Then my mother, who happens to be the CEO of Sweet Heaven. Then my best friend. Then I sat on it all for another month." She took a deep breath. "And then I called my Realtor friend and asked him to keep an eye out for me in a handful of cities I love."

Adley had no idea where this was going, but she was riveted now, so she waited for the rest of the story. Sabrina's voice had gotten softer and softer as she spoke, and now, it was just above a whisper.

"Two months ago, he texted me with some possibilities, and one of them was right here in Northwood."

Adley's whisper matched Sabrina's. "Possibilities for what?"

"Ice cream shops. Or buildings that could be converted into one."

"Oh." What? Ice cream shops? "I…oh."

"It's weird, right? I know." Sabrina shifted in her seat, turned a bit, and brought one leg up onto the bench so she was facing Adley. And this time, she looked right at her face, right into her eyes. "Listen. You and I have one very important thing in common: We've both been in ice cream for years. We both love it. We both *know* it." She paused there, maybe to see if Adley was following? Which she was trying hard to do, but found herself just blinking a lot. "I know how to run an ice cream business. I've done it my entire adult life. I've been around the best."

"Your mom," Adley said, finally finding her voice.

Sabrina nodded. "Yes. But what I don't know is the creation part. The invention. The experimentation. Flavor. I haven't the first clue how to handle any of that." She swallowed audibly, her nervousness showing once again. "But you do."

Adley flinched and sat back slightly, as if Sabrina had pushed her. "Me?"

Nodding. "You. I've never seen anybody who can create flavor combinations that work so remarkably well. You have a gift, Adley. And I want to hire you for it."

She was so confused. "Wait, what? You want to hire me to work in a Sweet Heaven shop?"

"No. No, no." Sabrina shook her head. "I told you, I don't work for Sweet Heaven anymore. No, I bought a shop that's just mine. Here in Northwood. In fact…" Sabrina glanced down at her hands and cleared her throat. "In fact, I bought yours."

Adley stared. Blinked. "What?"

"I bought the building Get the Scoop was in. I want to open a new shop in the same space, update the place, invest in new, more modern equipment. And I want to focus on the *artisan* part of it, and I want to add desserts. Make them an experience in and of themselves. I figure adding desserts to the ice cream will lend itself to off-season business. People eat ice cream in the summer, but they eat dessert all year long." She held Adley's gaze for a heavy moment before adding, "And I want to hire you as my business partner."

More staring. More blinking. "What?" Apparently, that was the only word in her vocabulary at the moment. "I mean…what?"

"It's a lot, I know. But I have so many ideas, Adley. So many." She could see, hear, and feel Sabrina's excitement just by watching her talk now. "I would take care of the money, all the financial stuff, the ordering, the payroll, the marketing and advertising—which is my favorite part. And you would be in charge of the product itself. All of it." She studied Adley. "You'd be the face of the business. This town knows you. I'd stay behind the scenes."

Seemingly done with her pitch, Sabrina went quiet. Adley sat there with everything Sabrina had said floating around her. She was completely confused...and she wasn't. What Sabrina wanted was pretty clear. She wanted to hire her to go back to work in the place she loved doing exactly what she loved. It really was as simple at that.

"I know this is a lot," Sabrina said again. "You don't have to answer right away. Roll it around. Sleep on it. I'm looking to open July first, so don't, like, wait a month to tell me." Her soft laugh was tinted with uncertainty. She seemed to take a beat to collect herself, and when she spoke again, her tone was firmer. More confident. "Look. Like I said, I've been in this business my entire adult life. I've seen a lot of shops. I've seen a lot of others in this business. But I've never seen anybody with your talent and dedication. You're fantastic at what you do. I'd offer you a more than competitive salary, plus options to co-own. And to be honest, I think we'd make a great team."

Seriously? Was she just going to gloss over the other part?

"How does your mother feel about you coming here to compete with her business?" Yeah, there was some snark in her tone. She couldn't help it. Didn't think she had to—the question was legitimate, regardless of its snottiness.

Sabrina nodded slowly and gazed off into the distance. "Sweet Heaven isn't really on the same level as something artisan. They do cheap, fast, loud, family. It's what they've always been good at, and they use it." She turned to look at Adley. "That's not what our place would be."

Our place. Adley had trouble even absorbing that. "What about our..." She searched for the right word. "History?"

Sabrina exhaled and nodded. "Yeah. There is that."

"There is that." They sat quietly for a while then. Adley felt like her head was overstuffed with too much information, pretty sure it was seeping out her ears as she sat on a bench in a dog park. "So, you, like, live here now?"

"Yeah. I bought a little house over near Jefferson Square. In the same neighborhood where I rented that Airbnb." Adley must've made some kind of shocked face because Sabrina laughed then. "I know, I know. Like I said, it's a lot."

"It's so much. God, Sabrina. It's *so much*."

Sprinkles sprinted back to them and collapsed at Sabrina's feet, clearly wiped out. The poodle had been leashed, and his mom was walking him to the exit. She tossed a wave in their direction, and Sabrina waved back.

"So," Sabrina said as she reached down to pet Sprinkles, "I'm fine with you thinking it over. Take some time. Talk to…whoever you need to talk to." And her tone right there on that last line? Her slight stumble? Adley almost laughed because it was so utterly clear Sabrina had only realized in that second that maybe Adley had somebody. A partner. A girlfriend. A wife. What was also clear? She hated the idea.

Interesting.

Adley felt a little spark of something ignite in her belly.

"Well. I certainly can't answer this now. I'm definitely going to need to think it through. Talk to some people." She left that vague on purpose.

"That's all I ask." Sabrina seemed excited, and Adley wondered if she'd expected her to say no right off the bat. Maybe she should have, but something about sitting there next to Sabrina again was so surreal. And looking into her big blue eyes right then? Yeah, that had her world standing still. *Okay, she still has the power to make time stop. To make me feel…Yep. Good to know.* "What do you say, buddy?" It took Adley a second to understand Sabrina was talking to the dog. "Ready to go home?" With a glance up at Adley, she added, "Still have some unpacking to do." She clipped the leash onto Sprinkles just as the goldens in the big-dog area started barking. Sabrina stood, then looked down at Adley—pretty much the only time she was ever taller than her, which made Adley smile. "Thanks for meeting me," Sabrina said softly. "I wasn't sure you would."

"I wasn't either," Adley said.

"I'll wait to hear from you, okay?" And with one nod, she gave Sprinkles a little tug, and Adley watched them walk away. Even when they turned the corner and walked out of sight, she continued to sit there feeling a mix of surprise, irritation, confusion, and about a million other things. Because, seriously, what the hell had just happened?

She pulled out her phone and texted Scottie.

❖

"You have *got* to be fucking kidding me." Scottie's eyes went wider than Adley had ever seen them, so much so that it made her laugh.

"I kid you not."

"But she…but then…you have *got* to be fucking kidding me."

"Nope."

One of the happy things that had come of Adley's hostessing job at Chumby's was that it was closed on Mondays. So was Trio, Scottie's hair salon. So the two of them often met up on a Monday for breakfast or lunch or happy hour or whatever. They sat on Scottie's back patio in the bright May sunshine, eating an early dinner of salads that Scottie had whipped up for them. Scottie had had a forkful of lettuce and a cherry tomato hovering in the air near her mouth for a long time now as she sat there and looked at Adley in shock. Finally, she put it in her mouth, chewed, and set down her bowl. Turning in her chair so she faced Adley and gave her all her attention, she said, "Tell me everything. Start to finish. Don't leave anything out."

Adley did exactly that. Spilled it all, from the initial text to how irritatingly beautiful Sabrina still was when she saw her in the dog park. And also how nervous she seemed to be. The offer of a job, but not just a job. Sabrina had mentioned the phrase *business partner*. How she hadn't ignored their history. "We didn't really get into it, just acknowledged it was there."

Scottie nodded and, to her credit, said nothing the entire time Adley relayed the story. But she watched her face with rapt attention as she spoke. When she finished, Scottie sat quietly for a moment before finally asking, "So? What did you say?"

"I told her I wanted to think about it."

Scottie's eyes went comically wide again. "What? You do? Seriously?"

Strangely, saying the words out loud to Scottie only solidified them in her mind. "I do. I am. Thinking about it." She sighed loudly. "I miss ice cream, Scottie. I miss it so much."

"You can make it at home," Scottie said, then wrinkled her nose. "Can't you?"

It made Adley laugh. She couldn't help it. "I can, yes, but only in tiny batches and I can't share it beyond, like, you."

Scottie lifted a shoulder in a half shrug as she shook her head. "I'm not opposed to that, and I don't see the problem." They both laughed softly, and then Scottie closed a hand over Adley's forearm. "I understand. I do. I know you, and I see how sad you are lately. I know how much you miss your shop. I just…" She pressed her lips together in a thin line and held Adley's gaze.

"It's okay. Go ahead and say it."

Scottie leaned forward and tapped a finger against Adley's chest. "I worry about this. Right here. I know how you felt about her last year, and I know you've probably promised yourself that you'll be careful, that you'll keep things strictly business if you decide to say yes, but… is that possible?"

It was Adley's turn to half shrug. "It'll have to be. Right?" Scottie still had a slightly skeptical edge to her expression, so she went on. "If this is what I want to do, if I want to get back into ice cream, I don't think I can turn down an opportunity like this. It has literally just fallen into my lap."

"Or been placed there gently by somebody you find devastatingly attractive. Oh, and that you've had sex with. The best sex of your life, if I remember correctly."

A nod. "Yeah, there is that." She had to give it credence. Didn't she? Scottie was not wrong. But she'd been rolling it all around in her head for hours. And it was true, she'd need to take more time before she made a definite decision. "I just…I miss it so much."

"I know you do."

"And this is an opportunity that I'm not going to get anywhere else. Artisan ice cream maker isn't exactly a common category on job search sites, you know?" She gave a bitter chuckle. "Believe me, I've looked."

Scottie pushed the remaining salad around in her bowl for a moment, and when she looked back up at Adley, her face was dead serious. "Just please promise me you'll watch out for your heart. Okay? Don't make me worry about you."

Adley made a *pfft* sound. "Who are you kidding? You're going to worry no matter what. It's what you do. Look at you. You've already started."

"Truth."

Eventually, they shifted to other topics. The end of school approaching, which would leave Jaden to visit different family members and would free up much of Marisa's time to teach more dance. How much Scottie was looking forward to their first vacation together, just the two of them. They talked about Trio, the salon Scottie co-owned, and Scottie gave Adley's dark hair a tug and let her know her ends were fried and it was time to make an appointment.

By the time Adley got home, she felt lighter. She always left Scottie's place feeling that way. Happier. Calmer. She'd promised Scottie that she'd give herself until the end of the day on Wednesday before she made a final decision. That way, her brain would have a chance to examine both sides, the good and the bad, the pros and the cons. It was a reasonable request, and Adley agreed to it, even though she was pretty sure of her answer.

She woke up Tuesday feeling the same way but went through her day like normal. Stopped in to see her mother at her office in the morning. Did some long-overdue grocery shopping to fill her empty cupboards and barren refrigerator. Went for a walk around Black Cherry Lake just to soak in the spring air and play peekaboo with the sunshine as it hid behind clouds here and there. She went to work at Chumby's and still felt lighter. There was a little spring in her step that she could feel, and she knew she was smiling more than usual—or at least more genuinely than usual. She ate a dinner of chicken French that was the night's special—and insanely delicious—in the kitchen as she chatted with the cooking staff. When she finally got home, just before eleven o'clock, she found herself not at all disappointed that she hadn't heard from Sabrina. She was giving her space, and Adley appreciated that more than she'd realized at first. It was clear Sabrina didn't want to push her. Adley poured herself a glass of cabernet and took it to the bedroom with her. She did her nightly routine, slipped under the covers, and clicked on the television to the Food Network. She watched three episodes of *Chopped* before her eyes started to get heavy. With one last glance at her phone's screen—nothing from Sabrina—she turned everything off and went to sleep, dreaming of freshly made waffle cones and big tubs of ice cream and Sabrina smiling at her.

CHAPTER TWENTY-TWO

Waiting until Wednesday evening was very nearly torture for Adley. When she woke up on Wednesday morning, she knew with every fiber of her being what her answer was. But she'd promised Scottie she'd wait. And she had to admit that no matter how unlikely, it was still possible she might change her mind before the day was over.

"Fat chance," she muttered as she took her morning walk, this time up and down and around her neighborhood. The day was a bit cooler and a little grayer than yesterday, and she zipped up her hoodie as she went. She tried to simply be in the moment, to look at the spring flowers popping up through the soil, to feel the dampness in the air, to notice birds singing. Anything to stay in the present and not get mired in the decision she was trying to make.

Unsurprisingly, it didn't work. All she could think about was getting back to what she loved. Being creative again. Making little kids smile. Being a vital part of the community in which she lived. Her brain wouldn't shift to anything else, and that was a pretty big clue, as far as she was concerned.

By the time she was ready to head in to work that afternoon, she couldn't take it any longer. She typed out a quick text to Scottie.

I'm gonna take it. My mind hasn't wavered a millimeter since we talked. She sent it and didn't have to wait long for a response.

I just want you to be happy. And a smiling emoji and a heart followed. Scottie was worried about her, she knew, but she was also the most supportive person in Adley's life, so getting her okay was freeing.

She got ready for work, trying to formulate exactly the right text to Sabrina. She went around and around and hit every possibility there was. Overly grateful. Too snarky. Too distant. Vague. By the time she'd seated her fifth table that night at Chumby's, her brain was exhausted. She returned to her hostess podium near the door, sighed as she thought *fuck it*, and took out her phone.

I'm in.

That was it. Simple. Emotionless. To the point.

She sent it.

Cassandra allowed her to have her phone up front with her but didn't like seeing her on it, understandably. So as soon as she sent the text, she put the phone back under the podium and focused on the large party of eight that was walking through the front door.

The restaurant got extra busy after that, and by the time things were wrapping up for the night, Adley remembered the phone, the message. Interesting how, once she'd made a decision, she'd been able to set it all aside—finally!—and not have it consuming her every moment. She grabbed her phone and took a look at the text response that had just come from Sabrina.

Seriously? That's fantastic! I'm so glad! I promise you won't regret this. It's going to be amazing. I'm so happy...I'm thrilled. Dancing around my living room right now. Sprinkles is also dancing. Let's meet at the shop tomorrow and we can go over details. There was a pause and the gray dots bounced for a moment before the next words came. *Thank you, Adley. I mean that.* The message was followed by several celebratory emoji, including but not limited to smileys, champagne bottles, and party horns.

Adley grinned. She couldn't help it. The image of Sabrina dancing around with her dog just made her happy, and if Scottie knew that, they'd probably have to sit and analyze it. Good thing Scottie wasn't there.

She smiled as she drove home and felt lighter somehow. She called Scottie from the car.

"I did it. I told Sabrina I'd take the job."

"OMG, what did she say?"

"Well, it was all through text 'cause I was working, but she seems really happy about it."

"And you? How are you feeling?" Scottie's voice was soft. Kind and curious.

"I feel...so much, Scottie. So much." She took in a deep, slow breath and understood that she needed to talk all this out. "I mean, part of me still can't believe I lost the shop. I'm so embarrassed, Scooter. So incredibly embarrassed that I couldn't keep it afloat. I feel like I let my grandpa down in the biggest of ways. And then there's the hostessing. I mean, is that what I want to do for the rest of my life? Lead people to their dinner table? And through all of this, I was still mourning the loss of what might have been with Sabrina."

"That all makes perfect sense," Scottie said, her voice soft and understanding.

"And then Sabrina shows back up with this offer." She shook her head. "And I wanted to scream at her. *You tank my business? You ruin my life? You humiliate me and now you're back and you want to save me? Fuck no. Fuck that. No.* But..." She took a moment, took a breath, let herself calm down again. "But the weird thing is, I still trust her. After all that she did, after all that happened, I still trust her." She hadn't actually said that out loud, and hearing the words now, actually *hearing them* for the first time, didn't freak her out the way she was afraid it might. "I didn't tell her that, of course." She gave a little chuckle. "But the reality is that it's true. I still trust her, and I feel like a weight has lifted. Isn't that weird?"

"I mean, does it feel weird?"

"Not even a little bit. It feels right. It feels exactly right."

"Well, there you go then. I think the Universe is telling you that you made the right decision."

Adley sighed and turned into her driveway, then shifted the car into park. "I think so, too."

"And you feel okay about the rest of it? The...history?"

"I do right now. I guess we'll have to see how it goes when we're both there, you know?"

They signed off shortly after, and Adley went inside. As she poured herself a glass of wine, there was a part of her that wanted to call Sabrina now, talk to her, listen to her ideas, and share some of her own. But she gave herself a shake, reminded herself that's not who they were anymore.

Sabrina was going to be her boss for the time being, and she'd do well to remember that little fact.

❖

Sabrina's nerves were shot.

She woke up Wednesday morning feeling jittery and buzzing, like she'd had too much caffeine…except she hadn't had any yet.

Today was the day. Adley had accepted the job she'd offered, and today, they were going to meet. She'd texted her an hour ago to set the time. They were going to meet at noon at the ice cream shop and go over all the pertinent details. Sabrina also wanted to pick Adley's brain about some equipment preferences and also wanted to let her in on the plans she had for the grand opening and the summer in general.

And she wanted to see her. Just…see her.

She had to put that in a box on a high, high shelf, and she knew it. But still.

The meeting was five hours away, and Sabrina needed to burn off some of the frantic energy she had or she might burst into a pile of ash from the nerves.

A run.

That always helped. She called Sprinkles in from the backyard where he was giving the perimeter his morning sniff-down. She laughed at how quickly he'd understood the yard was his now. They'd been there less than a week, but he'd already established a morning routine of sniffing along every inch of the privacy fence, nose to the ground, tail up in the air. She'd taken to sipping her first bit of coffee at the window while watching him do his thing. It felt shockingly domestic and homey, and she wasn't sure what to do with that.

Now, she held the back door as he trotted inside and looked at her expectantly. She'd filled his Kong with peanut butter and some treats to keep him busy while she ran. She'd tried running with him once, but he was such a terrier. All he wanted to do was sniff every blade of grass, and her run had become a casual stroll, which burned off zero energy for her but completely pooped her dog out.

She ran until her lungs burned. Then she walked until her breath returned to normal. Then she ran again until her lungs burned. It was a chilly morning, and sucking in the cool, damp air made the run harder, but she pushed on, not stopping until she felt better. Less electrified. More herself.

Back home, she made herself some breakfast—running in the morning always famished her—and turned on *Today* so she could focus on something other than her noon meeting. It worked for a short time, and then she gave up, showered, dressed, and headed to the shop a full ninety minutes before her meeting with Adley.

Bobby Unger was already on the premises, along with another of his guys. A small speaker sat on the counter playing classic rock. Bobby was the contractor she'd hired to do some updates, a local guy who'd lived in Northwood his whole life and who had his own small contracting business. His Yelp reviews were stellar, and she'd done extensive research on him, along with a phone interview, before hiring him.

"Hey, Sabrina, how's life treating you?" He stepped off the ladder he'd been perched on to give her his full attention, something she really liked about him.

"Can't complain, Bobby. Can't complain." She almost laughed at how much she'd sounded like her father just then. "What news do you have for me?"

He gave a small shrug and shook his head. "Not much. Everything's on schedule. Once Jay and I finish rewiring the electric and patch the drywall, I think we'll be ready for fresh paint."

"Fantastic. And you'll take care of that?"

Bobby nodded. "I work with a gal who's been painting since she was a teenager. She's good. We'll need to meet with her about colors, but then she'll take it from there."

"Great." She gave him a wave. "Okay, don't let me disturb you. You do you. I'll be in my office."

Another nod and Bobby got back to work.

Because Sabrina had actually purchased the building, she'd been able to make some structural changes, and they included walling off some of the back area so there was a small office. It was the first thing Bobby had done so that she had somewhere to work even while the renovations were still in progress.

Her office was small, but cozy. She had a tiny window, so she could get some natural light. She'd purchased herself a nice desk and a top-of-the-line laptop and put all her accounting software and business applications on it. This was her thing, the business end. It was what she loved. The numbers and the profit/loss reports and the marketing.

She'd been able to do little bits and pieces of those things here and there at Sweet Heaven, but there had been an accounting department. And a marketing department. And a new business department. And Sabrina couldn't work in all of them. Once upon a time, all that travel had been appealing.

She'd had no idea how tiring it would be after so long.

But this? Right here? Her own office in her own shop that she owned? This was her version of very sweet heaven. And she was about to have the best ice cream maker she'd ever seen as her right hand. Did it get any better?

Her phone pinged a text and she saw it was Teagan. Opening it, she read, *How's the hideously inappropriate crush on your soon-to-be employee who's pretty much an ex going? Good?* That was followed by a slew of laughing emoji, and Sabrina shook her head and couldn't help but smile.

She'll be here in 1/2 an hour. I'll let you know then.

She sent it back. Teagan let it drop and sent four baby photos instead. She was still looking at them and mentally oohing and aahing over them when there was a knock on the back door. All the nerves she'd worked all morning to subdue came back to life as if she'd plugged herself into an electrical outlet and suddenly had power.

She smoothed her hands down her thighs and stood up. Three deep breaths later, she headed out to the back door and pushed it open.

Adley looked gorgeous.

Uncertain and skeptical and a little ticked off. And gorgeous. Her dark hair was down around her shoulders, wavy and sexy. She wore cropped jeans, white sneakers, and an orange V-neck shirt that complemented her skin tone beautifully. It was hard for Sabrina not to stare.

"Hi," Sabrina said and stood aside. "Come in. Come in."

Adley looked around quickly, then returned her gaze to Sabrina's face.

"Is it hard for you to be here?" she asked before she could stop herself.

"It's weird," Adley said, glancing down at her feet.

"I guess that would make sense." There was a beat while they just stood quietly, but before Sabrina could find the right thing to say, Adley spoke instead.

"Okay." She seemed to bolster herself. "Show me around."

"Yeah. Okay. Um...here's the kitchen." She did a little arm flourish like Vanna White.

"That's new." Adley pointed toward Sabrina's office, then walked that way.

"My office. I like to be in the midst of things. I'm having a camera installed later this week, so I can see out front while in here. In case there are any problems with customers or whatever."

Adley nodded as her eyes moved over the desk, the window, the chair. "It's nice."

"Thanks." They turned back to the kitchen. "I didn't make a whole lot of changes here. Just updated the countertop. I wanted to get your input on some new equipment, so we'll look at that in a bit." That seemed to brighten up Adley's expression a bit.

"My input?"

"You're the ice cream maker. I want to have equipment that works for you."

"But you're the boss."

Sabrina tipped her head and studied Adley. Her face wasn't quite readable, and she knew that Adley was likely shuttering her expression for Sabrina's benefit. *You don't get Open Me anymore.* It made her sad, but she pressed on. "I would really like this to be a partnership." Wincing internally at the choice of words, she waited for Adley to balk, but she didn't. She just gave a small nod and moved toward the front.

Bobby and Jay were up on ladders still, but like earlier, Bobby saw them and came down. "Hi there," he said, holding out a hand to Adley. "Bobby Unger. Nice to meet you."

"Bobby, this is Adley Purcell, my business partner. If you have questions and I'm not here, she can answer them." She felt Adley's surprised expression more than saw it as she and Bobby shook. "He's bringing in his painter to go over colors this week, and I'd love it if you could be here, give your opinion."

Still clearly surprised, Adley nodded. "Sure."

They talked with Bobby about the electric—Adley commented about how great it was that it was all rewired—and the display cases in the front, which were also new.

"I'll have those hooked up and good to go before the end of the month," Bobby said. "That's when the light fixtures should be here."

"Once that stuff's all done, we'll be ready to paint," Sabrina informed Adley. "New tables and chairs, indoor and outdoor, will be here the first week in June. I could use your help on art and decor. I loved the stuff you had hanging on the walls."

"I still have some of it," Adley said, and Sabrina could tell she was starting to get excited, even if she was trying to hide it. "I can bring it by."

"That'd be great." Back in the kitchen, they talked about utensils and dishes. "I'm hoping you'll still make waffle cones. I'd like to advertise those more. They're a big deal."

"You think?" Adley asked, running her hand across the door to the new walk-in freezer.

"Are you kidding? Best I've ever had. And I've had *a lot* of waffle cones in my line of work." Adley's smile made her keep going. "I don't know what your secret is, but they're amazing."

"I'd tell you, but then I'd have to kill you."

Oh, playful Adley had arrived! Sabrina tried not to jump up and down with glee. Instead, she held her hands up, palms forward, and said, "I don't need to know. Just keep making them."

"I can do that."

"Okay. Come into my office and let's talk numbers."

❖

"And? How'd it go?" Brody's voice was curious and worried and skeptical and hopeful all at once, and Adley loved her for that. She was in her car on her way to her shift at Chumby's and talking to her sister through the Bluetooth.

"It went…great. Super. Like, really, really well."

"Yeah? Tell me."

"It's almost too good to be true, which is the only thing that has me worried because what's that saying? If it seems too good to be true, it probably is?"

"I get that, but give me the details anyway."

"The pay is generous. Very. There will be health care and eventually some kind of retirement benefit. Those things seem important to her, even if the business is a small one. I get the impression that being good to her employees is a big deal."

"I like her already."

"She kept referring to me as her business partner."

"Seriously?" She could picture Brody's dark eyes going wide with surprise.

"Yeah. She wants me to get a feel for the place and the job, and if I decide I'm happy, she wants to talk partnership. Like, me owning part of the business."

"Wow. How do you feel about that?"

"It feels fantastic. And weird. And scary. And awesome. And I'm honestly waiting for the other shoe to drop."

Brody was quiet for a long moment.

"What?" Adley prodded.

"I mean, the other shoe's already dropped, don't you think? It's your past with her. Can you set it aside?" Her voice went softer. "Do you even want to?"

Goddamn it, Brody knew her so well. Sabrina had looked beautiful today. Stunning. Gorgeous. As always. Seriously, did the woman ever look messy? Unkempt? Even Casual Sabrina was more beautifully put together than anybody else she knew. She gave a shrug, even though Brody couldn't see it through the phone. "Well, I'm gonna have to, aren't I?"

And that was it and all about it. That was the fact of the matter. Yes, they'd had a thing. Yes, it had been incredible while it lasted, but it *didn't* last. It had crashed and burned and that was life. Now, they had to leave their past in the rearview mirror and look forward instead. Simple.

She could do that.

Couldn't she?

They ended the call just as she pulled into Chumby's parking lot. She was going to need to talk to Cassandra and put in her notice this week. She wasn't looking forward to that, but only because she hated to be an imposition, not because she'd miss the job. She wouldn't. In fact, she'd already been rolling around different flavor combinations.

Later that night, when she was home from her shift and texting with Scottie, she thought about that again, about the flavors running through her head.

You know, it's like after the Scoop closed, I put a lid on my creativity and stored it in a dark corner someplace because I couldn't bear it. She squinted into the dim light of her bedroom as she thought about it. *And now that this job is here, the lid has popped off and all those ideas have just come flowing back out. I can't stop them.*

The gray dots bounced as Scottie typed her response. *I'm so happy to hear this! You sound so much better than you have the past few months…and I have missed being your taster.* That was followed by several ice cream cone emoji and a tongue.

Adley laughed. And Scottie was right about her sounding better. She felt better. Like she'd been tightened into a ball and had suddenly been loosened up, finally able to stand and stretch and reach again. It was delicious. And she owed it all to Sabrina.

Which was something she grappled with a bit. Because the tightening was also owed to Sabrina. Sort of. Kind of. Okay, not really. Something else she'd been grappling with.

I can't wait for you to be my taster again. Soon… And she sent back the tongue emoji, then signed off with a good night, and set her phone on the nightstand. She was tired, but her brain wouldn't settle, so she clicked on the TV and snuggled down into her covers. Then she grabbed up her phone again, opened the notes app, and jotted down the flavors that had been on her mind the past couple of hours.

Chocolate and cherry and cayenne, oh my…

Chapter Twenty-three

Sabrina sat at her desk in her small office off the kitchen and smiled. In the monitor before her, she could see Kirby Dupree up on a ladder, painting the interior wall out front a happy, soothing peach color. Across from her, the other wall was going to be more of a rust orange. The idea was to make the interior of the shop feel earthy and comfortable and joyous, all at once. She and Adley had chosen happy colors. At least, that's what Kirby had called them.

In the kitchen, Adley was flitting about, grabbing different ingredients from shelves and the fridge and the freezer. She was mixing and blending and grinding, and Sabrina found herself mesmerized by her in ways that went far beyond just how beautiful she was.

"Taste this." Suddenly, Adley was right there. Next to her desk, holding out a spoon piled with something that appeared to be chocolate ice cream. Dutifully, she opened her mouth, and Adley spooned it in, then waited, watching her face carefully.

"Mm," Sabrina said, giving it a minute. She'd learned quickly this week that when Adley asked her to taste something, it meant she wanted her to *taste* it. Slowly. Deliberately. Then give her opinion. "It's good," she said, rolling it around on her tongue. "Chocolate and…cherries? And oh. Wait. *Ooh.*" A spice hit her then on the back of her tongue. Something hot with a little smokiness. Then hotter. "That's got a kick."

"Too much of one?"

Sabrina tipped her head one way, then the other, and felt her nose start to run, before nodding. "Maybe a little bit, yeah."

"I was afraid of that. Okay." She turned on her heel to head back to the kitchen. "Toning it down!"

Yeah, Adley Purcell in her element was a sight to behold indeed.

It had been three weeks since Adley had accepted the job Sabrina'd offered, and it was now Thursday of her first full week in the shop. The first day had been a bit awkward, the two of them trying to find their footing with each other, and it still surprised her how quickly that had passed. And now? Adley was running the kitchen with the precision of the pro she was. And what was more, she was happy. Sabrina could see it on her face, in the way she carried herself confidently around the room. In the way her dark brow would furrow when she tasted something that wasn't quite right and she was trying to figure out why. Watching her work was fascinating to Sabrina.

Her phone pinged with a text, interrupting her daydream. She glanced at it, then pushed to her feet, a wave of excitement washing through her.

"Come with me," she said to Adley as she passed her and headed out into the front of the shop.

"Bossy," Adley said, but her voice was light, and she tossed the towel that had been draped over her shoulder to the counter and followed Sabrina out.

At the front door, she turned and said to Adley, "Okay, close your eyes."

"What? Why?"

Sabrina tipped her head. "Please? Just close 'em."

Adley sighed loudly, like she was so put-upon, but there was a ghost of a grin on her face as her eyelids closed.

Sabrina grabbed both her hands and slowly walked backward out the front door. "Keep them closed. Just walk. I've got you. Okay, step down. One. One more." Adley followed her instructions until they were out of the shop. Sabrina led her a little farther into the parking lot, then turned her around by her shoulders so she was facing the front of the building. Just for added security, she put her own hand over Adley's eyes.

"Okay. Ready?" she asked, her voice soft. God, she hoped this had the effect she intended.

"Ready," Adley said.

Sabrina nodded to the guys in front of her who had just finished their job. She removed her hand from Adley's face and said, "Open. Ta-da!"

Adley opened her beautiful dark eyes, took in the front of the building, complete with its brand new sign. Above the door and across the entire front of the building were the words *A Second Scoop*. Underneath it in smaller letters was *Artisan Ice Cream and Dessert Experience*. It was all done in a lovely peachy-orange that was both bright and summery, but with a touch of earthiness, just like the walls inside.

Adley said nothing.

She just stood and looked, and just when Sabrina started to feel slightly ill, Adley's eyes welled up. She blinked rapidly until her tears spilled over and ran down her cheeks.

Sabrina grabbed her hands again. "Hey. Hey. I'm sorry. I thought you'd like it. I meant it as a sort of sequel to your old place. Please don't cry. We can change it. No problem."

That's when she felt Adley's hands grip hers back. "No," she said with a sniffle. "No, no, don't change it. I love it. I *love* it." Her gaze shifted and captured Sabrina's, and she felt it all the way down to her center. "I love it, Sabrina," Adley said one more time, this time as a whisper. "Thank you."

And then she was wrapping her arms around Sabrina, pulling her into a hug, and it took Sabrina a second or two to realize what was happening. When she hugged Adley back, she held on tight, inhaled the creamy, nutty, chocolatey scent of the ice-cream-making version of her, squeezed, took her in, and tried not to think about how long it had been since she'd had Adley in her arms.

"Wow, that looks incredible." It was Kirby, who had clearly come outside to see the final mounting of the sign. "Nicely done," she said to Sabrina, who had to work to keep her smile from being comically wide. All she'd wanted was for Adley to love the new name, and it seemed like she'd gotten her wish. Her relief was, well, a relief. And seeing Adley so happy… Sabrina didn't want to dwell too long on just exactly how that made her feel.

"This is so awesome," Kirby was saying now, and Sabrina forced herself out of her own head and back to the present. She liked Kirby, had liked her right away, her kind, fun energy emanating from her constantly. Sabrina had learned it was hard not to smile with Kirby around. She stood now in jeans that were spotted with countless different colors, work boots, a sleeveless red T-shirt that had clearly had sleeves at one time, and a baseball hat backward on her head, tufts of blond hair sticking out the fastener hole. "I remember coming here as a kid with my dad." Her voice took on a slightly dreamy quality. "Lotta good memories here for me. I'm glad it's back."

"Me, too," Adley said, and when she turned those dark, dark eyes to Sabrina, there was more in them than Sabrina was ready to analyze.

"Listen," Kirby went on as she glanced at her watch, "it's almost five. I've got some cleanup to do in there and then I'm meeting my girlfriend out for happy hour. You guys interested in grabbing a drink? I know how hard you've both been working this week because I've seen it with my own eyes. Meet me out? First round's on me."

Adley looked at Sabrina, and they had a silent conversation that basically boiled down to *It's impossible to say no to Kirby Dupree. She's too nice.*

With a nod, Sabrina answered for the both of them. "Sure, we'll meet you. Where?"

"It's a cool bar in Jefferson Square called Martini's. My girlfriend's cousin owns it."

Well.

That was a twist she hadn't seen coming. The very bar where she and Adley had first seen each other, had first met, had first made out in the ladies' room. She glanced at Adley, and there was that ghost of a smile again. For some reason, it made everything that had tensed up in Sabrina release, and she knew what the answer was, just like that. She gave Kirby a nod. "Sure. We'll meet you."

❖

"Do you want to ride together or—?" Sabrina's voice was close. Adley hadn't heard her approach, so absorbed in jotting down notes for the Chocolate Cherry Bomb ice cream she was trying to get right. And it sent pleasant chills across her skin.

It was a good question. But things had been really great this week, and she felt less stressed around Sabrina. Less frustrated. Softer. That new sign? Calling the shop A Second Scoop? Yeah, that had been a big freaking deal. Many, many points to Sabrina for that.

"Sure, we can ride together. Just let me make myself presentable." She'd already cleaned up her equipment and supplies and such, and now she put her notes away in the small filing box on the shelf. She'd transfer them to the computer later, but she found that writing stuff down by hand somehow solidified things in her mind better. It's how she'd always done it, and digging out her little box with the ice cream stickers on it had given her a thrill she hadn't expected. She'd revisit the Chocolate Cherry Bomb tomorrow and get the cayenne just right. She gave the box an affectionate little pat.

"Okay. Let me know when you're ready." Sabrina gave her a smile, then headed back into her office, and yes, Adley watched her walk away. Yes, she watched that ass, the way it moved, the way her hips swayed. Thank God it was a short walk, and she could refocus on the job at hand after a few seconds.

In the small bathroom, she took off her white coat and tossed it into the small hamper. Sabrina had made sure she had five of them, and there was one clean one left. Time to do some laundry, and she made a mental note.

Had she known they'd be going out, she'd have dressed a bit nicer than the jeans and black T-shirt she wore, but that was okay. She didn't want to dress up to go out with Sabrina, especially to Martini's. That would definitely send the wrong signals, which made her laugh internally as she fixed her hair in the mirror, touched up her mascara, and applied lip gloss, and wondered what kinds of signals *that* would be sending.

She had so many feelings around this new working environment. So many.

Joy. That was first and foremost. She'd had zero idea just exactly how happy it would make her to be back in ice cream. She woke up each morning thrilled to get to work. There was an element of relief around having somebody else take care of the numbers and the money and the workmen and the marketing. Somebody who was not only good at those things but enjoyed them. All she had to do was create the ice cream, which was her favorite thing in the world to do anyway. How had she gotten this lucky?

Fulfillment. That was another one. She felt like she was doing what she was meant to do again. And Sabrina was totally hands-off. She wasn't an ice cream maker and she knew it, left it all in Adley's more-than-capable hands, had undying faith in her abilities. She was also a fabulous taste tester, Adley had discovered. As good as Scottie.

Maybe better, though she wouldn't tell Scottie that. Sabrina was really good with the critiques. Gentle, insightful, suggestive. But still hands-off. Adley appreciated that more than she could put into words.

Contentment. She was settled here. Much more so than she'd been when she was running things alone. Much more so than she'd ever expected to be. She was exactly where she was supposed to be, doing exactly what she was supposed to be doing, and she knew that. Felt it, deep down in her very core. Some people were never as lucky as she was at thirty-five. Every day, she counted her blessings.

And then there was Sabrina.

Oh, what to do about Sabrina.

True, it had only been a week that she'd been working full-time, but the two of them? They looked. Oh, yeah, they looked. She'd caught Sabrina several times. Sabrina had caught her as well. Looking. Staring. In some cases, ogling. She could only speak for herself, but it was hard not to stare at Sabrina. The way she carried herself, the way she spoke to vendors and contractors and potential employees alike, kindly but firmly, never hesitant, always in control. The way she smiled every time she caught Adley looking. Equal parts flattered, shy, and knowing. God, it was sexy. She was sexy. Adley could admit that.

And she was softening, she could feel it. Softening to Sabrina. Leaning into forgiveness. She understood that, regardless of the way things had gone with them last year, it wasn't intentional. They said business wasn't personal, that you had to take the personal away when dealing with business, but she was pretty sure most small-business owners would disagree with that. When you owned a small business, your business was personal. It was your life and your livelihood, and if those things weren't personal, she didn't know what was.

But.

She was back now, in the same place, doing what she loved but with less pressure and less stress and still, there was Sabrina. Beautiful, kind, sexy Sabrina.

Adley gave herself one last look in the mirror and blew out a breath. Gave her head a shake. She knew where her thoughts were headed, and she needed to nip them in the bud. Things were different now.

Weren't they?

She took a breath in slowly, let it out slowly while watching herself in the mirror. She counted to five, then left the bathroom.

Fifteen minutes later, Sabrina was holding the door to Martini's open for her to walk through. The place was jumping, and Adley noticed at least three different softball teams, based on the colors of T-shirts. It was mid-June, and recreational softball in upstate New York had begun a couple weeks ago.

"Softball," Sabrina said, as if just discovering it was a thing. "We need to sponsor a couple teams. Maybe one adult and one youth?" She looked to Adley. "You think?"

"I think it's a great idea. Good way to connect to the community."

"Exactly." Sabrina pulled out her phone and typed. Adley could see the Notes app open on the screen.

Kirby spotted them and waved them over to the bar where she sat. "Saved you a stool," she said happily, then indicated a pretty woman with light brown hair and striking eyes sitting next to her. "Sabrina, Adley, this is my girlfriend, Amelia. Babe, these are the awesome women I've been working for that I was telling you about." Handshakes and smiles all around and soon everybody had drinks.

"You sit," Sabrina said to her, indicating the stool. "You've been on your feet all day while I've been at my desk." Adley nodded and slid onto the stool, Sabrina standing close.

It was something Adley really loved about her hometown, the openness, the welcoming atmosphere. Kirby kept her hand on Amelia's back, rubbing in circles, and it was clear to anybody who looked that they were together. Adley found herself enjoying the closeness of Sabrina, inhaling the clean, fresh scent of her, even after a full day's work.

She felt herself finally start to relax as time went on and alcohol went down. Kirby was cheerful and funny and just fun to be around. Amelia was quieter but threw a zinger into the mix every so often that had everybody laughing. The bar got louder, and Sabrina got closer as the crowd grew, and pretty soon, she was pressed up against Adley's back, and Adley wasn't mad about it. At all.

"Is this okay?" Sabrina breathed near her ear, and Adley could only assume she meant her proximity. "It's a little tight in here."

She nodded and looked into Sabrina's blue eyes. "It's the only time we're the same height," she said with a grin.

"True." And Sabrina smiled back. "It's nice."

"It is."

There was a moment and it was charged. Definitely electric, like a current ran between the two of them. A heat. And instead of being completely freaked out by it, Adley felt oddly comforted.

The evening went on, laughter and cocktails, and Sabrina never left her spot. Adley could feel her even when she wasn't looking and couldn't actually see her. Amelia was telling a story about a client of her dog walking business, and the whole time Adley was looking at Amelia, listening to her words, she could feel Sabrina behind her. And the best word she could come up with in her head to describe the feeling was *perfect*.

"Gotta hit the ladies' room," Sabrina said in her ear. "Feel free to follow me." Then she winked and walked away, and Adley had to consciously force herself to stay sitting. Because Sabrina was just teasing. Right?

"So," Kirby said as she leaned in. "You two together?"

Adley blinked at her. "Who? Me and Sabrina? No." She shook her head, probably too vehemently.

"No?" Kirby actually looked disappointed. "That's too bad. You've got off-the-charts chemistry."

"You think so?"

"Please." That was Amelia, sitting two stools away. "I can feel it all the way over here. You're getting it on me." She made a show of brushing some invisible substance off her arms.

"And me." The bartender, a tall brunette with tons of hair gave her a grin as she pulled a tap to pour a beer.

"Seriously," Kirby said as her eyes found Sabrina heading in their direction, and she lowered her voice. "You should see the way she looks at you."

And before she could process those words, Sabrina was back and in the exact same spot that had become so cold when she'd left. Adley could feel the warmth again up against her back. Welcome. Wanted. Desired.

Jesus. This was bad.

But so very, very good.

They stayed later than Adley had intended, and it was nearing eleven o'clock by the time they were in Sabrina's car and headed back to the Scoop parking lot for Adley's car. They'd both switched to water a while back, and that pleasant buzz that Adley had been headed toward was gone now. Still, though, sitting in the car mere inches away from Sabrina, their attraction was palpable. Comfortable and not, both at the same time.

"You're okay to drive?" Sabrina asked as she guided her car into the spot next to Adley's.

"Oh yeah. Totally okay." The interior of the car was dark, and her hand was on the door handle, but she made no move to get out.

"Kind of a bummer. Drunk Adley is fun."

"Drunk Adley is reckless," she said with a laugh. "She makes bad decisions."

"And does lots of kissing."

"Exactly." And even though it was dark, their gazes held, and Adley could feel the intensity of Sabrina's. God, it would be so easy to kiss her now. Just a slight lean toward her was all it would take. Time ticked by. A second or a minute or an hour, Adley wasn't sure. But finally—finally—she managed to pull on the door handle. The overhead light was rude, bright. They both blinked several times. "I'll see you tomorrow, Sabrina," Adley said softly.

"Good night, Adley." Sabrina's smile was tender, and Adley could feel her watching as she got out of the car and into her own. She stayed there until Sabrina pulled out of her spot and headed home, then followed her until her turn came and watched as her taillights disappeared.

Lying in bed a little while later, she replayed the night in her head. Hell, she replayed the week. Scottie had warned her about this very thing. About the attraction showing up again. And honestly, she'd known it was a possibility—she and Sabrina had too much of Kirby's aforementioned chemistry for it not to pop up again—but she hadn't expected it to happen so fast. It was only the first week!

She lay there in the dark, her mind spinning, her body buzzing. Sleep seemed far away, and she could think of only one good way to release the tension and push herself toward rest. Eyes closed, she slipped a hand into her panties and found herself unsurprisingly wet, as she had been for pretty much the entire time that Sabrina's body was pressed up against hers in the bar. Her mind tossed her images of Sabrina in various states of undress as her fingers moved through her own wetness.

She came in less than three minutes.

CHAPTER TWENTY-FOUR

That night at Martini's had shaken something loose. Sabrina could feel it as the days progressed toward the grand opening. They were lighter around each other. More relaxed. She didn't understand why or how—all she knew was that she loved it.

"Taste this." Adley came at her with a spoon, as she did so often lately.

Sabrina dutifully opened her mouth, tasted. "Mm." She rolled the ice cream around and said it again, louder. "Mm. Oh my God, what is that?"

"What do you taste?" It was Adley's standard question. She never told Sabrina what the flavor was. She wanted to know that it was recognizable in some way.

And Sabrina had discovered that she enjoyed this little exercise. "Nutmeg? No, wait. Yes. Nutmeg. Cloves? No. Something warm. Pumpkin? Pumpkin pie. Is it pumpkin pie?" She knew she got it right when Adley's face lit up.

"I'm playing with some fall flavors. I know it's June, but the summer always flies by, and I want us to have a plan for autumn."

"I like the way you think," she said, and Adley smiled at her for a beat before heading back to her workspace. "It's delicious," she called after her. And she did love the way Adley thought. She'd known she was good at her job, but honestly? She'd been blown away by how diligent she was. How precise. How very creative. In Sabrina's mind, Adley wasn't any different than any master chef working on new meals in their kitchen. She was focused and determined. She slammed things and banged stuff around when something didn't come out tasting the way she'd hoped. She was passionate. Sabrina wasn't sure why that surprised her, having experienced Adley in a more…intimate way. Her passion bled into every part of her, and it was a characteristic Sabrina found fascinating.

Later on that day, Adley appeared in her office again, this time with a clamshell container. Without saying a word, she pushed Sabrina's laptop away, cleared a space in front of her, set the container down, and opened it. A glorious-looking burger and a huge mound of french fries, seasoned with rosemary if her nose was correct, were revealed, and the aroma instantly made her stomach growl. Loudly.

"I haven't seen you eat a thing today," Adley said. "You can't run our business successfully if you faint from hunger. Eat." She ran a hand down Sabrina's arm and left, going back to her kitchen.

That? The incidental touching? Yeah, they did that now. It was a thing.

And had she said *our business*? She had, hadn't she? Sabrina could ask herself why that phrase warmed her heart, but she didn't have to. She knew.

The alarm on her phone sounded, surprising her. She had a meeting with a local TV reporter in an hour, hoping to get some coverage for the shop on grand opening day. But Adley was right. She hadn't eaten at all today, and the smell of the burger and fries kept her tethered to her seat.

She clicked over to the schedule on her laptop and went over it in her head as she took a bite of the burger—oh my God, so good—summarizing the things she had left this week to prepare for their big opening, which was barely a week away. A final meeting with the company creating their Second Scoop app, which would allow people to order ahead of time for quick pickup. A contract with DoorDash needed to be finalized—she had found nobody in all of Northwood that would deliver dessert to your door, so she was jumping all over that. Uniform shirts and hats for the employees should arrive tomorrow. She had one more interview to do, and then they'd have a full staff. Kirby's girlfriend had sent another friend who was planning a fall softball team her way for possible sponsorship. Sabrina kicked herself for hopping on the train too late for this summer. Next summer, though, she'd be ready.

"I don't hear any chewing going on in there." Adley's voice came from…somewhere. Sabrina looked around, and her eyes landed on the security monitor, which showed Adley up on a chair out front in the shop, staring right into one of the cameras, shaking a finger and looking mock-disappointed. Sabrina laughed.

"If you can hear my chewing from way out there," she called out loudly, "then I have some issues to work on."

Adley's face broke into a smile. "Valid." Sabrina watched her climb down and put the chair back.

There was a knock on the back door, and Sabrina knew from experience who it was. She got up from her chair, called out to Adley, "Scottie's here," and let her in.

"Hey, Brina, how's the ice cream biz?" Scottie said. Nobody called her that but Scottie, and she was okay with that. Sabrina liked Scottie, even though she wasn't yet sure the feeling was mutual. Scottie was super protective of Adley—the main reason Sabrina liked her so much—which meant there was always an element of suspicion when she looked at her. Like Sabrina was an animal she was uncertain of so expected her to take a swipe with sharp claws at any moment. Understandable. That was her role as BFF—suspicion and protection. It made Sabrina happy to know that Scottie had that kind of loyalty to Adley.

"Ask me in a week and a half."

"Fair enough. Where's my BFF?" Scottie's eyes landed on Adley as she came from up front.

"Your BFF is right here, my BFF."

"You're bouncy," Scottie said, pointing at her with her brow furrowed.

"I'm bouncy?" Adley asked, then looked to Sabrina and back to Scottie.

"You are. You just bounced in here." Scottie turned to Sabrina. "Does she bounce everywhere now?"

Sabrina lifted a shoulder and nodded. "Pretty much."

Adley swatted her playfully. "I do not. Go finish your burger, Boss Lady. You've got a meeting shortly." She said it with affection, and Sabrina could see that Scottie noticed. She looked from Sabrina to Adley and back. "I'm gonna show Scottie the front now that it's finished."

Sabrina gave a mock salute. "Yes, ma'am. Good to see you, Scott

Free." Back in her office, she sat down and resumed her meal, trying not to notice how happy it made her that Adley knew her schedule.

Adley had led Scottie out front, and she could see them on the monitors. Out of respect, she turned down the volume, feeling weird about eavesdropping, though she continued to watch as she ate. Adley pointed out different things to Scottie, and Scottie reacted. It was clear when she recognized the art that Adley'd had in her former shop, old photos her grandfather had hanging when he'd owned the place. But the thing that really stood out for Sabrina was the pride on Adley's face as she pointed out different things to her best friend. Her smile never left her face. Her exuberance was clear, even without sound.

Sabrina sat there, chewing a french fry, and realized that for the first time since she'd started on this business venture, she felt one hundred percent certain she'd done the right thing. Like she could take a deep, full breath for the first time in months. Like this was exactly where she was supposed to be. In this very spot, in this very building, with this very person. The realization was so strong, it brought tears to her eyes. So she sat there in her Boss Lady chair, eating the food that had been ordered for her, and cried silently at the joy she felt right then.

Adley must've said something funny because Scottie threw her head back in laughter—it was silent on the monitor, but Sabrina could kind of hear it from her seat—then threw her arms around Adley and they hugged for a long moment. Sabrina realized things had gone from playful to serious in the span of a few seconds, and she forced her gaze elsewhere, feeling like she was intruding on something personal. When she glanced back at the monitor, both women were gone, and she heard them in the kitchen again.

"This place looks fab, Brina," Scottie called out.

It was time to head to her meeting with the TV people, so she closed up the clamshell on what was left of her burger—not much— and picked up her purse as she went out to the kitchen.

"It does, doesn't it?" She gestured at Adley with her chin. "I owe it all to this chick. She's got a great eye." And did Adley blush as she looked down at her feet? Sure seemed like it. "Okay, I've gotta run." She glanced at her watch as she headed for the back door. "Shouldn't be longer than an hour or so. Bye."

When the door clicked shut behind her, she blew out a breath and leaned back against it, needing a moment to get her bearings. Again, she wanted to wonder what that was about, to be indignant about the interference, but she did neither. Because she knew exactly what was happening. Her feelings for Adley, the ones she'd so carefully tucked away in their secret compartment, had picked the lock somehow and were sneaking out, oozing into her brain, her body, her heart.

If only she had the first clue what to do about them…

❖

"You're different." Scottie didn't say the words until the door had clicked shut behind Sabrina and they heard her car start up.

"I know, I know," Adley said with soft laugh as she scrolled on her phone for the notes she'd made about a new flavor. "I'm bouncy."

"No. No, it's something else." And then Scottie scrutinized her, which Adley hated because she could never hide anything from her. Not one thing. Ever. Scottie gasped. "Wait. Are you sleeping with her again?"

"What?" Why was her voice suddenly an octave higher than usual? She cleared her throat, hoping to get it back down to normal. "No, why would you think that?"

"Do you *want* to sleep with her again?" Adley swallowed, but before she could answer, Scottie went on, "'Cause you shouldn't sleep with your boss."

"Well. I mean, she's not really my boss."

"You called her Boss Lady."

"Yeah, in jest."

"In jest? Are we in nineteenth century England? Nobody says *in jest.*"

Adley frowned. "What? Lots of people say in jest."

"No, they say joking or kidding or screwing around or yanking somebody's chain or busting somebody's chops. Nobody says in jest."

An eye roll. "Fine. I called her Boss Lady *jokingly.*"

"Better. And it's cute that you think this will distract me from the original question, which is do you want to sleep with her again?"

Yes. The answer to that question was a loud and exuberant yes. Adley knew that. Watching Sabrina in her element, handling vendors and interviewing potential employees and doing interviews for the small local paper? It was something to see. She was confident and in control and oh so sexy that it set Adley's body to buzzing. And now that she'd been working here closely with Sabrina for a few weeks, it seemed like her body was *always* buzzing.

"God, I don't know," she said honestly. And she explained the buzzing. "It's like a low-key humming that runs through my entire body anytime I'm in the same vicinity as her. Like I'm plugged in or something. It's so weird."

"But in an awesome way, right?" Scottie got a slightly dreamy look on her face. "I remember when that started for me. Anytime I was around Marisa, I felt turned-on." She laughed and shook her head. "Not like that. I mean, yes, like that, but I meant like somebody flipped a switch inside me every time she came into view."

"Yes," Adley said, thrilled that somebody got it. "Like we're those fluorescent light bulbs they have in school, remember? The long skinny ones? And the teacher turns them on, and they buzz slightly at all times? Like that. Just like that."

They basked for a moment in the knowledge that they both understood what Adley was dealing with. But then Scottie slid in with the obvious, unanswerable question. "So, what are you gonna do?"

Adley blew out a breath. "Fuck if I know."

She didn't think she'd ever spoken truer words in her entire life.

❖

The grand opening of A Second Scoop was one day away. One day. Tomorrow. It was tomorrow.

Holy shit.

Teagan and her wife and baby were coming today and thank God because Sabrina was nervous. Beyond nervous. She'd been through countless grand openings for Sweet Heavens in the past, and while there was always an adrenaline kick of excitement around them, she'd never been this nervous. Not once. Not ever. Because this? This was her baby. Its success or failure was all on her. No big corporation to blame. No headquarters taking decisions out of her hands. No ability to eschew this one and look on to the next. Nope. It was her. All her.

Holy shit.

She had no reason to be nervous. Everything was in order. All the finer details of the shop had been taken care of. The cute little dishes and the standby flavors—your vanilla and chocolate and strawberry—as well as those that were unique to A Second Scoop, Chocolate Cherry Bomb and lemon rosemary sherbet and the reinstitution of Baby Bear, were all ready to go. Adley had planned her time perfectly, finished making all her ice cream this morning, so that this afternoon, this last day before the grand opening, all she needed to do was make fresh waffle cones and bake brownies for the brownie sundaes. She'd decided to flavor some of the waffle cones, so she'd seeded a couple vanilla beans and was simmering them on the stove. Apparently, buying vanilla extract was out of the question when you knew how to make it yourself, and Sabrina loved that about Adley, loved that she was creative and, again, passionate. Right then, she was busy chopping dark chocolate, the rhythmic tapping of the knife on the cutting board filling the kitchen. It was early in the afternoon, and the employees she'd hired were due in for a meeting at three. About two hours from now. Until then, it was just her and Adley.

They were ready.

She could hardly believe it. They'd gotten everything done, everything set. She'd been so right when she told Adley several weeks ago she thought they'd make a great team. They did. The best. They were flawless together.

From her seat at her desk, she could see Adley. Not on the monitors, but through the open doorway, at the counter in her white coat, soft classical music coming from the speaker on a shelf behind her, enormous knife glinting in the overhead lighting. God, she loved to watch Adley work. It was like a dance, choreographed and graceful—

Adley cried out and dropped the knife.

Sabrina was up and out of her chair before she even had time to think about it. "What happened?" she asked as she reached Adley, who was holding her hand, blood on the counter and running down her wrist. "Oh my God." Sabrina grabbed her and dragged her to the sink, shoved her hand under the running water, at which Adley winced. Sabrina felt her arm tense under her hands. Her own heart was pounding in her chest. "Oh my God," she said again. "What happened are you okay this is a lot of blood lemme see how deep you might need stitches did the knife slip is it too dull we can get you a new set, if you want, a better set."

A squeeze on her shoulder stopped the words, and she turned to look at Adley, who was pale, but also smiling. "That was the longest string of words I've ever heard."

Sabrina felt sheepish and gave her a small grin, then took a breath and forced herself to calm down. "Sorry. I do that when I'm scared. I babble. When I was fourteen, I broke my wrist, and the poor guy who put my cast on had to listen to me talk nonstop about the entire season of *Buffy the Vampire Slayer*. Every episode. Every plotline. The poor guy's ears must've been bleeding by the time he finished with me." She grabbed a nearby towel and wrapped Adley's finger with it.

"I mean, it was Buffy. How could you not share?"

"Right? And the very last season. It was important." Their gazes held, and Sabrina felt that now-familiar stirring low in her body that Adley had caused since the first time she'd seen her. She didn't need to keep holding her hand, but somehow, she couldn't let go.

After a long moment, Adley cleared her throat softly. "I think it's okay now," she said, her voice quiet. She did not pull her hand away.

Sabrina blinked rapidly, like she'd been in a trance, and turned off the water. She opened the towel and examined the cut. "It's not as deep as I thought it was, it's just long. I don't think it needs stitches, but let's get it bandaged up good, okay?" She met Adley's gaze again and whispered, "You scared me."

A tender smile and a soft voice as Adley said, "I work in a kitchen. Cutting myself is an occupational hazard. This won't be the last time."

"Well, I'm gonna need you to be more careful because—" She caught herself before she said the words running through her head.

"Because why?"

The sound of Sabrina's phone ringing startled them both, and she felt Adley's body flinch, even while her own felt a wave of relief. The phrase *saved by the bell*, clichéd as it was, zipped through her head, and she gave Adley an apologetic smile. Slowly, they parted. Sabrina let go of Adley's hand, and she took it back, peeked under the towel, and grimaced. Sabrina slipped her phone out and glanced at the screen. Teagan.

"Hey," she said, watching Adley as she found the shop's first-aid kit and rummaged through the bandages.

"Just letting you know our flight landed, and we're at your lovely airport. Just gotta grab the rental and we'll be over." They sounded tired, but happy.

"Are you sure you don't want me to come pick you up? It's not a problem."

"For the nine hundred seventeenth time, thank you, but no. We're fine. I'll get the car seat all hooked up, and we'll be good to go." There was a pause, and Sabrina could hear a muffled conversation. "Waze says twenty minutes to your house, once we've got the car. See you then."

Sabrina said good-bye and hung up.

"That your bestie from home?" Adley asked, trying to put some antiseptic cream on her forefinger. "Did they make it okay? Is the family with them?"

Sabrina so appreciated Adley for paying attention, and she felt a warm glow of gratitude. "They did and yes. I have to run home to meet them, get everybody settled."

"No worries. I can hold down the fort."

Sabrina took the cream from her hand. "Here, let me." They stood quietly, their heads nearly touching as Sabrina doctored Adley's finger, wrapped it neatly, then taped it to keep it secure.

Adley sighed as she looked at the counter. "Well, that's a waste of good chocolate. Glad I ordered extra."

"You sure you're gonna be okay here if I go?"

Adley tipped her head and regarded her, then said softly, "Sabrina, I cut my finger. It's no big deal. I'll be fine."

She nodded once. "Yeah. Okay." She grabbed her purse from the office. "I just need to get them settled, and I'll be back in time for the meeting. I promise."

"Bri." At the sound of her name from Adley's lips, she stopped in her tracks and her eyes met Adley's. "I'm fine. I promise. Don't worry so much." Sabrina gave another nod. "And thank you. For helping me with this." She held up her bandaged finger and wiggled it. "See? Still works."

"Good." And they stood there for a beat, just looking at each other, and that subtle electric sizzle that was always there between them seemed to kick up several volts. "I'll be back."

CHAPTER TWENTY-FIVE

"O h. My. God." Sabrina turned the lock to the back door, locking it after the last employee headed home. Then she spun to face Adley and punched her arms up into the air. "Oh my God! We did it!"

"That was amazing!" Adley said, throwing up her own arms, and they danced around in a circle before collapsing into each other.

Man, nothing sobered Adley up like being so close to Sabrina, and usually she fought internally with herself to keep a healthy distance between them. But this? This was special. This was a celebration, and being in Sabrina's arms felt exactly right.

"We did it!" Sabrina said again. "No bumps. Without a hitch. And we raked in the sales. I am so happy!" They hopped around in a circle like two happy kids, and it seemed like Sabrina didn't even give it a second thought when she pushed up on her toes and kissed Adley on the mouth. It was quick. Not much more than a peck, but it froze both of them. Like statues. Sabrina's blue eyes went from wide surprise to heavy-lidded in a split second. Adley watched it happen, and it was sexy as hell.

"We, um, probably shouldn't." Adley cleared her throat. "You know?"

Sabrina nodded and made zero attempts at removing herself from Adley's arms. "Yeah. It's probably a really bad idea."

Adley stood there, looking into those eyes, and Sabrina stared back at her. Adley's gaze dropped, and Sabrina's lips were glossy and full, and Adley couldn't pull her eyes away and then all her control just melted. Vanished. She couldn't stop herself. It wasn't possible. She leaned forward and kissed Sabrina again. Not a peck this time. *So* not a peck.

They kissed like their lives depended on it. They kissed like they hadn't kissed another human being in years. They kissed like they couldn't get enough of each other. Lips and tongues worked overtime. Hands came into play. Adley couldn't touch Sabrina enough. She wanted all of her. Every inch. Every single inch. Without even thinking about it, she tugged Sabrina into the small office and pushed her against the desk, then kissed her some more.

The entire shop was quiet, the only sounds those of ragged breathing and smacking lips. Adley unfastened Sabrina's pants, quickly pushed them down to her ankles, and then helped lift her so she sat on the desk. Adley pushed her knees apart so she had room to stand, and she pulled Sabrina's body as close to hers as she could.

And they kissed.

There was nothing in the world sexier, nothing more exciting than kissing Sabrina James. Adley had figured that out the very first time they'd done so, in the ladies' room of Martini's more than a year ago. Part of her wondered if it had just been a fluke, a result of the situation, of the clandestine sexiness of it, but now she knew it hadn't been that. It was Sabrina. She and Adley were meant to be kissing. Adley was sure of it.

But she wanted more, and she wanted it right here in their shop, and she didn't care that it was impractical or hurried or whatever else it might be, because it was also fucking sexy and Sabrina seemed to think so, too. Sabrina parted her legs farther, as if anticipating Adley's next move, which, of course, was to push Sabrina's underwear aside and swipe her fingers through the wetness there.

God, so much wetness.

She must've made a sound because Sabrina whispered, "It's all you. That's all you."

And then Adley pushed into her. Not gently. This wasn't about gentle. It was about pairing. It was about lost time. It was about claim. And while she didn't say the words, didn't even let herself dwell on them in her own mind, she knew they were true. Without a shadow of a doubt, she knew they were true.

Sabrina was hers. Always.

Fingers gripped her shoulders, and Sabrina threw her head back, allowing Adley to nuzzle that spot where her neck and shoulder met as she pushed in and out of her. She withdrew and focused on the hot, wet folds of flesh, stroking and caressing, and it didn't take more than a couple minutes before Sabrina whispered her name and Sabrina's whole body tensed, spasmed, and she tightened her grip on Adley as a low hum issued from deep in her throat.

As Sabrina's body began to slowly relax, Adley dropped her forehead to Sabrina's shoulder, kept her fingers pressed to the hot, wet flesh between her legs, and let herself bask in the beauty that was Sabrina.

"We probably shouldn't have done that," she whispered, then looked up into Sabrina's eyes and grinned.

"Nope. Definitely shouldn't have."

There was a beat of silence, and then they both burst out laughing. Not just laughing. Cracking the hell up. They were living, breathing laughing emoji, tears leaking from their eyes, snorts coming from noses, stomachs hurting from so much.

Adley pushed a lock of blond hair behind Sabrina's ear and touched her forehead to Sabrina's. "What are we gonna do about us?"

"Well," Sabrina said, "I think you should make us a Decadence sundae to share, and we can talk about it while we eat. Yeah?"

"I like that idea." But Adley didn't move. Not right away. Instead, she took the moment and gazed into those blue eyes, studied the exact shade of blue, noted the black circle around the irises that made that blue pop. She slowly removed her fingers from where they were still tucked inside Sabrina's panties. And then she kissed her. Slowly. Softly. Smiled at her. Then headed out to the kitchen.

❖

Sabrina watched Adley head out to make them a sundae, and she could feel her own pulse still pounding between her legs. She hadn't expected that, for Adley to fuck her on her own desk. Not that she hadn't fantasized about exactly that, because she totally had. Many times. Many, many times. She could admit now that she'd totally underestimated how sexually frustrating it would be to have Adley in the very next room all day long. And watching her in her element—in her white coat in the kitchen, floating around and creating deliciousness, happy and humming to herself—was more of a turn-on than she was prepared for. She clearly hadn't thought it through, which she was certain she'd hear all about from Teagan when she got home and recounted her evening.

All that being said? She was stupidly happy right now. Like, *stupidly*. Was that good? It was bad, wasn't it? Was it? Giving her head a shake, she pulled herself together, fastened her pants, fluffed her hair, and followed Adley into the kitchen, where she had a bowl on the table and a small pan on the stove, warming up some hot fudge.

Sabrina didn't think she'd ever get enough of watching her work. Even just making a sundae for the two of them, Adley took her time, was precise and creative at the same time. She sliced one of the thick, fudgy brownies she'd made that morning through the center so it was like a sandwich. The bottom went into a bowl, and she topped it with the peppermint mocha chip ice cream she knew was Sabrina's favorite. The top of the brownie went on, then she added homemade whipped cream, then drizzled the hot fudge over the top. The finishing touch was a dusting of cocoa, and it was ready. She looked over at Sabrina and held up two spoons.

"Doesn't really get any better than my own personal ice cream chef," she said, taking a spoon. She popped herself up so she was sitting on the counter.

"And sex on your desk." Adley grinned and dug her spoon into the brownie.

"And sex on my desk. This will go down in history as a perfect day."

Adley held her gaze as she chewed. "Yeah?"

"Absolutely."

And that really was the truth of it. They ate the sundae and talked about the day, what went well, what could use tweaking, and it was like they'd been doing exactly that for years. Sabrina had a strange flash then, an image in her mind of the two of them doing exactly this years down the road…and being ridiculously happy while doing it. Settled. Content.

It was wonderful and weird. Slightly uncomfortable, which made sense to her. And mostly, it was just the best. Perfection. And exactly what she wanted…and *that* was the real realization.

"You look like you just saw a ghost or something," Adley said, startling her back to the present. "You okay?"

And those dark eyes on her, the note of concern in Adley's voice… Adley had her. Sabrina just knew that. Adley had her and wouldn't let her fall, and she knew *that*. She smiled at Adley then. "It might've been the ghost of ice cream future."

When Adley returned her smile, Sabrina could have sworn the room lit up. Seriously. Like the sun came out. "Yeah? What did it show you?"

"Us." Sabrina didn't hesitate. In fact, she was done hesitating. Just like that. Finished. "Years from now. Right here, running our business. Together."

"Oh yeah? Was there sex on the desk?" Adley's tone was playful, but when she scooped up a spoonful of the sundae and met Sabrina's eyes, the smile faded and her expression went serious.

"There was. And so much more."

Adley swallowed audibly. "Like what?"

"Like love." Oh, sweet baby Jesus in a hot air balloon, she'd said it. Out loud. And…it was okay. More than okay. It was right. She felt a relief she hadn't expected, and she kept talking. Couldn't stop, even if she'd wanted to. Which she didn't. "There was love. So much love. I love you, Adley. I'm sorry. I do. I think I have since the first night I met you." She set down her spoon and braced. Teagan would kill her when they found out what she'd said. That she'd just blurted it out. But she'd had to. She knew it in that exact moment. She had to. There'd been no choice. Adley deserved to know, didn't she?

Adley's eyes went wide, but her face softened, and her eyes filled with unshed tears. She held Sabrina's gaze for what felt like a year and a half before she finally spoke. And her words set Sabrina free. "Well, thank fucking God because I love you, too."

And then they were in each other's arms and kissing and crying and laughing and kissing some more. Sabrina had Adley's face in her hands, looked in her eyes. "I'm never letting you go. You should know that right now. Never. And I can't believe how these words are just spilling out of me, but I can't seem to help it. This is it for me. You're it for me. I want you to know that. I'm sorry."

Adley was laughing, but not at her. With her. The most beautiful sound in the world. "You did warn me that you babble when you're scared. This is the second time I've seen it in action."

Sabrina sighed and looked down at her feet. "It's true. I'm sorry."

And it was Adley's turn to lift Sabrina's chin and hold her face in both hands. "For what? For loving me? Don't you ever, ever be sorry for that. I don't know where you came from, Sabrina James, but I'm so glad you landed in my town. In my shop. In my life." Her voice went very soft. "In my heart. I love you, baby."

More kissing. But soft. Sweet. Gentle. Loving.

Sabrina pulled back with a start. "Oh, damn it."

"What?"

"Well, we've just admitted our love for each other—fucking finally." They both laughed and then Sabrina continued, "And I want more than anything to take you home with me and make love to you all night long."

"That sounds incredible," Adley said, burying her face in Sabrina's shoulder, nuzzling her neck, their positions putting them at an equal height.

"Except there's another couple and a baby at my house."

Adley's head snapped up. "Oh, crap. I forgot."

"Me, too."

They held one another's gaze for a beat before they both burst into laughter. Deep belly laughs that came with tears and snorts and playful shoves. It was several moments before they became serious again.

"There's good news, though," Sabrina said.

Adley tipped her head. "That I own a vibrator and can take care of myself when I get home? I suppose…"

She smiled at this beautiful woman who'd changed her life in so many ways. "I mean, yeah. But that's not what I was talking about. The good news is this." She grasped the belt loops on Adley's jeans and pulled her between her knees so their noses almost touched. "We have all the time in the world."

Adley's smile blossomed across her face like the sun coming out after a rainstorm, big and bright and gorgeous. "We do, don't we?"

And this time when they kissed, instead of a fluke or a test or a questionable decision, it was a beginning.

It was a beginning.

EPILOGUE

Early December

A Second Scoop wasn't open on Sundays in the offseason, but that was okay with Adley. That meant her kitchen was quiet, and she could concentrate on the holiday dessert for next Friday's dessert special. It was a fun thing she'd instituted in the fall, a revolving dessert special every Friday, made fresh that day and only available until they ran out. It had ended up being a hot product, and since the first one in October—a Halloween pumpkin and chocolate cheesecake sundae—they'd sold out every single Friday.

The cranberry compote was cooking down nicely on the stove, and the entire kitchen smelled lovely, warm and inviting and rather Christmasy. She gave it a stir to keep it from sticking to the bottom of the pan, then picked up her phone and scrolled to some holiday music, turned on the speaker on the shelf to her left, and soon Kelly Clarkson was singing about being wrapped in red.

Adley took a moment then. Just stopped moving, stopped working, put her hands on the counter and just inhaled. Closed her eyes. Felt what was so prevalent in the air around her lately.

Happiness.

She'd always thought she was fine. When she'd owned Get the Scoop on her own, she'd been stressed, of course, but happy. Or so she'd thought. The reality was, she'd had no earthly idea what true happiness was, because she was living it now. What she'd done in some other life to deserve what she had now—a thriving business and an amazing woman who was also an amazing partner in every way—she had no idea, but it must've been something. She gave the cranberry compote another stir. No, life couldn't get much better than it was right now. She was an incredibly blessed woman.

The back door opened then, startling her, and in walked that amazing woman herself, stomping snow off her boots.

"Hi, babe," Sabrina said, giving Adley a peck on the lips. "Cold out there." She peeked over Adley's shoulder. "Ooh, that smells divine."

"I'm trying to come up with next week's dessert special," Adley said. "I think they all need to be holiday themed in some way from here until the first of the year."

"Agreed." Sabrina had a big manila envelope with her, and she held it up. "Got a minute? I'd like to go over something with you."

"Oh. Sure." She clicked off the burner, the compote pretty much done, wiped her hands on her apron, and turned to Sabrina. God, she'd never get enough of simply looking at her. Sabrina had let Scottie cut her hair last month, taking some of the length, and it only made it look thicker and more lush, and it seemed to catch the various colors of the Christmas lights Adley'd strung around the kitchen and toss them back. She wore jeans and cute black ankle boots with a sherpa lining. Her sweater was black and hooded, her puffy vest cream. She looked like the cover model on any given winter clothing catalog, and Adley often had difficulty understanding that this woman was hers. Hers alone.

"Why are you looking at me like that?" Sabrina asked with a soft smile.

"'Cause you're gorgeous."

"You're biased."

"True. I also have eyes." She indicated the envelope. "Whatcha got?"

Sabrina opened the envelope and pulled out a small stack of papers. Without a word, she handed them over to Adley, who scanned them quickly, then let out a little gasp. Her gaze snapped up to Sabrina, who was grinning widely. "This gives me half ownership."

Sabrina nodded. "Doesn't feel right for you not to be a legal owner of this place. It just doesn't. Plus, it's been six months now, and I'm pretty sure you're not going anywhere."

Adley laughed. "Not in my plans, no."

"Good. We share everything, fifty-fifty, right down the middle. The building, the business, and everything in it." Sabrina produced a pen with a flourish. "Brian put little highlighted X's everywhere you need to sign." Brian was their lawyer, and Adley realized that Sabrina had been working on this for a while. She took the pen and held her girlfriend's gaze for a moment.

"Thank you, Sabrina," she said quietly. Spreading the forms out on the counter, she flipped through and signed where each X was, not bothering to read any of it because she trusted Sabrina that much. If she said it was split right down the middle, it was. She signed her name several times, and when she finished and straightened the papers back into a neat pile again, she said, "There. You're never getting rid of me now." She turned to look at Sabrina and gasped.

Sabrina was down on one knee, a black velvet box open in her hand, the ring inside sparkling in the lights. "I never, ever want to get rid of you." Her voice was trembling, as were her hands, and Adley's heart warmed. Sabrina wasn't a person who got nervous, but it was clear she was now. "I know it's fast. I know it's soon. But I've never been more sure of anything in my entire life. I love you, Adley, more than I ever thought I'd love anyone. I don't know how it's possible to feel this much joy with somebody, but you…you're the whipped cream on my sundae. You're the sprinkles on my cone. You're the very best part of everything, and if you'll let me, I want to spend the rest of my days standing next to you and making you the happiest you can possibly be." Her blue eyes shimmered with unshed tears. "Will you marry me?"

It *was* fast. It *was* soon.

It didn't matter because it was also perfect. More perfect than Adley ever could have imagined her life to be.

"Yes," she said without hesitation. "Yes, yes, yes." She leaned down, took Sabrina's face in both hands, and kissed her, and part of her worried that her heart might burst from so much joy. From this much love. She pulled back slightly so she could look in Sabrina's beautiful blue eyes. "I was literally just standing here before you came, trying to figure out what I'd done in some other life to deserve what I have in this one. You are everything I've ever hoped for but never thought I could have. I am the luckiest woman on the planet, and I love you more than you'll ever know."

Lips met again, they kissed softly, and then Sabrina stood. She took the ring out of the box and grasped Adley's hand. "I can't wait to be your wife," she said as she slid the ring onto Adley's finger. "I love you," she whispered, and just as their lips were about to meet again, there was a shockingly loud pounding on the back door.

"Can we come in yet?" Scottie's voice rang through the air. "It's freaking freezing out here!"

Adley looked at Sabrina in surprise.

"Yeah, I brought a few friends," Sabrina said as she pushed the door open and shouted, "She said yes!" into the back parking lot.

And suddenly, a flood of people—an actual wave—flowed into the kitchen from the back lot. Scottie threw her arms around Adley before she could even say anything, and then she was grabbing Adley's hand and holding it up for Marisa to see.

"See? I knew it would look perfect on her," Scottie said to her girlfriend. To Adley, she explained, "I helped Sabrina pick it out." And then Adley was enveloped in another hug. "I'm so happy for you, Ad," Scottie said softly in her ear. And this time, when she pulled back, her eyes shimmered.

Then Marisa hugged her and told her the same thing, and then it was an endless line of hugs and congratulations. Teagan and Kyra were there—how and when they'd arrived from Atlanta, Adley had no idea. And her parents. And Brody and Nathan, her sister still carrying that shadow of sadness that Adley worried had become permanent. But she hugged Adley tightly and kissed her cheek and brushed her hair behind her ear, and her love was clearly written on her face. Mandy was next, as were the rest of the Second Scoop employees, and then there was a loud pop, followed by another, and suddenly champagne was being poured.

It was crazy and busy and loud and happy, and Adley felt like she was floating on a cloud. A rhythmic tinging sounded, and Adley's gaze landed across the kitchen where Sabrina was standing on a chair, asking for everybody's attention. When the hum of a dozen conversations died down, she smiled that smile, and Adley felt her heart swell with the love she had for this woman.

"Thank you all so much for coming today. It means so much to me, the support you've given me as I put this plan together." She locked eyes with Adley. "You are so loved, baby. You have no idea. Everybody here knew I was proposing today, and they all dropped whatever plans they had to come celebrate with us. A year and a half ago was my first trip to Northwood. I fell in love with the city immediately, but I was here for work. I had no idea what was in store for me or that less than two years later, I'd be down on one knee, asking the love of my life to be with me forever. Life is funny like that. I'm not a person who's at all experienced at following my heart, but I'm so glad I did this one time because it led me to you." She held up her plastic cup of champagne. "To my beautiful bride to be, I can't wait to be your wife. I love you, Adley."

"Hear, hear!" somebody shouted. Cups were raised in salute as Adley felt the tears that had been threatening finally spill over and track down her cheeks. Scottie had an arm around her and gave her a squeeze and then there was Sabrina, moving through the throng of people until she was standing in front of her. She lifted her plastic cup, the smile on her face glowing with joy.

Adley touched her cup with her own and wondered if anyone had ever been as happy as she was in the moment. She couldn't speak. She tried, but the lump in her throat was preventing words, but Sabrina seemed to get it because she simply nodded and whispered, "I know, baby. I know."

And then they were side by side, the way they'd face the rest of life. Leaning against each other, surveying their business and their loved ones, and Adley had a flash-forward of toddlers running around, then kids, then teenagers, and she knew this was it.

She turned to Sabrina, who looked up at her with such love and adoration, it made Adley's chest ache in the best of ways. *I love you*, she mouthed, and Sabrina's smile grew.

This was her life.
This was her love.
This was exactly where she was supposed to be.
This was home.

About the Author

Georgia Beers lives in Upstate New York and has written more than thirty-five novels of sapphic romance. In her off-hours, she can usually be found searching for a scary movie, sipping a good Pinot, or trying to keep up with little big man Archie, her mix of many little dogs. Find out more at georgiabeers.com.

Books Available From Bold Strokes Books

Crush by Ana Hartnett Reichardt. Josie Sanchez worked for years for the opportunity to create her own wine label, and nothing will stand in her way. Not even Mac, the owner's annoyingly beautiful niece Josie's forced to hire as her harvest intern. (978-1-63679-330-6)

Decadence by Piper Jordan, Ronica Black & Renee Roman. You are cordially invited to Decadence, Las Vegas's most talked about invitation-only Masquerade Ball. Come for the entertainment and stay for the erotic indulgence. We guarantee it'll be a party that lives up to its name. (978-1-63679-361-0)

Gimmicks and Glamour by Lauren Melissa Ellzey. Ashly has learned to hide her Sight, but as she speeds toward high school graduation she must protect the classmates she claims to hate from an evil that no one else sees. (978-1-63679-401-3)

Heart of Stone by Sam Ledel. Princess Keeva Glantor meets Maeve, a gorgon forced to live alone thanks to a decades-old lie, and together the two women battle forces they formerly thought to be good in the hopes of leading lives they can finally call their own. (978-1-63679-407-5)

Peaches and Cream by Georgia Beers. Adley Purcell is living her dreams owning Get the Scoop ice cream shop until national dessert chain Sweet Heaven opens less than two blocks away and Adley has to compete with the far too heavenly Sabrina James. (978-1-63679-412-9)

The Only Fish in the Sea by Angie Williams. Will love overcome years of bitter rivalry for the daughters of two crab fishing families in this queer modern-day spin on Romeo and Juliet? (978-1-63679-444-0)

Wildflower by Cathleen Collins. When a plane crash leaves eleven-year-old Lily Andrews stranded in the vast wilderness of Arkansas, will she be able to overcome the odds and make it back to civilization and the one person who holds the key to her future? (978-1-63679-621-5)

Witch Finder by Sheri Lewis Wohl. Tasmin, the Keeper of the Book of Darkness, is in terrible danger, and as a Witch Finder, Morrigan must protect her and the secrets she guards even if it costs Morrigan her life. (978-1-63679-335-1)

Digging for Heaven by Jenna Jarvis. Litz lives for dragons. Kella lives to kill them. The last thing they expect is to find each other attractive. (978-1-63679-453-2)

Forever's Promise by Missouri Vaun. Wesley Holden migrated west disguised as a man for the hope of a better life and with no designs to take a wife, but Charlotte Rose has other ideas. (978-1-63679-221-7)

Here For You by D. Jackson Leigh. A horse trainer must make a difficult business decision that could save her father's ranch from foreclosure but destroy her chance to win the heart of a feisty barrel racer vying for a spot in the National Rodeo Finals. (978-1-63679-299-6)

I Do, I Don't by Joy Argento. Creator of the romance algorithm, Nicole Hart doesn't expect to be starring in her own reality TV dating show, and falling for the show's executive producer Annie Jackson could ruin everything. (978-1-63679-420-4)

It's All in the Details by Dena Blake. Makeup artist Lane Donnelly and wedding planner Helen Trent can't stand each other, but they must set aside their differences to ensure Darcy gets the wedding of her dreams, and make a few of their own dreams come true. (978-1-63679-430-3)

Marigold by Melissa Brayden. Marigold Lavender vows to take down Alexis Wakefield, the harsh food critic who blasts her younger sister's restaurant. If only she wasn't as sexy as she is mean. (978-1-63679-436-5)

A Second Chance at Life by Genevieve McCluer. Vampires Dinah and Rachel reconnect, but a string of vampire killings begin and evidence seems to be pointing at Dinah. They must prove her innocence while finding out if the two of them are still compatible after all these years. (978-1-63679-459-4)

The Town That Built Us by Jesse J. Thoma. When her father dies, Grace Cook returns to her hometown and tries to avoid Bonnie Whitlock, the woman who pulverized her heart, only to discover her father's estate has been left to them jointly. (978-1-63679-439-6)